W9-CFL-272

Murder on the Switzerland Trail

MURDER ON THE SWITZERLAND TRAIL

MIKE BEFELER

FIVE STAR

A part of Gale, Cengage Learning

GALE
CENGAGE Learning·

Farmington Hills, Mich • San Francisco • New York • Waterville, Maine
Meriden, Conn • Mason, Ohio • Chicago

GALE
CENGAGE Learning·

LIBRARY OF CONGRESS CATALOGING-IN-PUBLICATION DATA

Befeler, Mike.
   Murder on the Switzerland Trail / Mike Befeler.
   pages ; cm
   ISBN 978-1-4328-3050-2 (hardcover) — ISBN 1-4328-3050-3 (hardcover) — ISBN 978-1-4328-3047-2 (ebook) — ISBN 1-4328-3047-3 (ebook)
   1. Murder—Investigation—Fiction. 2. Boulder (Colo.)—History—20th century—Fiction. I. Title.
PS3602.E37M87 2015
813'.6—dc23   2015012953

First Edition. First Printing: October 2015
Find us on Facebook– https://www.facebook.com/FiveStarCengage
Visit our website– http://www.gale.cengage.com/fivestar/
Contact Five Star™ Publishing at FiveStar@cengage.com

Printed in the United States of America
1 2 3 4 5 6 7 19 18 17 16 15

To Sandy Stewart, Chuck Klomp and Mac for our many hikes along sections of the twenty-first-century Switzerland Trail.

ACKNOWLEDGMENTS

Many thanks for the assistance from my online critique group, Michael O'Neill, the librarians at the Carnegie Library in Boulder, my wife Wendy, and support from Alice Duncan, Tiffany Schofield, Tracey Matthews and Gretchen Gordon at Five Star. I'm also grateful to Forest Crossen, who wrote the definitive historical book *The Switzerland Trail of America*.

Switzerland Trail

Sunset ○———————○ Coppe

Hill
○
Silver Lake Siding ○   ○
Glacier Lake

○ Blue Bird
○ Anson

○ Lakewood

○ Wolfram
Cardinal ○

Eldora
○
Lake Eldora   ○ Sulfide

of America

-ock

Salina

Black Swan

Wall Street

Crisman

Sugar loaf

Tungsten

Orodell

Boulder

N

CHAPTER 1

I am the Switzerland Trail. My full name is the Switzerland Trail of America, a title my publicists loved to use, accompanied by panoramic pictures of me winding my way along the backdrop of the majestic Rockies. My name was given to me in 1898 by the superintendent of public schools for Greeley in Weld County, Professor J. E. Snooks, and he won a cash prize of ten dollars for his suggestion. Can you imagine? Ten dollars? I, of course, thought he deserved more, but I'm sure the good professor was delighted to receive the additional remuneration. I like to think that Professor Snooks used his winnings to take a group of children for a ride in one of my forty-six-person-seating-capacity Barney and Smith coach cars, but he probably spent it on books, tobacco or food.

I was born in the blood, sweat and pain of the hardy souls who dug, blasted and built my track bed. I lived a short but glorious life as events unfolded in Colorado at the end of the nineteenth and beginning of the twentieth century. I carried coal to hard-rock miners, ore down my twisting route to the smelters on the plains below, produce from farmers to market, and passengers thrilled to view the mountain vistas. And the passengers gave me the most pleasure as they stopped to collect wildflowers, sang my praises and admired the stunning beauty of the jagged peaks to my west.

At one time the Lions Club even erected two ten-by-twenty-foot billboards to advertise me along with the other attractions of Boulder, Colorado.

My muscles and sinew were a collection of rails, ties and rolling stock, but I was also the heart and soul of the foothills leading into the Rockies. I witnessed derailments, huge snow storms that blocked my way, floods that destroyed my trestles, and death. I also promoted romance, as young lovers and honeymooners used me to escape to the privacy of mountain meadows. Much as a stream brings precious water to the land below, I provided a flow of commerce and entertainment, moving in both directions.

I remember so many times when passengers filled my Pullman cars with laughter and song. But one day I will never forget is Sunday, June 29, 1919, a morning that started as normal as grandmother's apple pie. Now, let me give you a hint of how, by the afternoon of that same day, the world for a group of my passengers changed in a way they never expected.

Picture a man staggering out of the woods, leaving a trail of blood behind him. He is well-dressed, but he has lost the hat he'd worn in the morning, and his clothes are now rumpled and dirty. As he approaches the back ladder to my Pullman car number nineteen, he stumbles and falls to his knees, coughing and spewing blood into the dirt. The whistle blows from my locomotive, and the wheels begin to turn. The man grasps the handrail of my passenger car and drags himself up to the metal platform, pausing to catch his ragged breath as the train leaves the station. After another cough of blood, he uses his last bit of strength to reach up to open the door and crawl through the doorway. With a shaky hand he points to the group of eight people gathered in the front of the compartment, and with his final breath shouts, "You assassin!" At the sound of this accusation, all sixteen eyes turn in horror as the man collapses to the floor. A knife juts from the center of his back.

CHAPTER 2

Early on Sunday morning, June 29, 1919, Harry McBride stepped out his bungalow door on Eleventh Street in Boulder, Colorado, and lent an arm to help his wife, Susan, over the single cobbled step. He had a momentary urge to kick a pebble against the stone rubble wall surrounding the porch. Silly thought for a policeman on his day off, acting like one of their children, now grown and living with their own families. Harry couldn't help feeling joyful, escorting his hard-working wife away from her household duties and away from their small, ten-year-old, gable-roofed bungalow with the partially finished second floor they'd never completed.

He knew he'd pay for this day off. More unpaid hours to work. Chief Lawrence Bass was laid up again after a relapse from the influenza that had struck every country in the world. Probably more time patrolling the streets, as well, to allow George Savage, the other cop, to take a day off.

Harry and George had become good friends working alongside each other over the last few years. They made arrests together, swapped stories and shared meals. True, they hadn't seen much of each other this year, what with Chief Bass's illness and having to work nonoverlapping long shifts, but that would be resolved once the chief recovered.

At the railroad station on the corner of Ninth and Water Streets, Harry passed under the arched entrance to purchase their round-trip tickets. A dollar-fifty each, but he could save

13

that much skimping on lunches for a couple of weeks. Wouldn't hurt his waistline either.

For the train ride he'd selected a sack coat with matching waistcoat; contrasting trousers, ankle-length with cuffs, creased front and back; a stiff bowler; and round-toe boots. Susan wore an outfit with a V-neckline over a camisole with accompanying belt. A blue bonnet shaded her smiling face. They blended in with the crowd of sightseers waiting to board the train.

Susan hugged his arm. "It's about time for us to have a day together."

"You're right." Harry smiled, realizing her enthusiasm dispelled all concerns regarding the expense. "This will also give my feet a rest for one day."

Harry hoped one of these days the chief would purchase a motorcar for the police department to alleviate patrolling only on foot, but so far the city council refused to approve the request. This posed an increasingly difficult problem—the challenge of apprehending a speeding automobile on foot, on horseback or with a horse cart. He wondered when the council would come to its senses and provide improved police transportation such as existed in their larger neighbor, Denver.

Harry regarded the station building. The solid stone structure of the depot was covered by a shingled roof that led to a pointed spire. He put his hand on one of the brown stones, sensing the lingering warmth from the ninety-four-degree heat of the day before and the unusual warmth overnight. He checked his pocket watch. Ten minutes after nine. The train from Denver would soon arrive with passengers transferring to the Switzerland Trail. The narrow-gauge passenger cars of the Switzerland Trail would take them into the mountains, also his and Susan's destination today.

The day had started out at a bearable temperature, but it was expected to end in the mid-nineties again. That's why this would be an excellent opportunity to escape to the cool breezes of the mountains. He had patrolled in the heat all day on Saturday. His feet could take it, but the rest of his body was starting to have more trouble on hot days. At the age of forty-eight. After twenty-four years as a policeman, the work was starting to take a toll on him. Susan had commented on how red and tired he looked when he returned home last night, and he definitely felt exhausted by the heat after a long day of patrol. But today, he planned to relax and enjoy a ride on the railroad.

Shining black locomotive number thirty-three hissed impatiently as if anxious to start its journey. A small stream of smoke emerged from the smokestack. The attached tender was heaped with coal, and behind it rested two green Pullman cars.

Three young people stood on the platform: an attractive blond-haired woman in a yellow and white summer frock accompanied two men. Her tiered skirt displayed a raised hemline, now becoming popular among the younger set. Of her companions, one stood close to six feet tall, skinny with a vacant look on his face. His black hair was cut short, and he had a neatly trimmed moustache. He wore a tweed Norfolk jacket with paired box pleats over his chest and back, and a fabric belt. Matching breeches, polished boots, and a flat straw boater completed the outfit. The young man looked vaguely familiar, maybe someone Harry had seen on patrol.

The other man was younger, shorter, gaunt, with sunken cheeks and darting eyes. He wore simple brown breeches, a long sleeved-shirt, scuffed leather boots and a cap.

The three people appeared to be traveling together, but their demeanors indicated separate thoughts. Harry eyed them warily. His policeman's sixth sense gave off a warning. The younger man continued to look around wildly and began to wring his hands. Would there be problems today?

Harry shook off his concerns. He was taking a day off. No

patrol duties for him. The young man might be troubled, but that wasn't Harry McBride's concern on this fine morning. He planned to spend a pleasant day with his wife.

Susan, always the socialite, went up to the three and introduced herself. Harry realized he should join in as well.

"Harry, meet three of our fellow passengers," Susan said.

The younger man ducked behind the woman and averted his eyes. Harry decided there was definitely something wrong with him.

"I'm Allison Jacoby," the woman said. "Behind me is my brother, Michael. He's . . . kind of shy, so don't take offense."

Harry was used to the variety of reactions from people. He dealt with friendly, angry, boisterous and reticent citizens every day. This young man obviously suffered from more than shyness, but it was interesting how his sister protected him. "No offense taken."

Allison raised her large brown eyes. "And meet my fiancé, Frederick Hammond."

Harry held out his hand. The taller man shook it crisply, but maintained his vacant stare. *Interesting.* Harry sensed a problem here as well. Allison struck him as a Florence Nightingale, taking care of her brother and fiancé, two damaged souls.

"Frederick is a war veteran," Allison said. "He was invalided home with shrapnel wounds after fighting in France and is recovering from influenza."

Harry smiled inwardly at his insight that this young man also had problems. The war to end all wars had returned many who held the same vacant stare as Frederick. "Thank you for upholding our country's honor," Harry said. "It's young men like you who have protected our freedom."

Frederick nodded, his eyes looking as dull as the stone surface of the depot.

Harry had encountered this reaction once before. On one occasion, he arrested a returned soldier for drunk and disorderly behavior. Once in jail, the soldier curled up in a fetal position and spent the night crying. The next morning Harry released the prisoner, whose eyes were lost in memories of a troubled past. The war had sucked life out of that jailed man and the man standing in front of him today.

"What brings the three of you out on this Sunday?" Susan asked.

Allison said, "Frederick's old professor invited him to go on the train. He was reluctant at first, but I thought it would be an excellent outing. I also try to bring my brother along as often as possible. He needs . . . to be out in public more often."

The younger man made no eye contact with anyone.

Harry had also encountered people like this before. He had once been called to a grocery store where a man was violently waving his hands. Harry ordered him to stop, but the man became more agitated. Harry raised his billy club to strike the recalcitrant man and then thought better of it. It turned out the man suffered from brain damage and didn't understand Harry's orders. Harry finally calmed the disturbed man without resorting to physical violence.

"How far will you be traveling today?" Allison asked Susan.

"We're going to Eldora."

Allison's eyes lit up. "So are we. I want to collect some wildflowers when we get there. I understand we stop for several hours before the train returns."

"An hour and forty-five minutes," Michael Jacoby said from behind Allison, his voice high-pitched but authoritative.

Harry was surprised to hear the young man speak.

"Thank you, Michael." Allison faced Susan. "He may not speak often, but he's very precise in what he says."

While the conversation continued, Frederick closed his eyes as if not listening.

"I'm sorry to hear that you suffered from influenza," Harry said to Frederick.

The young man gave a start as his eyes shot open. "Uh . . . yes. I'm almost fully recovered."

"The sunshine and mountain air should be good for you," Susan said.

"I suppose," Frederick replied.

Allison leaned close to Frederick. "It's the perfect cure. We're going to have a lovely trip and see all the mountain sights. I've never taken the railroad before."

"I want to collect some wood," Michael said from behind Allison, still not looking at anyone.

"Yes, Michael. I'm sure you'll be able to find a good supply." Allison smiled at Susan. "He likes to whittle. You should see the beautiful things he makes."

"I'm going to carve a mountain lion," Michael said.

"And they're so realistic. I have a wolf on my mantel that looks as if it's alive."

Michael let out a growling sound.

"Michael likes to act out what he carves," Allison said. She reached into the carpetbag she carried and pulled out a carving of a bear. "Here's what Michael gave me this morning."

She handed it to Susan who turned it over in her hand. "How intricate."

Harry leaned over to see. *Amazing.* The bear looked like the one he chased out of a garden on Fourth Street a week ago. Once in a while, a bear moseyed out of the foothills into town, and he took care of the situation, which usually entailed making noises to scare the creature away. Harry regarded the carved animal again. It appeared to come alive, ready to attack. What a contrast to the retiring demeanor of the carver.

"I don't know why your brother wastes his time carving," Frederick said to his fiancée.

Allison's eyes flared. "Watch what you're saying, Frederick Hammond. My brother has his talent."

"Sometimes I wonder about the two of you." Frederick's face turned into a snarl.

Michael ducked out from behind his sister and waved a shaky fist at Frederick while averting his eyes. "Wa . . . wa . . . watch what you say."

Harry wondered if he might have to intervene in a family quarrel, but Frederick turned his back on them and limped away to the east side of the platform.

Michael scampered in the other direction, stopped and looked toward the mountains.

"I have to apologize for the behavior of my fiancé and brother," Allison said. "I can't excuse Frederick, but you have to make exceptions for Michael. He was a delicate child, not speaking until five years of age, and, even now, barely talks. Other children teased him unmercifully in school, but he got by with his wonderful artistic ability."

A whistle sounded, and the train from Denver pulled in. People began to exit the passenger cars. Harry sniffed the earthy aroma of coal and steam that permeated the air. Most people headed into town, but a few stayed on the platform to transfer to the Switzerland Trail railroad.

"All aboard," came the call as a husky, red-nosed conductor leaned out of the first of two mountain-bound Pullman cars resting on the tracks behind the engine and tender.

"Michael, let's go select our seats." Allison brushed a strand of hair away from her forehead. She stepped toward the second Pullman car, and her brother followed her.

People were streaming into the first car so Harry took Susan's hand, and they headed toward the open door to the second passenger car.

He felt a strange twinge—he sensed this would not be a casual trip into the mountains.

CHAPTER 3

The green Pullman cars appeared newly painted. Harry helped Susan up the stairs and stared at the Janney coupler that connected the two passenger cars with a firm metal handshake. He had heard of runaway cars and felt thankful that the coupling appeared secure.

He opened a windowed door, and they passed through the vestibule and into the compartment. The gray carpet, overhead chandeliers and plush burgundy velour seats for two on each side of the aisle promised comfort, as did a Baker heater for winter travel. The car interior was bright from the dozen windows on each side. Metal armrests jutted out on the aisle side of the seats, and wood veneer lined the sides of the Pullman below the windows.

Susan took the front window seat on the left forward-facing side of the passenger car, and Harry slid in beside her. He took a moment to admire his wife. Light filtering in from the small skylight in the tiered ceiling danced across her shoulders. Although she had aged along with him, she still possessed the perkiness of a young woman and a smile that made his body pulse with warmth. With their two children grown and living elsewhere, Harry and Susan had each other as they entered their older years.

Once he retired from the police force, they planned to visit their son in Colorado Springs and their daughter in Fort Collins. After raising the children, he felt no qualms about mooching off them for a while. Then they would use the savings they had accumulated from his police salary and years of frugal living to buy a small farm somewhere in the western part of the state. Harry could picture himself as a gentleman farmer, working part of the day and relaxing during the remainder.

He noticed Michael and Allison Jacoby sitting on the right side, one seat behind. Michael pressed his face against the window. His left arm flapped like a wounded pigeon.

Harry wondered what it must have been like for the boy's parents to deal with this peculiar behavior. He and Susan were fortunate their children never had problems more serious than sibling arguments, episodes of sulking and minor tantrums. Both children survived childhood and emerged into adulthood as contributing citizens.

Allison took a book from her carpetbag and read. She appeared unfazed over Michael's idiosyncrasies. There was still no sign of Frederick Hammond.

A boisterous crowd clambered aboard and headed to the back of the passenger car. The women wore long, dark traveling dresses, and the men tan pants, long-sleeved shirts, boots and tan hats. They carried walking poles and rucksacks and appeared ready to explore the mountains.

A thin man approximately five-foot-seven, in his fifties, with thick glasses stepped aboard. He wore a crumpled jacket; a checkered, single-breasted vest from which hung a prominent watch chain; a wing-collared shirt; a bow tie; and patent-leather boots. He removed his felt homburg to display a head of gray hair to match his full beard.

An attractive, dark-haired woman in her late thirties accompanied him. Her large brown eyes, slightly rouged cheeks, upturned nose, and immaculate hair gave her the appearance of a society woman. She wore a day walking suit; a loose, belted jacket with fur-trimmed sleeves and lappets; a large black hat;

and black bulldog toe-button boots. Harry squinted at her. He recognized her face but couldn't think where he had seen her before.

The couple stopped alongside the seat behind Harry and Susan. The man stated loudly, "If it's all right with you, Lucille, I would appreciate having the window seat."

"I don't mind at all, Benjamin," she replied in a demure tone.

"Thank you," Benjamin said. "You are a most accommodating woman."

"That's why we get along so well."

"Ah, there's Daniel." Benjamin waved forward. "Take the seat at the front of the car so we'll be close together."

A short young man with dark complexion and moustache acknowledged the command with a wave of his hand. He wore a navy blue blazer with brass buttons and a Panama hat. He bowed to Allison, and dropped into the seat across from Harry. Once in place, he stretched his arms as he nervously tapped his foot against the wood in front of him.

"Now we're only missing Frederick Hammond," Benjamin said.

"He should be here soon." Allison craned her neck to look at Benjamin. "We're traveling together."

"Ah, you must be his fiancée, Miss Jacoby," Benjamin said. "Allow me to introduce myself. I'm Professor Benjamin Sager. I invited Frederick to join this expedition today. This young woman with me is Mrs. Lucille Vickering, a widow who runs the Vickering boarding house on Pearl Street. And up there in front meet Daniel Compton, a former student of mine, as was Frederick."

"I know Daniel," Allison said with a clipped tone.

"Good, good," the professor announced. "We're almost all assembled. I must say, Miss Jacoby, that Frederick has excellent taste. You have cheeks like peaches. Which reminds me, there is an exceptionally good peach crop on the western slope of Colorado this year. Now, who are these fine people in front of me?"

Harry turned. "I'm Harry McBride, and this is my wife, Susan." He reached a hand back to shake the professor's.

"You heard our names," Benjamin said. "I'm a history professor at the University of Colorado. Have taught there for fifteen years."

"And educated many young people who are contributing to society today," Lucille added.

"Ah, yes, my dear. Thank you for the endorsement. And you, Mr. McBride. What is your profession?"

"I'm a police officer here in Boulder," Harry said.

Benjamin let out a loud laugh. "I guess we'll have to be careful not to commit any crimes today. I promise to keep my flask hidden so you won't have to confiscate any booze." He pointed toward the front of the compartment. "Finally, there's Frederick. Young man, take the seat next to your old classmate Daniel."

Frederick came to an abrupt halt. He focused his brooding gaze on Allison before he sat next to Daniel, across the aisle from Harry.

"Always the last to arrive, just like when he attended the university," Daniel said. "We called him 'Can't Get Out of Bed, Fred.' "

"You're as pleasant as you used to be," Frederick replied. "I'm sure it serves you well as a lawyer. Too bad you weren't patriotic enough to support your country during the war."

"I left that to you fanatics," Daniel answered as if the insult didn't concern him.

In a lightning-fast motion, Frederick thrust his hands around Daniel's throat.

Allison screamed, "Stop it! Don't you two start quarreling again."

Harry stood to intervene, but was beat to the scene by the conductor. "Break it up. There will be no fighting on my train." He pulled the two men apart.

Daniel coughed and rubbed his throat. "You're insane."

Frederick snarled at the conductor and pushed him away. "You. I should have known. Interfering as you used to."

"And you still causing trouble as you did in our neighborhood. Will you behave yourself, or do I have to throw you off the train?"

Frederick gave a snort and crossed his arms. "I'd like to see you try."

"Gentlemen, I think it's time for everyone to calm down." Harry remained standing. He noticed the conductor wore a nameplate that read Theodore Shultz. "Mr. Shultz, I'm a police officer. I'll keep my eye on the combatants. I know you have work to do to prepare the train for departure."

Theodore tipped his hat. "Thank you. We have a full passenger car with the group from the Rocky Mountain Climbers Club, and I need to help them stash their hiking and camping equipment." He retreated to the back of the car.

Harry regarded Frederick and Daniel. "I'd suggest finding separate seats, but the car looks completely full. Can the two of you control yourselves on the trip?"

"Sure." Daniel dusted off his jacket. "If he doesn't try to choke me again."

Frederick sat like a stone statue.

"Mr. Hammond?" Harry focused on the young man.

Frederick lifted his gaze toward Harry, and the vacant eyes showed a small sparkle for the first time. "Yes. If he doesn't place his throat in my hands again."

Harry suppressed a smile. "Good. I sense a lot of history

among the passengers here."

"Although I invited Frederick and Daniel, I didn't know they held animosity toward each other," Professor Sager said. "They were two of my best history students. I expect good citizenship from them for the rest of the trip."

"And your teaching helped me, Professor," Daniel said. "When I went on to get my law degree, I was well prepared. I found that I was sager than many of the other students."

The professor rolled his eyes. "Still telling your awful puns, Mr. Compton. You were always one for juvenile jokes and wisecracks. And you, Mr. Hammond. Have you put my teaching to good use?"

"I can't say it helped me much in the trenches in France." Frederick glared at Daniel.

"No, I imagine not," the professor replied. "But some European government leaders could have benefited from being better students of history. Western civilization has a propensity to repeat the same mistakes over and over again."

"Mr. Hammond, you know our conductor," Harry said. "How so?"

Frederick took a deep breath. "He lived in the same neighborhood where I grew up. He was older and took it upon himself to tell my parents whenever I did something he considered wrong. A busybody who interfered all the time."

Harry faced Allison. "And, Miss Jacoby, you made a reference to Frederick and Daniel fighting before."

Allison reddened. "Uh . . . yes. Daniel was a suitor before I became engaged to Frederick. They once had an altercation in a restaurant."

"Are there any other relationships we need to settle before having a calm and peaceful trip?" Harry asked.

Allison looked thoughtful. "Frederick used to live in a boarding house. Was that by any chance the one you run, Mrs. Vickering?"

Lucille Vickering cleared her throat. "Yes. Your fiancé was one of my boarders when he attended the University of Colorado. He and several of his classmates enlisted when the United States entered the war."

Allison opened her book again.

"What are you reading, Miss Jacoby?" Lucille Vickering asked.

Allison tapped the cover. "*My Ántonia* by Willa Cather. It was published last year."

Lucille wrinkled her brow. "I've heard the name of the book but haven't read it. Are you enjoying it?"

Allison eyes brightened. "Yes. It's written from the perspective of the narrator, Jim Burden, a lawyer."

Daniel swiveled in his seat. "Obviously a good person who doesn't want to be a burden on anyone else."

Professor Sager gave a croaking cough. "Mr. Compton, please desist from telling your atrocious puns."

Daniel smiled. "Only trying to liven up the conversation."

At that moment a man weighed down with a large rucksack staggered into the compartment and stumbled into Harry, who had not yet returned to his seat.

"Pardon me."

Harry steadied the small man struggling with his load. "Looks like your companions are aboard and waiting for you."

The man gasped for a breath. "I think I'm the last one to arrive. We'll be hiking and camping overnight."

"You should have excellent weather for your expedition," the professor said. "You've chosen the right time of year."

The man wiped his forehead. "Yes, after the warm weather here in Boulder, it will be a pleasant escape to the mountains." He regained his hold on the rucksack and continued up the aisle to join his group.

Harry sat, and Susan patted his arm. "Never a moment of peace for a policeman."

"No. It seems troublesome situations must be dealt with even on the Switzerland Trail."

CHAPTER 4

Hissing steam escaped from the engine, and a piercing whistle sounded as the passenger car surged forward.

Harry looked out the window toward the south to take in the sight of a number of wooden structures and a few trees along Boulder Creek; in the middle distance, the buildings of the university; and off in the far distance, the hills surrounding Chautauqua, the summer retreat for educators from Texas. He and Susan had attended several concerts in the wooden auditorium, one of the largest structures in Boulder. Susan enjoyed music, but Harry often nodded off. He tried to catch himself in time, but on occasion suffered a sharp elbow to the ribs as a reminder to pay attention.

"Ah, our adventure has begun," Professor Sager announced. "The mountains await us. This will be a nice respite after an exceptionally busy week. On Wednesday, I took part in commencement. Dr. Livingston Farrand, former president of the university, gave a rousing address to the class of nineteen-nineteen."

"A pontificator probably sandbagging the unsuspecting graduates," Frederick muttered.

Conductor Theodore Shultz returned and stood in front of the passengers, tweaking his moustache as his rheumy eyes scanned the car. "We're on our way, ladies and gentlemen. Everyone settled in?"

Frederick Hammond glared at him, and the conductor met

his gaze with an equally intense scowl, as if they were two junk-yard dogs faced off.

"We're all quite ready," the professor said. "I'm sure this will be an extraordinary day. We have sunshine and good company. What more could be asked for?" He pulled out his watch. "We're leaving right on time. Exactly nine-thirty."

Conductor Shultz removed his watch from his vest pocket. "You have the correct time, sir."

"I pride myself on having a mechanism that keeps exact time." The professor tapped his gold watch and snapped it shut.

Allison looked at her wristwatch. "Oh, good, I have the correct time, too."

Daniel pulled a watch from his vest pocket. "Looks like I'm five minutes slow." He adjusted the stem to the correct time.

"You were always slow," Frederick growled.

Harry prepared to intervene if necessary, but the two men looked away from each other.

"What can you tell me about the mechanical behemoth pulling our passenger car, Conductor?" Professor Sager asked.

"What would you like to know?"

"I'm a man of facts and historical significance," the professor replied. "Tell me what you can."

Theodore Shultz tipped his cap. "I'm glad you asked, sir. Our locomotive runs on thirty-six-inch narrow-gauge track and was manufactured by the Brooks Locomotive Works in nineteen-oh-six, the newest engine in our rolling stock. It's designated a two-eight-zero, which means two leading wheels on one axle, followed by eight powered wheels on four axles, with no trailing wheels. Our tender can carry up to nine tons of coal, and the water tank has a capacity of four thousand gallons."

The professor whistled. "Quite a piece of machinery."

"Yes. It can easily manage the grade through the mountains with the two cars attached today."

A whoop came from someone in the hiking group at the back of the passenger compartment, followed by a cheer.

"Good to see so much enthusiasm. I'll see if anyone back there needs further assistance." Shultz headed along the aisle toward the back.

The train picked up speed as it moved through the railroad yard. They passed a pile of railroad ties and a stack of rails. Boxcars lined the siding. In the doorway of one car sat two men in ragged clothes.

"We're approaching a historic site," the professor announced.

"Oh," Lucille Vickering replied from beside him. "Something you will undoubtedly educate us on."

"Yes, indeed. On February tenth, nineteen-oh-seven, right here at the corner of Tenth Street occurred the largest explosion in Boulder's history."

"I remember that," Lucille said. "Something to do with Mrs. Kiser's boarding house. That old biddy always tried to take business away from me."

"I'd hate to be on your bad side, my dear, since I know you hold a grudge. Irrespective of the friendly competition between you and Mrs. Kiser, her son, Frank, was involved in this unfortunate event. It started because of a switchman's strike. The railroad company brought in Pinkerton scabs to break the strike and that infuriated John W. Reeves, a brakeman. Some of the strikebreakers were staying at Mrs. Kiser's boarding house—"

"Typical that she played a role in questionable activities," Lucille said. "That woman let any unsavory character stay in her boarding house. Whereas, I only have the highest clientele—businessmen and conscientious students."

"Yes, my dear. As I was saying, John Reeves, with Frank Kiser in tow, made the rounds of saloons on the night of August ninth—"

"That's why I'm glad temperance has finally passed," Allison Jacoby said from across the aisle. "Whiskey leads to all kinds of trouble."

"Harrumph. If you young ladies will allow me to finish my story."

Lucille broke out in laughter. "Oh, Benjamin, you so hate having one of your lectures interrupted."

The professor cleared his throat. "I'm not lecturing. I'm merely recounting one of the highlights of the dynamic history of our town. May I finish?"

"Oh, don't act so indignant," Lucille said. "Of course you can complete your lecture."

"It's not . . . oh, bother." He waved his hands in the air. "Now to continue. So Reeves in his intoxicated state, with the assistance of young Kiser, set fire to a caboose where some of the Pinkerton men were sleeping. Luckily, some boys returning from the mountains came along and doused the flames."

"If the fire was put out, how did an explosion occur?" Allison asked.

"My, I do have some inquisitive listeners," the professor said. "I'm glad you're paying attention. After Reeve's first unsuccessful attempt to set a fire, his still not clearly functioning brain came up with the idea to start another fire. Frank Kiser pointed out a boxcar he said contained merchandise. Unfortunately, the boxcar's merchandise was two thousand, four hundred pounds of dynamite. This boxcar full of explosive material was destined for the Boulder County mine at Cardinal, but it had remained in Boulder for several days because it wasn't allowed to be attached to a train with passenger cars—during the summer all the trains took passengers into the mountains, just as ours is doing today. In fact, we'll be going past that very mine on our journey. It's still a source of gold and tungsten. The mill at Cardinal processed ore to be carried down to Boulder on the

Switzerland Trail railroad."

Lucille adjusted her hat. "Are you going to pontificate on mining as well as explosions? Do I detect the good professor going off on a tangent?"

"Only because you distracted me, my dear." He patted her on the arm. "To continue. These two scalawags, Reeves and Kiser, started their second fire of the early morning. Unfortunately, the boxcar fire was not put out in time, and the resulting explosion carved a crater thirty feet across and ten feet deep. Three men died."

Allison regarded the professor. "Were the two culprits some of those killed in the explosion?"

"No. They had left the scene by then. The victims were people trying to extinguish the blaze, men trying to assist. But, fortunately, the perpetrators were brought to justice."

"And rightfully so," Harry said, joining the conversation. "A fellow policeman apprehended both Reeves and Kiser. Reeves confessed, claiming whiskey and his hatred of the strikebreakers led to his crime. They were found guilty of second-degree murder later that year and pulled ten to fifteen years at the Colorado State Prison."

"Which means they might be out by now," Susan said. "I had forgotten about that arrest."

Harry nodded to his wife. "One of the major crimes during my tenure with the police department. I certainly hope that Reeves and Kiser don't come back to Boulder. They were a bad lot. We don't need their types here again."

"You have a point there, Officer McBride," the professor said. "People like those two, in addition to killing innocent citizens, hurt business in downtown Boulder. And that explosion didn't help the railroad one bit. The company paid for windows blown out throughout the Boulder business district. Caused quite an amount of damage. Two years later, as a result

33

of those expenses, the panic of nineteen-oh-seven and a decline in business, the railroad ownership changed after a forced sale to the present owners—Denver, Boulder and Western."

Daniel chuckled. "Known affectionately as 'Drink Beer and Wine.' " He opened his hand toward Allison. "Pardon, if that offends you."

Allison's lips pinched into a tight line, but she didn't respond.

"And we face another debacle with our beloved railroad," the professor said. "Once again economic problems may force the Switzerland Trail either to close or find new owners. This line has always been a financial challenge."

"Look at all the passengers today," Susan said. "How can the railroad be having money problems?"

"Ah, an astute observation, Mrs. McBride," the professor said. "If it were summer all year, there would be no fiscal problems. Unfortunately, the passenger traffic declines during the winter and isn't made up by enough shipments to and from the mines anymore. The motorcar is taking business away, and the expenditures to keep the line open during the winter have become excessive. Do you know what's required to clear snowdrifts from the railroad tracks? That alone causes the DB and W to lose money. It's a shame, but one of the problems of running a railroad in the mountains."

Daniel Compton faced the professor. "The real problem is the railroad executives pay themselves too much money."

Benjamin Sager chuckled. "Ah, my young socialist friend. If that were only the case. A succession of owners has been bearing the losses of the Switzerland Trail for years. It's a rare year that this narrow-gauge railroad actually makes a profit."

"There's a huge disparity between what the president of DB and W makes and the wages for our conductor," Daniel said.

"True, but our conductor, Mr. Shultz, hasn't invested his own money in making the railroad successful."

"Even with the risk, the capitalists make too much money. I would have defended Reeves and Kiser if I had been a lawyer at that time. I could have gotten them off."

Frederick gave a snort, which Daniel ignored.

"I doubt it, young man," the professor said. "As Officer McBride stated, they confessed, and the evidence was clear. They received the punishment they deserved."

Daniel Compton muttered. "We need to change our economic system. Too many poor people and a handful of excessively rich men."

"I beg to differ," the professor said. "That's the beauty of our capitalist system. You must take the risk but can also reap the rewards of financial success. Right now the owners of this railroad are losing money. It doesn't bode well for the future. You as a lawyer, Mr. Compton, succeed by your skill and ability to represent your clients. You are adequately compensated for your abilities and should not disparage our industrialists."

"Lawyers are as bad as the robber barons," Frederick Hammond growled.

"Ah, we have another antagonist entering the discussion," the professor said. "I have a comment directed at you, Mr. Hammond. It's unfortunate that you never applied yourself. You had great potential but haven't lived up to it."

Frederick Hammond jumped up and shook his fist at the professor. "You old fraud. You're nothing but an arrogant loud-mouth."

The professor's voice turned cold. "Case proved. Only anger and no results. Apply yourself, Mr. Hammond. I hate to see young people waste their lives. The fine education I provided for you should launch you into a successful career. It's survival of the fittest. Some make it and some fall along the side of the road."

CHAPTER 5

The train crossed Boulder Creek west of Fourth Street over a trestle firmly implanted on both sides of the stream. The passengers were jostled as the car sped up over tracks curving around a rock outcrop and hillside stretching to the south, dotted with sprigs of grass, a few trees and bare spots of dirt. A higher ridge led to Flagstaff Mountain basking in the morning sunlight. To the right on the other side of the canyon, Anemone Hill looked down over Boulder Creek.

The temperature in the passenger car increased due to the day's heat. Harry took out his handkerchief and mopped his brow. His mouth watered, anticipating a bowl of ice cream, one of his favorite treats. If he could eat ice cream every day, he would put on even more weight. He patted his belly. It was a good thing he walked so much when on patrol.

Lucille looked toward the back of the passenger car. "Oh, there's my friend Mary. I didn't know she was in the climber's group. I'll have to go say hello." She stood and bustled toward the boisterous group, grabbing seat backs as the train rumbled and wobbled.

"Look how low the creek is," Susan said. "Usually at this time of the summer it's running close to full."

"Boulder Creek was only running one-fourth its usual amount during the peak runoff period," Harry replied. "And this summer there hasn't been much rain."

Susan tapped the window as the train approached a water

tower. "We needed the moisture that fell this last week. My daisies were getting thirsty."

"You and your flowers." Harry nudged Susan. "You certainly have a green thumb, my dear, whereas, as you know, any plant I touch immediately dies."

"That's because you had that black ink all over your finger all summer long. It probably kills plants, to say nothing of the mess it makes in our sink."

"But the ink is useful for taking fingerprints."

"I don't know why you get it all over your hands, though. I thought the ink was for the suspects, not the police officers."

Harry shrugged. "I can't help getting it on my fingers as well."

Professor Sager tapped Harry on the shoulder. "I hate to eavesdrop, but I heard you mention fingerprints. Is your police department employing that technique to catch criminals?"

"Back before the police chief suffered his relapse, the other police officer, George Savage, and I practiced fingerprinting each other. We also held objects such as forks, knives and glasses to accumulate prints and compared them to the ones we inked for each other."

Susan arched an eyebrow. "Is that why I found soot on some of my silverware?"

Harry gave a sheepish grin. "You caught me. I borrowed a few pieces for us to use for our experiments. Both George and I have become pretty good at matching fingerprints."

"But have you used fingerprinting for real cases?" the professor asked.

"Yes. We now collect fingerprints at the scene of major crimes and compare them to the prints we ink from suspects. It's proven to be an effective tool for law enforcement. Much better than the Bertillon system of using different measurements of bodily limbs."

The professor nodded. "The Bertillon system has been discredited. In nineteen-oh-three two prisoners in Leavenworth Prison named Will Smith and William Smith had identical Bertillon measurements. They were later found to be identical twins. Each fingerprint is unique, even between identical twins."

"My, my," Susan said. "You're quite the expert, Professor Sager."

"As a historian, it's my duty to understand what has transpired in any part of our society. I must stay current on economics, war, judicial outcomes and even the world of a policeman. Back to the subject at hand. Are you aware, Officer McBride, that Edmond Locard developed a technique last year to definitively identify a person with twelve specific points of a fingerprint?"

"That's correct. I've seen it work on several occasions," Harry said. "I'm surprised you know so much about fingerprints, Professor. Not many people are familiar with the topic."

At that moment, Lucille returned and slid back into her seat.

The professor waved his hands, almost striking Susan's bonnet. "It's amazing what this modern technology can do. Have all of you been paying attention to the development of the airplane?"

"They certainly played a role in the Great War," Daniel said.

"You're correct, young man. The airplane will eventually be taking passengers much like our Switzerland Trail is today. And someday we'll even have telephones that people can carry with them."

Harry laughed. "I don't think so. It's not possible for someone to move around with telephone wires attached."

"You obviously haven't been paying attention to wireless telegraphy. Messages can be sent through the air without wires. There's no reason we won't eventually have telephones that operate without wires attached. Think of the possibilities. Within the next fifty years we'll see all kinds of new inventions."

"I agree with Officer McBride," Lucille said. "I can't imagine a telephone being carried around, even without wires. You'd need a trunk to transport it. And speaking of telephones, I have to watch my boarders. They try to use the boarding house telephone whenever I'm not paying attention."

"I'm sure you keep them in line, my dear. You run a tight ship."

"Of course. I have the best boarding house in town. And I never put up with rude behavior or slovenliness."

Frederick looked at Lucille. "When I lived in your boarding house, the place was a mess, and you served atrocious food."

Lucille jumped up and pointed a finger at Frederick. "And you, young man, didn't know how to behave yourself. Always insulting the other boarders. What made you think you were so high and mighty compared to everyone else?"

Frederick looked away in disgust. "Your boarding house was a pig sty, and the other boarders were pigs. I don't know why I put up with living there."

"And I don't know why I let you room there in the first place."

"Hah. You know why." Frederick crossed his arms and slumped into his seat.

"Can you believe the insolence of that young man, Benjamin? Did he misbehave in your class as well?"

"As I mentioned earlier, Mr. Hammond showed great promise, but his inherent laziness doomed him never to achieve his potential. It's a shame he hasn't emulated Mr. Compton and pursued a meaningful career."

"Don't disparage Frederick," Allison interjected. "He has gumption and will make a success of himself. He was a patriot for our country and paid the price. No one else in this group went off to fight in Europe and had to put up with the conditions he did. Now he has an injured leg and still suffers the aftereffects of influenza."

"Now, now, Miss Jacoby." The professor bowed in Allison's direction. "I'm not saying your Mr. Hammond isn't a hero. I'm only suggesting that it's time for him to stop feeling sorry for himself and to get on with his life."

"We are getting married, you know."

The professor smiled. "And a fine institution marriage is. I wish the two of you the best for a long and fruitful life together. I'm only implying your fiancé will need to find a profession to support you in the manner which, I assume, you've become accustomed."

"He will do fine, Professor." Allison gave a determined bob of her head and turned toward her brother, who was whittling on a piece of wood. "How is your carving coming, Michael?"

He held up the end of a chunk of wood with an intricate head of a mountain lion. "R-r-roar," Michael said and returned to his carving.

The hiking group in the back of the passenger car broke out into a loud chorus of "Hinky, Dinky Parlez-Vous," accompanied by a harmonica and much hand-clapping and stomping of feet. Professor Sager and Lucille Vickering joined in, but the others in the front of the car only listened.

After they repeated the same verse three times, the singing died out. Then a loud voice announced, "Another song."

The hikers proceeded into a liberal rendition of "How Ya Gonna Keep 'Em Down on the Farm." At the conclusion of this song, one voice bellowed out, "How ya gonna keep 'em down on the plains after they've seen moun-tains." This led to a round of cheering. The concert concluded with a rousing interpretation of "Over There."

The singing, rather than appealing to Frederick Hammond, appeared to sink him into a darker mood with each song. After the hikers concluded, Frederick slipped a flask out of his coat pocket and took a long swig.

"Frederick, put that away," Allison shouted.

"This is none of your business," he said with a growl. He took another swig, put the stopper back in the flask and slipped it into his coat pocket.

"Of course it is. You know how I oppose whiskey, and, besides, it's illegal. Do you want Officer McBride to arrest you?"

Harry tried to make light of the situation. "We're nearly out of the City of Boulder jurisdiction, so Frederick is safe from me. Since we're entering Boulder County, we'll have to call the sheriff if anything needs attention. Besides, I'm off duty today, so I won't be arresting anyone."

Frederick stared ahead.

Allison pursed her lips. "I don't care where we are. Frederick, remember what happened last time you drank? I don't want to deal with you all sulky and morose again. We're trying to have fun. It wouldn't hurt for you to smile a little and, by all means, leave the liquor alone. We're here for a pleasant day in the mountains."

"Maybe for you. It hasn't been that pleasant for me, particularly with some of the people here today. You can have the lot of them."

Allison shook her index finger at the back of Frederick. "If you will give the day half a chance, we'll have a wonderful time."

"Yeah." He closed his eyes.

My train progressed toward the mouth of Boulder Canyon carrying the troubled lives, past encounters, and future hopes and dreams of the passengers.

CHAPTER 6

The train crossed Boulder Creek again over the number two trestle, hugged the cliff on the north side of the slowly moving stream and disappeared into shadows.

"Notice the track off to the side," the professor said. "It's a two-car powder spur. Since the nineteen-oh-seven explosion, the railroad has been required to keep any cars with dynamite here out of the city."

"It might be safer for the city, but if an explosion occurred here, it might bring down an avalanche of rocks," Daniel said.

"True," the professor replied. "The railroad is willing to take that chance rather than risking the lives of citizens. A tradeoff on what provides the most benefit."

"Why don't people just decide to give up using dynamite?" Allison asked. "You men with your whiskey and explosives."

"Ah, Miss Jacoby, you support nonviolence as well as prohibition," the professor said.

Allison crossed her arms. "Look what the war did to Frederick."

The professor nodded. "I understand your concern about wars. They never seem to solve the problems in society, but they are inevitable. Dynamite, on the other hand, has a most important use. That's what blasts rock so our industrious miners can retrieve the gold, silver and tungsten stored in our hills."

A slight downslope breeze in the canyon caused cinders and black smoke from the engine's smokestack to swirl along the

42

windows on the left side. The combination of the breeze and the shadows dropped the temperature within the Pullman car, and all the passengers became silent as they studied the stark canyon scenery through the windows.

A few minutes passed, and the smoke cleared, breathing life back into the car's occupants.

A mule deer scampered along the edge of the stream. It came to an abrupt stop, sensing the power of the mechanical beast surging up the canyon.

Susan perked up and pointed. "Our first wildlife sighting."

"I'm glad it's on the other side of the train so Michael didn't notice it," Allison said. "He becomes agitated when he sees deer."

Harry leaned across Susan to catch a glimpse of the set of antlers. "At least that one isn't trying to eat your garden."

"No, but they can sure be a nuisance. I enjoy seeing them when I don't have to chase them out of our yard."

Harry patted her hand. "You'll have a chance to find other creatures. We'll see lots of chipmunks and squirrels in Eldora."

"As long as we don't have to deal with any bears or mountain lions."

Harry stared back across the aisle where Michael Jacoby continued to carve. What a strange young man. He carved animals but became upset when he saw a real one in nature. "I think the only mountain lion will be the one being whittled."

Michael worked intently on his art. He seemed to pay no attention to anyone around him, the picture of complete concentration. His ebony-handled knife pared away wood chips to reveal the shape of a mountain lion.

Harry gazed at Frederick Hammond. This young man fidgeted, clenching and unclenching his fists. As opposed to Michael's focus, Frederick's demeanor gave off the sense of a caged animal, ready to lash out. Suddenly, he jumped up.

"Where are you going?" Allison asked.

"I need to stretch my wounded leg."

"Do you want company?" she asked.

"No." He limped past her toward the back of the car, holding onto the edges of the seats as he went.

"Frederick is off on a rampage," Daniel Compton said.

"He just needs some time to himself," Allison said.

"Why do you put up with his bad behavior, Allison?" Daniel asked.

"That doesn't concern you, Daniel." Allison clenched her teeth before leaning toward Michael. "I like what you're carving."

Michael ignored her as a few more chips flew.

Harry looked at Daniel, and their eyes met. "What type of law do you practice, Mr. Compton?"

"Call me Daniel. Please." He straightened his shoulders. "I mainly represent renters threatened with eviction. My practice is in Boulder. It's small but growing. I've only just begun to build my clientele, and it takes time to gain a reliable reputation in the world of law. It's slow progress, but I'm able to support myself and work my way up to the more important cases."

"I guess that's why I haven't seen you in court before," Harry said. "I run up against many of the old-time lawyers."

"I imagine you do, but soon enough we'll encounter each other there. Today I may be representing mostly students and the poor, but tomorrow I'll be defending those accused of burglary or even murder." Daniel chuckled. "And prohibition violators. That law will generate new sources of income for all sorts of people, including lawyers."

Harry grimaced. "I'm sure it will. I'm seeing more homemade and bootleg whiskey coming through our town these days, a lot of it by motorcar. I'm going to be busier than ever."

"I don't know what this country is coming to," the professor said. "The anti-saloon law we passed in Boulder in nineteen-oh-seven did no good. Neither did prohibition in the state of Colorado in nineteen-sixteen. And now the country has ratified a constitutional amendment doing the same. It's a sad state of affairs. A shame. A shame."

"Now everyone wants to be a bootlegger," Harry added.

"When the government enacts stupid laws, entrepreneurs will jump in," the professor said. "And all a waste of your time as a law enforcement official. You should be catching real criminals and keeping those crazy motorcar drivers from running over peaceful citizens."

Susan snuggled against Harry's arm. "That's why it's so important to have this day in the mountains. I don't know when I'll have you to myself again."

"It's going to be tough until Chief Bass regains his health. Maybe then the city council will realize we need more policemen. Our little town is growing, and growth leads to more crime . . . and more business for you, Daniel."

"And I'll be happy to represent any of the accused."

Allison leaned forward. "Daniel, doesn't it bother you to go to court knowing a client is guilty?"

Daniel shrugged. "It's not my duty to determine if someone is innocent or guilty. Our legal system provides for anyone accused of crime to have his day in court with legal defense. I'm providing a needed service. If I ever come up against Officer McBride in court, it's his responsibility to show evidence of guilt and my job to convince a judge or jury that a reasonable doubt exists. It's as simple as that."

Harry knew it wasn't as simple as that. Juries usually saw through the bluster of a self-involved lawyer, but once in a while, they succumbed to emotional arguments. Good lawyers might convince a jury to let a guilty man off, and a bad lawyer might miss an important argument when his client was innocent. Still, the system worked the majority of the time.

Allison regarded Daniel quizzically. "I think it would be difficult to represent someone who committed a heinous crime such as murder. If you knew your client killed another person, how could you live with yourself if you let him out of jail to do it again?"

"Things aren't always black and white. There may be mitigating circumstances—a witness who falsifies information, a wrong identification, and even, although I'm sure it doesn't happen often, an error by the police." Daniel winked at Harry. "It's a defense lawyer's obligation to look for any of these inconsistencies."

"And it's my job to collect the evidence. I need to demonstrate the suspect's guilt so not even a finagling attorney can get the culprit off." Harry winked back at Daniel.

"*Touché*, Officer McBride. I look forward to presenting our respective views in court one day."

"I'm sure we'll meet there."

Daniel smiled. "Then we'll have an opportunity to represent our different opinions."

Harry narrowed his gaze. "I only give the facts."

"Facts can be interpreted very differently," Daniel replied.

Frederick reappeared from the back of the compartment. He limped up and stood in front of Daniel. "I can see you lying and cheating to defend criminals who should be taken off the street. It's people like you who cause problems in our society."

Daniel jumped to his feet and poked Frederick in the chest. "Me? You're the one causing problems. Look at you. I know you've been through some difficult times, but you come back from the war full of anger, resent everyone, and mistreat your fiancée. You have no respect for her. She's too good for you. I don't know why she puts up with you."

Frederick made a fist and pulled back his arm.

Harry shot out of his seat and pushed between the two men. "Both of you calm down. No more altercations on this trip."

Frederick dropped his arm.

Harry looked back and forth between the two combatants. "Well?"

Daniel inspected his sleeve and removed a piece of lint before regarding Harry. "If forty-four nations can set aside their differences to sign the League of Nations covenant as they did yesterday, I can get along with Frederick." He held out his hand.

Harry stepped aside.

Frederick glowered at Daniel but finally shook his hand.

"There," Harry said. "That isn't so difficult."

The two men returned to their seats. Daniel rested his shoulder against the window, and Frederick moved as close to the aisle as possible.

Harry waited a moment and sat down.

Susan leaned over and whispered in his ear. "The Germans may have signed the peace treaty, but I'm not convinced they are really any more ready for peace that these two young men across the aisle."

Harry whispered back. "Unfortunately, I believe you're right. I don't think we've seen the last of the personal war to end all wars either."

CHAPTER 7

The train rounded the bend at Goat Rock. Conductor Shultz stopped by and pointed toward the stream. "Right here in eighteen-ninety-one, engine sixty went over the stone wall into the creek on a return run to Boulder."

"Oh, my," Allison said. "Was anyone hurt?"

"The engine landed on the cab, but the engineer and fireman escaped."

Allison shivered. "Traveling by railroad sounds dangerous."

Shultz tugged on the lapel of his coat. "Most of the time it's extremely safe. We've experienced few wrecks. The next scenic sight, ladies and gentlemen, Lover's Leap, that sheer rock formation that dominates the other side of the creek."

Allison asked, "Why is it called Lover's Leap?"

The professor tapped the back of the seat in front of him. "You've never heard the legend?"

"No, I haven't."

"The story goes that a young Indian maiden and a white boy were lovers. This led to problems from both sets of parents. To end the tension the young woman climbed to the top of the cliff and jumped to her death on the rocks below." The professor raised his hands and brought them together in a loud clap. "That was the end of the young maiden."

"My goodness." Allison put her hand to her cheek.

"Whether truth or fiction, it's nothing more than a retelling of Shakespeare's *Romeo and Juliet*. Boy meets girl. They fall in love. The families disapprove. Tragedy results. I assume your families approve of your and Frederick's engagement."

Allison let out a deep sigh. "My parents would have approved of Frederick. Unfortunately, all of our parents are dead."

"I'm sorry to hear that, Miss Jacoby. Who will give you away?"

"I have an uncle who lives in Denver. He'll fill in for my father."

"That's good." The professor tweaked his beard.

The train rumbled around another bend.

Shultz pointed out the right window. "We're passing Maxwell Pitch. Notice the water flume and old stage road. On the railroad we also refer to this as Windy Point."

"I can see two pine trees shaking in the breeze," Allison said.

Theodore Shultz rubbed his red nose. "You should have seen this in the blizzard of nineteen-thirteen. The trains couldn't get through in the mountains, and even this close to the city, we encountered huge snow drifts."

"Ah, yes," the professor said. "The year for record snow. Not like the minimal snowfall of this last winter. Quite a contrast."

"Snow began in early December of nineteen-thirteen," Shultz said. "On the run of December third, the storm unloaded, and the train with attached plow barely made it back to Boulder. The next day it got stuck back near Lover's Leap. We added another engine and reached as far as the mouth of Four Mile Canyon. Then we had to return to Boulder."

"That was some blizzard," Lucille said. "I hired a boy to climb up on the roof of my boarding house to clear off the drifts."

"A wise move, my dear. That storm caused damage throughout the city. The records show that forty-three inches of snow fell in Boulder during one week of December."

"And we didn't get the line to Eldora opened for a week," Shultz said. "At the end of December we couldn't even reach

Glacier Lake and were forced to back down to Sunset. The wind whipped the snow into huge drifts, some up to twenty-five feet deep in the cuts along the way. The railroad borrowed a rotary to clear the tracks to Eldora in mid-January. It went off the track west of Hill's siding. How we struggled to get it back on the rails. On the other leg of the railroad from Sunset toward Ward, a train didn't reach Puzzler until May ninth of nineteen-fourteen, a four-month period without railroad service. I've never seen so much snow."

"And an economic nightmare for the railroad owners," the professor added. "It's amazing the havoc old man winter can cause."

"But today we can enjoy the sunshine with no concern about bad weather," Lucille said. "I don't see a cloud in the sky."

The train crossed a trestle supported by sturdy stone bridge emplacements to the south side of the creek.

Professor Sager tapped the back of Harry and Susan's seat as if impatient to say something. "Officer McBride, have you investigated any murders?"

"No. Fortunately, we don't have many in Boulder, and when we do, the police chief takes those. I mainly get involved in smaller types of crimes."

"And what are those?" the professor asked.

"As I mentioned earlier, a lot have to do with whiskey, either transporting it or consuming too much. We must also deal with all types of robberies and thefts. A week ago Friday after nine p.m. two boys robbed the Allen and Eaton grocery store in the Kirkbride block. They stole several dollars' worth of candy, tobacco and cookies. I didn't get there in time to catch them. If something isn't nailed down, someone will try to steal it."

"Isn't that the truth," Lucille Vickering said. "Someone is always trying to beg, borrow or steal. Last month a man tried to snatch a chair from my front porch. One of my boarders saw the pending crime and ran the man off."

"Probably one of your clients, Mr. Compton," the professor said.

"Or one of your students inspired by your lecture, Professor," Daniel replied.

The professor harrumphed. "I doubt that. What other kinds of crimes do you encounter, Officer McBride?"

Harry thought of the earlier altercation between Daniel and Frederick. "Breaking up arguments and fights. A good number of those turn out to be good folks who have indulged in too much whiskey. The worst involve a husband and wife."

"Ah, yes," the professor said. "Holy matrimony often leads to strife."

Lucille swatted him. "I beg your pardon. My late husband and I never resorted to violence."

The professor rubbed his arm. "I don't know, my dear. I seem to have a bruise from your nonviolence. Women can be vindictive."

Lucille raised her chin and looked away from the professor.

Harry remembered the one time he was almost knocked out while on duty. Summoned to a house where neighbors heard loud cursing, he knocked on the door and was met with a string of swear words, foul enough to make a hard-rock miner blush. He stepped inside to see a man holding a hammer and a woman raising a frying pan. He tried to calm them down. Finally, the man dropped the hammer.

Harry made the mistake of stepping between them to put a hand on the man's arm when the woman landed a blow to the side of Harry's head with her frying pan. He reeled but recovered in time to fend off another blow from the woman, who shouted, "Leave my husband alone!"

Harry's recollection was interrupted by a man in tan shorts and hiking boots who came forward and doffed his broad-brimmed hat. "Good morning, ladies and gentlemen. Do any of you enjoy hiking?"

"I have a passion for all things outdoors," the professor said.

"Excellent," the man replied. "Let me give all of you brochures on our Rocky Mountain Climbers Club."

He handed them to the professor and Lucille. Allison and Harry took one, but Frederick and Daniel waved the man off.

The professor skimmed through the brochure. "I've heard of your group but never attended a meeting. Tell me more."

A broad smile crossed the man's tanned face. "We have a club house at Chautauqua that opened last year for our meetings, and we go on regular expeditions into the mountains. Today, we'll be getting off at Glacier Lake to hike and camp overnight."

"So you won't be returning with us this afternoon?" Allison asked.

"No, miss. We'll be spending the night under the stars."

The professor studied the brochure intently. "Didn't your group have a different name at one time?"

"Very astute. We were founded as the Chautauqua Climbers Club in eighteen-ninety-eight and changed our name to the Rocky Mountain Climbers Club in nineteen-oh-eight." He chuckled. "We wanted a larger name to represent that we covered the Rocky Mountains and not just the hiking area around the Boulder Chautauqua."

"I enjoyed your animated singing," Susan said.

The man rolled his eyes. "What we lack in musical ability, we make up for in enthusiasm. We welcome any of you to come to one of our meetings. We're encouraging new members to join. Climbing is an invigorating activity. It requires persistence and perseverance—you have to keep going no matter what the terrain." He tipped his hat again and returned to his companions.

"How come you never suggest going hiking?" Susan said to Harry.

He regarded his wife with a raised eyebrow. "With all the walking I do while on duty, you can understand that in my spare time I have no desire to further test my feet."

"I promise to not make you hike too far in Eldora."

The train recrossed the creek over another trestle to the north side of the canyon and continued its steady climb upward.

"How steep is this grade?" Lucille asked.

Conductor Shultz heard the question and replied, "The roadbed was dug for a three-percent grade—a three-foot rise for every hundred feet of track. That allows the engine and tender to pull three fully loaded cars and a caboose without slipping. We have a few places that exceed that grade and have to be careful through those. We have to make sure we don't stop on too steep a section where we'll have trouble starting again."

"It's bad enough to have Professor Sager pontificating all the time," Frederick said with a growl. "Now we have the conductor giving lectures as well."

"I beg your pardon." Shultz stepped in front of Frederick. "We don't need any snide comments from the peanut gallery."

Frederick shot to his feet and put his face inches from Shultz's. "Are you trying to insult me, you interfering busybody?"

Harry let out an exasperated groan and stood to separate the two men. "Gentlemen, once again I suggest you temper your emotions. We have entirely too much threat and posturing going on. This is a Sunday outing, not a brawl. I don't care about your past arguments. It's time to put those to rest."

"I'll say," the conductor replied. "I have work to do." He pushed past Harry and headed to the back of the passenger car.

Frederick's eyes followed Shultz's departure, flaring with intense anger. Then he dropped back into his seat.

Harry waited a moment and also sat down. He whispered to Susan, "There's enough heat in this compartment to keep the engine's boiler going all the way to Eldora."

The train rattled across another trestle to the south side of the creek.

"Frederick, I wish you'd control your temper," Allison said.

"I want to be left alone."

"Does that include from me as well?" she asked.

Frederick crossed his arms and remained silent.

Michael flicked a shaving that landed on Frederick's shoulder.

Frederick spun to the right to stare at Michael. "Don't go throwing your refuse at me, you imbecile."

"Frederick, don't you dare use that word with Michael. He meant you no harm. It was an accident."

The train jolted and traversed another trestle back to the north side of the creek.

Another chip flew right onto Frederick's shoulder. For the first time on the trip, Michael actually smiled.

CHAPTER 8

The train continued up Boulder Canyon hugging a rock face on the north side of the creek. A large protrusion of rock appeared with a discernible forehead, large nose and receding chin.

Michael looked out the window and pointed. "Face."

Allison leaned across Michael and laughed. "That's Profile Rock. It does look like a face. I think it's an Indian chief."

Daniel Compton looked out his right-side window as well. "I think it resembles a man deep in concentration. Look at the furrowed brow, closed eyes and set mouth. I imagine a distinguished professor."

"Please," Benjamin Sager said. "That hunk of rock doesn't remind me of anyone at the university. It has too much life to it."

Lucille cocked her ear. "Benjamin, you surprise me. I didn't think you ever made fun of your profession."

"Of course I do, my dear. You can't imagine the people I have to put up with. We have numerous stuffed shirts in the academic world."

"Including the present company," Frederick said.

"Ah, what am I hearing? Has the young man with the chip on his shoulder entered the conversation?"

Allison giggled. "Actually, he did have a chip on his shoulder a few minutes ago. One of Michael's wood chips landed there."

"Deliberately." Frederick made an exaggerated motion of dusting off the right shoulder of his coat.

As if in response, Michael sent another chip flying from his carving that landed this time in Frederick's lap.

"See what I mean," Frederick said. "Michael is a menace. He shouldn't be allowed out in public."

"Frederick, what an awful thing to say." Allison patted her brother's arm. "He has as much right as anyone to be on this train. And, Michael, maybe you can next carve a face like the one on Profile Rock."

Michael shook his head vigorously as if to loosen something stuck in his hair. "Only animals, not people."

"That's fine. Your mountain lion looks wonderful."

Michael gave a low growl and returned to his work.

"What are everyone's plans for the Fourth of July celebration on Friday?" Lucille asked. "I know I'm going to watch the Highlanders' concert and drill at Chautauqua in the afternoon. They always put on a spectacular performance."

"And I hope you'll join me, my dear, for dancing in Pearl Street in the evening," the professor replied.

"Of course."

"I'll be in the baseball game at Gamble Field," Daniel said. "We'll be playing Aurora Recuperation Camp."

"Your team won a stunning victory last Fourth of July," Professor Sager said. "If I remember correctly, you beat Longmont."

Daniel turned to Allison, a broad grin on his face. "We won six to five. I had a double and single and made a catch to end the game. I also stole second base."

"I'm sure that's not all you stole," Frederick said.

Daniel glared at his seat companion. "It's too bad your tongue didn't get shot off in the war."

Allison banged her hand on the seatback between Daniel and Frederick. "Can't you two act decently?"

Daniel bit his lip for a moment. "I'll do better, but only

because you asked, Allison." His eyes twinkled. "Are you going to come watch me play in the baseball game on the Fourth?"

Allison patted her hair. "I don't know. It depends on what Frederick wants to do."

"Oh, don't wait for him," Daniel said. "He'll only want to mope around and feel sorry for himself. You need an interesting outing."

"I'm sure we'll go to the parade in the morning on Pearl Street and probably the basket picnic on the courthouse lawn at noon."

"You'll also be able to watch auto races and stunts at four p.m.," Harry added. "I'll be there not as a spectator but on patrol. We need to make sure it's a safe event."

Susan sighed. "Another Fourth of July where I'll have to spend most of the day by myself."

"We'll have the evening to celebrate like everyone else," Harry replied. "I'll be able to join you after the automobile race."

"Ah, those motorcars can get out of control, can't they," the professor said. "They certainly have changed our fair city with all the noise and smoke. Still, it's a sign of progress. Horses have their own way of fouling the city." He winked at Lucille, who turned her head away from him and wrinkled her nose.

"I enjoy the reading of the Declaration of Independence and the speech at the courthouse square," Susan said. "Last year Bishop McConnell gave a resounding address."

"And don't forget the aerial bombing," Harry said. "We'll have the fire brigade on duty in case a fire starts."

"And there will be a war picture, *Under Your Flag*, shown at Chautauqua at night. Frederick may not want to see that, though." Daniel elbowed his seat companion who ignored the comment.

Lucille said, "I'm more interested in the motion picture being shown at the Curren Theater this coming Wednesday and

Thursday, *The Unpardonable Sin*. It stars Blanche Sweet. Are you going to come with me, Benjamin?"

"I expect so, my dear, if you want to attend on Wednesday. I have a faculty meeting on Thursday evening."

"I thought you had the summer to yourself."

"I do. But several of us at the university have been asked to participate in lectures this summer, first for the twenty-second session of the Chautauqua, which runs from July fourth through the end of August, and second for an afternoon and evening lecture series that's open to the public. For that later series, I'll be speaking on the new spirit in industry, the task of industrial manufacturing and, for you ladies, the feminine revolution."

"How revolting," Daniel said.

Benjamin made a gagging sound. "Another atrocious statement from our supposed live wire, Mr. Compton."

Daniel smirked.

The professor continued, "So, my dear, the faculty participating in these two lecture events have a final planning meeting on the evening of Thursday, July third."

Lucille gave a pronounced pout. "Then you will find time for me on Wednesday. We can choose between shows at seven and nine."

"We'll attend the nine o'clock showing. That will give me time to complete my preparation for the next day's meeting."

Susan turned around to speak to Lucille. "I'm trying to get Harry to take me to see *Sunnyside* with Charlie Chaplin Monday or Tuesday at the Iris Theatre."

Harry grunted. "I'm not much for that little man with the moustache. I'd rather take in *The Knickerbocker Buckaroo.*"

"You do like those westerns with lots of shooting." Susan nudged him. "That will be fine as well. It stars the handsome Douglas Fairbanks."

"To say nothing of having Marjorie Daw as a leading lady." Harry wiggled his eyebrows at his wife.

"It's all right for me to notice the leading man, but you're not supposed to pay attention to the leading lady."

Harry groaned. "I supposed next you're going to become a suffragette."

"Well, of course. I hope all women in our country will be able to vote very soon."

"That will become a reality," the professor said. "In eighteen-ninety-three Colorado was the second state to allow women to vote, but I expect we'll have a new amendment to the constitution within a year to allow the fairer sex to vote throughout our country. England allowed a number of women to vote last year, and the United States won't be far behind."

"I'm already outvoted in my household," Harry said.

"Cheer up, Officer McBride. That's what we men have to look forward to. I'm sure Lucille will cancel out my vote as well."

"Only if you don't use it intelligently," Lucille replied. "Now don't forget that we're committed to the movie show on Wednesday."

"In addition to all the fine motion pictures, the Hagenbeck and Wallace circus is coming to town on July eighteenth," Allison said. "I'd take Michael, except seeing the live animals upsets him."

Smoke from the engine drifted past the windows on the left side of the train as it journeyed along Four Mile Creek and headed up Four Mile Canyon. The barren hillside here resembled that of Boulder Canyon.

"This is the last you'll see of Boulder Creek until we pass over it again right before reaching the Blue Bird mine," Conductor Shultz said. "Our next stop will be at Orodell."

The train disappeared into the shadow of the nearby hills. A chill ran through the passenger car as it continued on its mountain journey.

CHAPTER 9

The passenger compartment remained quiet, the occupants musing over their own thoughts. The car rattled, and Allison grabbed the seat in front of her. "Oh."

"There's no problem, Miss Jacoby," the professor said. "Only a section of track needing a little repair. It probably settled slightly."

Allison gave a wan smile. "That's reassuring."

The train slowed.

Conductor Shultz strolled up the aisle from the back of the car. "Orodell isn't a regular stop, but we have a signal, so there is probably a passenger to pick up to take to Sunset or Eldora. No station here, and there won't be enough time to get off to stretch your legs."

The train jerked to a stop as steam blew past the windows.

True to the conductor's word, the train started moving again within a minute.

"This railroad will stay on time," the professor said. "Very efficient."

"We stick with our schedule," Schultz said. "During the summer we have few delays. Unless a brown bear decides to block the tracks."

"Has that happened?" Allison asked.

"I'm kidding. We've had problems with animals standing on the tracks, but the sound of the whistle scares them away. No, we should have nothing to delay us today. Next stop, Chrisman." Shultz headed forward into the other car.

Lucille leaned across the aisle toward Allison. "I'm planning to pick wildflowers in Eldora. Are you?"

"Why, yes. I want to decorate my room. There's nothing like wild sage, yarrow and blue flax to liven up the decor."

"I'm hoping to find some columbines," Lucille said. "The soft bluish purple is delightful and adds to the reception area of my boarding house."

"Sounds like you've found some fellow flower lovers on this trip," Harry said to Susan.

Susan turned back toward the other two women. "I'll also be collecting flowers. I particularly like chiming bells and golden banner. To say nothing of wild roses. I plan to put a large bouquet in my dining room when we return today."

"It sounds like the poor hillsides around Eldora will be ravaged by these aggressive women," the professor said. "Can't you arrest them, Officer McBride? I want to enjoy the wildflowers in their natural habitat, not in a pot in a living room."

Harry chuckled. "I think anyone trying to stop them would require emergency medical treatment."

"A shame. A shame."

Lucille patted Benjamin's arm. "Don't be such a curmudgeon. You know you'll like to see all the bright colors we bring back."

"It's just that I prefer to enjoy them in their native setting, my dear."

"Do both of you garden?" Susan asked.

"I don't have time any longer with all the boarders I have to take care of," Lucille said. "I have a young man who takes care of the yard. One of these days I'll get back to planting and tending flowers."

"I garden when I have free time from the library," Allison said.

The professor snapped his fingers. "That's where I've seen you before. The city library on Pine."

"I've worked there for two years."

"Excellent," the professor said. "We're both in the book business. I write them and you help people find them."

"What have you written, Professor Sager?" Allison asked.

"Oh, don't get him started," Lucille said. "What hasn't he written?"

"Don't be so sarcastic, my dear. Just because I'm a prolific writer. I specialize in Colorado history. Our state has a most colorful history of how gold and silver lured men to comb the hills, a few successful, but most giving up after nearly starving to death. I've also written a great deal on the subject of societal trends. I've researched the development of the temperance and prohibition movement. I can assure you it won't last for long."

"How can you say that, Professor?" Allison said. "We've finally made progress on outlawing whiskey. I myself plan to attend the weeklong Woman's Christian Temperance Union conference at Chautauqua starting August seventeenth."

"Ah, the WCTU." The professor cleared his throat. "A group of women intent on reforming all of us profligate men."

Allison set her jaw. "I beg to differ, Professor. It's a fine group with good intentions."

"Yes, Miss Jacoby. But one of the lessons of history is that a movement of . . . uh . . . shall I say zealots can only last so long. The general population will object, and in a few years prohibition will be reversed."

"Z—zealots," Allison sputtered.

"Don't take it personally, Miss Jacoby. History has shown it is extremely difficult to legislate morality. Eventually, people will realize it's better to legalize whiskey again and collect taxes on it, rather than have people with stills in the woods race around in motorcars distributing it and trying to avoid Officer McBride.

Sanity will reign and the government will reverse its course. They have given in to the shrill chorus of temperance advocates but will reconsider in due time."

Allison sniffed and turned her head toward Michael.

Lucille laughed. "Oh, Miss Jacoby, don't be insulted by Benjamin's tirade. He does that to everyone and on all subjects. He loves to lord it over others and their viewpoints, which he considers inferior to his own. Right, Benjamin?"

Professor Sager stared at his seat companion for a moment as if trying to burn a hole through her forehead.

"Don't give me your professor's glare," Lucille said. "I'm not one of your students whom you can easily intimidate."

"He hasn't changed at all," Frederick said. "Trying to be the expert and disparage other viewpoints. I'm surprised the university puts up with the old codger."

"So your war experience makes you an expert on universities, does it?" the professor replied. "I would have hoped that you returned with some useful life experiences, but it appears you've only wasted your time as a doughboy."

"I've had my experiences." Frederick's voice vibrated with a deep menace. "You sit here in your safe little town with no understanding of trench foot and mustard gas. If you'd been with us in the trenches during the Second Battle of the Marne, you wouldn't act like such a pompous ass."

"My, I do detect some emotion from the scarred soldier," the professor said.

"Frederick has shrapnel in his leg, Professor," Allison said. "You're as bad as he at insulting people, but at least he has an excuse."

"Ah, well stated, Miss Jacoby. Frederick, you're a lucky man to have such a lovely defender of your erratic behavior."

"Can't we get back to discussing wildflowers?" Susan asked.

Allison bit her lip. "That would be preferable."

"I hope to find a place with cinquefoils," Lucille said. "You know they're a member of the rose family."

"Now look who's pontificating," the professor said.

"Oh, bother," Lucille said. "You can't stand anyone else being an expert on anything. Have any of you ladies tried the Hoover electric suction sweeper?"

Allison shook her head.

"I still use my trusty broom," Susan said.

"You must try it. It's absolutely amazing. I can clean the floors in the boarding house in half the time. I also got a gas stove waffle iron at the same time. My boarders love my waffles."

"You are a walking advertisement to all that the twentieth century has to offer for women," the professor said.

The train's whistle blew, and the conversation ceased. Sunlight streamed into the car. Harry turned his gaze to the window, only seeing the bare hills but anticipating the beautiful panoramas that awaited.

CHAPTER 10

Past Orodell, the train entered a narrow cut away from Four Mile Creek.

Allison shivered. "It looks like those rocks might tumble right down on us."

From across the aisle the professor said, "Have no fear, Miss Jacoby. Care was taken in digging this route through the rocks."

"I'm amazed at how few trees we see in the canyons above Boulder," Lucille said. "Look at the ravished hillsides."

"It's very simple, my dear," Professor Sager replied. "The trees have been cut and burned. You can blame it on mining."

"Oh, dear. I think I'm going to hear another lecture."

Susan turned around. "I'm curious, too. After living here all these years, I have the same question."

Lucille adjusted her hat. "Don't encourage him, Mrs. McBride. He'll talk for the whole rest of the trip. Once he gets started, there's no way to turn him off."

"Now, now, my dear. Since Mrs. McBride is also interested, I feel I owe it to both of you to give a good explanation." The professor paused, and once assured that both pairs of female eyes rested upon him, continued. "In the middle of the nineteenth century many more trees populated this canyon. Then the miners arrived looking for gold in the surrounding hills. They cut trees for firewood and for timber to hold up the mineshafts that they had dug into the mountainside. No need to import wood when so much was readily available right here."

"They didn't need so much timber as to leave these hillsides completely bare," Lucille said.

"That's correct, my dear. The sad part of the damage done to these hills resulted from another practice instigated by people searching for gold. They burned forests to expose rock outcrops. They sought quartz as an indicator of nearby gold, but it was difficult to locate rock outcrops in a forested area. Burning the trees allowed them to more easily spot the rocks."

"Seems like a very wasteful process," Susan said.

The professor adjusted his thick glasses. "Definitely for the forest, but the miners justified it. Burning down the trees provided a means to find their precious gold, and they had no concern for anything else. All a matter of perspective."

"But even after all the gold has been mined, it will be years before trees grow back," Lucille said.

"Very true, my dear. The price for the pendant on your neck."

Lucille's hand went to her throat, and she fingered her gold locket hanging from a gold chain.

"That is a lovely pendant," Susan said. "It goes well with your dress and highlights your creamy complexion. Have you had it long?"

"Yes. It belonged to my mother. She bought it in New York, so it didn't come from gold in these hills." Lucille thrust up her nose in Benjamin's direction.

The professor chuckled. "Don't be so sure. Colorado gold has been used in fine jewelry throughout the country." He reached into a sack on the floor and took out a handful of nuts. "It's time for my mid-morning meal. Would anyone care for my special mixture of walnuts, almonds and hazelnuts?"

All of them shook their heads.

The professor popped several nuts into his mouth and chewed.

"You and your health diet," Lucille said.

The professor patted his stomach. "It's kept me very fit, my dear. I might live to be a hundred."

"And be incorrigible the whole time," she said.

"Now, now. Just because I know the secret of long life doesn't mean you have to ridicule it. I've made my own improvements to the health teachings of Doctor John Harvey Kellogg."

Allison leaned across the aisle. "I've heard that name before. Isn't he the man who has that sanitarium in Michigan?"

"That's correct, Miss Jacoby. The Battle Creek Sanitarium run by Dr. Kellogg was founded by the Seventh-Day Adventists, the same religious organization that built our own Boulder Sanitarium in eighteen-ninety-five. Dr. Kellogg is an intelligent and wise man. I'm a staunch advocate of his health regime."

Harry also turned around to join the conversation. "I'm not familiar with his health program."

"Ah, Officer McBride. An active man like you would benefit from Dr. Kellogg's procedures. They do wonders for the body and soul. Dr. Kellogg developed techniques including hydropathy, electropathy, mechanotherapy, breathing exercises and radium cures. He's put together a whole series of methods to keep people healthy. I'm sure you'd also benefit from phototherapy, exposure to sunlight."

"I get enough sunlight during my daytime patrols," Harry said.

"Yes, you do have a solid complexion, Officer McBride. But the most important part is Dr. Kellogg's specified diet and bowel cleansing."

Susan crinkled her nose and turned away.

"This may offend some of the ladies present, but it's important to good health to cleanse the bowels regularly. Equally critical is the type of food we eat. Dr. Kellogg has found that ninety percent of illness originates in the stomach and intestines. You're only as healthy as the food you put into your mouth. I have become a strong advocate of Dr. Kellogg's recommendations to avoid meat and to eat grains, nuts, yogurt, vegetables and fruit."

"Didn't Dr. Kellogg start that cereal company?" Allison asked.

"He developed corn flakes, but his brother Will Keith Kellogg started the W. K. Kellogg Company, one of the providers of breakfast cereals."

"I ate a bowl of corn flakes this morning," Harry said.

"That's because we slept late and didn't have time for bacon and eggs," Susan said. "I know it's your last resort."

The professor frowned. "You will want to avoid bacon, Mrs. McBride. Beef and pork do you only harm. It congeals in the gut and causes distress and discomfort. Whereas the foods I've recommended aid continuous and healthy flow through your system."

"Oh, we can't give up meat. Besides, Harry loves steak and pork chops."

"It keeps me going for my long hours on duty," Harry said. "I don't think lettuce and spinach will suffice for what I have to do."

The professor smoothed his beard. "You'd have much more energy on Dr. Kellogg's diet. You most likely come home tired at the end of your shift."

"Of course. After I've walked for ten straight hours, that's understandable."

"It doesn't have to be that way. With proper diet, you can return to your loving wife in the evening as fresh as you started in the morning."

Frederick turned and gawked at the professor. "I doubt that. You're full of hot air like those observation balloons I saw hanging in the sky during the war."

"There you go, young man. Once again misinformed. If I taught you nothing else in my classes, you should have learned to get your facts straight. First of all, the balloons you witnessed were filled with hydrogen, not hot air. Second, I'm telling you the secret of a scientifically tested good diet. You can eat yourself to death on meat or follow a regimen that will allow you to live a long and full life."

"I'll take my chances," Frederick said. "I hope you choke on your hazelnuts."

"Frederick!" Allison shouted. "What a thing to say."

Michael looked up from his carving at the sound of Allison's loud voice. Agitated, he rocked in his seat.

"It's all right, Michael." Allison grabbed her brother's arm and tried to calm him. "I'm sorry I shouted."

He continued to rock and stared down toward his feet.

The train began to slow.

"Approaching Chrisman," Theodore Shultz called as he reentered the passenger car. "Milepost six point two, elevation six thousand, three hundred feet."

"I hope you get off and stay there, Shultz," Frederick called out. "And you can take the loudmouth professor with you."

Harry suddenly wondered if he should be back in Boulder arresting Saturday-night drunks who were sleeping off their hangovers in the alleys off Pearl, or chasing bootleggers, rather than being in the midst of this crowd. The only saving grace— this opportunity to spend the day with Susan. He looked out the window as the train pulled into the station, which consisted of the two-story wooden Farnsworth general store. He thought of suggesting they terminate their journey here, but Susan was intent on finding her wildflowers at the Eldora terminus. Maybe the rest of the trip into the mountains would be calm and peaceful.

In spite of his hope, his policeman's intuition told him that would not be the case.

CHAPTER 11

The train left the Chrisman station and continued up Four Mile Canyon, slowly gaining speed as the wheels click-clacked over the rails. A breeze kicked up dirt on the bare hillside and swirled like a tiny tornado. The sharp aroma of burning wood permeated the passenger car.

"In addition to train smoke, I smell a campfire," Lucille said. "Maybe set by another group of climbers."

"Or it might be a miner warming his coffee," the professor said. "People are still searching to this day for gold in these hills."

"Did many of those miners become rich, Benjamin?"

"No, my dear. Most gave up after finding little, if any, gold. Others were employed by mine owners and worked long and difficult hours. The gold rush had the same thing in common in California, Colorado and the Alaskan Klondike. Many men saw the chance for riches and suffered, died or returned as paupers."

"While their women waited for them," Lucille added.

"In some cases, or more likely gave up on them."

"I would wait for Frederick if he were a miner," Allison said. "I remained here for him after the Great War."

"A most noble gesture, Miss Jacoby. I'm not sure Frederick deserves it."

Frederick turned and glared at the professor.

Conductor Shultz stopped by again. "Ladies and gentlemen. We're approaching the most hazardous section of track on the whole Switzerland Trail railroad."

Allison clutched the seat in front of her. "Oh, no. Are we in danger?"

Shultz gave Allison an indulgent smile. "Not at all. We're going uphill. It's only a problem coming downhill at excessive speed through this stretch. Although I will warn you that the curve ahead at Black Swan was the scene of a fatal accident on July fifth, nineteen-fifteen. Given the sharp turn and the steep grade, one of the only sections of tracks exceeding four percent, locomotive number thirty was unable to negotiate the curve successfully on that fateful day."

Allison's eyes widened. "What happened?"

Schultz grinned at the young woman's attention. "The tender derailed. The combination baggage and coach car raced ahead, shearing the side of the engine where the engineer stood. Steam shot up. Everyone escaped except for the fireman, who died from either being crushed or scalded."

Tears formed in Allison's eyes. "That's horrible."

Shultz jutted out his chin. "I can assure you nothing like that will occur today."

"Did the passengers escape injury from the accident?" Lucille asked.

"One passenger car turned on its side. A number of people were treated for scrapes and bruises but no serious injuries. That train followed the same route back from Eldora you will take this afternoon. Another train was dispatched from Boulder to rescue the passengers. Everyone returned safely."

"Except for the unfortunate fireman," Daniel said. "Have there been many derailments on the Switzerland Trail?"

"Trying to figure out if you can sue someone?" Frederick asked.

"Just curious."

Shultz set his lips. "We have an excellent safety record for the number of trips taken through this winding mountain route. Infrequent derailments besides the Black Swan event and only a few deaths. I'd venture a guess that it's much safer to travel on this railroad than in any of those new fangled motorcars."

"That's true," Harry said. "We've dealt with a number of accidents where drivers went too fast and took out light poles, fences and even a livery stable. To say nothing of those who have too much whiskey before they drive an automobile."

"That goes to show why prohibition is so necessary." Allison raised her chin.

"The prohibition party has spoken again," the professor said. "I promise you, Miss Jacoby, I won't take a sip from my flask if I'm going to get behind the wheel of an automobile."

"You shouldn't be taking a sip at any time," Allison answered.

Professor Sager chuckled. "Medicinal purposes."

Allison shook a finger at him. "If your Dr. Kellogg is associated with the Seventh-Day Adventists, I'm sure he doesn't approve of whiskey."

"Astute observation, Miss Jacoby. You're right. Dr. Kellogg is equally adamant as you regarding prohibition. His one blind spot."

"Here's the Black Swan curve," Shultz said.

The car tilted and Allison grabbed the seat in front again. "Frederick, you'll save me if anything happens."

"I suppose."

"Not a ringing endorsement from your fiancé, I must say." Daniel tipped his hat toward Allison.

"He's in his grumpy mood right now," Allison replied.

"Which he seems to have been in since we left the Boulder station." Daniel nudged his seat companion. "Frederick, do you even remember how to smile?"

"Stay out of this." Frederick clenched his fists.

Daniel held his hands up. "All right. Don't be so testy."

Harry eyed the two men, making sure they weren't going to come to blows again. When all appeared calm for the moment, he reached in his jacket pocket and pulled out a packet of Camel cigarettes. Before he raised one to his lips, Susan placed a hand on his arm. "Please don't smoke today. You know I don't like it."

"There's nothing wrong with a little tobacco," Harry replied.

"Listen to your wife," the professor said. "That's another thing I've learned from Doctor Kellogg. Tobacco only leads to poor health."

"Tell that to half the population," Harry said.

"Hopefully people will start paying attention to Doctor Kellogg's advice. Much like putting bad food in your stomach, the lungs shouldn't be fouled with cigarette smoke."

Harry returned the cigarettes to his pocket. He knew when he was outnumbered.

"Thank you," Susan whispered.

Harry didn't know what this world was coming to. Whiskey outlawed, women soon voting throughout the whole country, and people objecting to tobacco. His life was changing so fast he couldn't keep up.

"I still have a package of nuts, Officer McBride," the professor said. "They will do you more good and will take your mind off cigarettes."

"No thanks." That's all he needed. To be carrying around a bag of nuts while on patrol. He'd be the laughing stock of the city. *Look, there's officer, McBride. His wife doesn't feed him well so he has to forage like a bear in autumn.*

"I'll try a few," Lucille said.

Benjamin handed her the sack of nuts, and she helped herself to a handful.

The train rattled past the Black Swan mine. One old man sat on a rock, sharpening a knife. "Someone else out there is getting ready to carve, like you do, Michael," Daniel said. "Maybe the guy wants your wood."

Michael looked out the window and started to twitch. The twitching became rocking and then arm flapping.

"It's all right," Allison said in a comforting voice. "Daniel is only making conversation. No one will interfere with your carving."

Michael's arms flapped more wildly.

Frederick turned around. "What's wrong with him? He looks like a wounded bird trying to take off."

Allison shot a dark glare at Frederick. "It's his way of relaxing." She turned to Michael. "You're fine. Take a deep breath."

Michael breathed deeply and dropped his arms to his side. He took another breath and started humming.

"There, that's better," Allison said.

"Most unusual behavior," the professor said.

"Michael often hums. It helps him calm down after being upset. He'll relax if Frederick and Daniel leave him alone."

"I apologize." Daniel bowed toward Allison. "I didn't realize I said something to upset your brother. You're up for an apology as well, Frederick."

Frederick stared straight ahead. The young man's intense gaze was strong enough to burn a hole in the wood, much as a focused beam of light through a magnifying glass could start a fire.

CHAPTER 12

The passenger car rattled from side to side as the train continued to climb, reaching a steep section below Salina. Light played through the compartment as the sun reappeared behind the surrounding cliffs. A strong aroma of Limburger cheese permeated the air from one of the climbers who opened a package of the pungent food to share with his companions. Background conversations drifted down the aisle as members of the climbing group told their stories, recounted recent events and impressed their friends with their latest accomplishments. For a moment the tension of the earlier part of the journey seemed to be relieved.

Harry had become used to the gentle swaying of the car, and his eyes closed. He could easily fall asleep after the hard work he'd done over the last week. He had chased a robber for five blocks before nabbing him in an alley off Pearl near Fifteenth. The man put up quite a fight before Harry subdued him with a nightstick. All that effort to recover fifteen dollars stolen from the Boulderado Hotel. Those incidents were rare. He preferred dealing with the regular complaints—a horse roaming in Mrs. Hendrick's garden or the Saturday-night drunks that needed to be cleared off the courthouse lawn.

He thought of all the patrols that lay ahead of him this coming week, in preparation for and during the July Fourth festivities. He'd have to be extra vigilant, as the holiday brought on more celebrations, drinking, fights and general rowdiness. In spite of the happy revelers, there existed the sad consequence of a large celebration—those who lost control and caused public outrage. The jail would be fully occupied by the end of next weekend. For a city, state, and soon country not allowing whiskey, there was sure a lot of conspicuous consumption and illicit liquor trafficking going on. As the professor had said, Harry also didn't know how long this whole prohibition ordinance could last.

"Next stop, Salina," Conductor Shultz announced.

"Ah, the town founded by settlers from the town of the same name in Kansas," the professor said. "And the Melvina mine near here produced tellurium valued at five hundred dollars a ton in the early eighteen-eighties."

"You know so much about towns in these mountains," Lucille said. "If I ever have any questions, I know who to ask."

The professor chuckled at the compliment. "As you know, that's one of my areas of expertise—history of mining towns."

As the train slowed, Harry opened his eyes to see the mountain desolation, offset by a few wooden shacks. This was a prime prospecting area, and miners still pulled gold out of the shafts dotting the hillside. He smiled to himself. He had never succumbed to the lure of searching for treasure. That's why he was a policeman. He liked having the run of Boulder, nodding to citizens as he strolled the streets, greeting children before they scampered away, and maintaining order. That was his calling, not the solitary life of one pursuing the allure of unreachable gold.

The locomotive pulled the two Pullman cars past the station, a twenty-by-thirty-foot wooden building with a wooden platform on all sides. The rails hugged a cliff, and a stream ran on the other side of the depot. Harry caught a glimpse inside the one-story frame station house, its wide open entryway leading into a darkened interior. Several passengers were waiting.

"Why is the train going past the depot?" Harry asked.

"Right by the station is a steep section of track," Shultz replied. "It's a more gentle incline above the station and easier for the locomotive to start again."

Once the train came to a complete stop, a man with a large drooping mustache helped a woman in a full white dress load a large valise aboard the passenger car ahead. No passengers disembarked. Conductor Schultz, who had gone to help the new passengers, stood on the dirt outside, took his watch from his vest pocket and checked the time.

Frederick and Daniel stretched. Harry used the opportunity to rise and loosen his stiff legs. He was used to being on his feet, but not sitting as he had for the last forty-five minutes— that is, except for the brief exertion he'd endured to break up altercations between Frederick and other people he alienated.

Frederick limped to the opening between their car and the one ahead and stood on the outside metal plate. Lucille stepped into the aisle and allowed Benjamin to join Harry and Daniel at the front of the car.

"Do either of you gentlemen own a motorcar?" Benjamin asked.

"Can't afford it on a policeman's pay," Harry said. "I hope to drive one periodically when the city gives the police department an automobile."

"I expect to be able to buy one within several years," Daniel said. "I've been saving toward a purchase."

"Your defense of poor miscreants must be more lucrative than I would have expected, young man."

Daniel sighed loudly. "Professor, you choose some of the most interesting words. But yes, I should soon have enough money to travel in style."

Benjamin placed his hand on the back of Harry's abandoned seat. "I have my eye on a Maxwell. I think I'll have to make the investment before the year is out."

Daniel imitated someone holding a steering wheel in his hands. "I can't imagine you driving through town like one of those bootleggers. Are you ready to scare off all the remaining horses in town?"

"No, my boy. I'll be a sedate driver. I'm sure Lucille will enjoy being taken for rides into the countryside. She can fix picnics, and I'll provide the transportation."

"That would be lovely," Lucille said from behind him. "How soon can we plan an outing?"

"Once I make my purchase, my dear. So, Daniel, what kind of motorcar are you interested in?"

"I'll go with a Ford. Nothing ostentatious for me," Daniel replied. "Simple transportation for a lawyer of the people."

"Automobiles are the wave of the future," the professor said. "In no time at all everyone will be driving them. And consider the impact they will have on other means of transportation. It's sad, but a trip like we're taking today may not be possible much longer. With the financial problems the Switzerland Trail railroad faces, by this autumn there might no longer be journeys like this available."

"Then it's a good thing we're here today," Harry said. "Enjoying the last of this way of life."

"True. True. After providing passenger service and supporting mines for the last thirty years, I'm afraid our little railroad may be destined for the scrapheap. We'll soon see motor trucks carrying essentials into the hills and bringing ore down to the plains."

"That can't be as economical," Daniel said.

"Not at first, but once roads are built, the motor vehicles will be able to move easily and inexpensively up and down through these mountains. Look at what those Stanley Steamers are doing on the trip to Estes Park. Quite remarkable. Yes, gentlemen,

I will join the motor set soon. And, Officer McBride, I hope the city council gathers their wits and finances a motorcar for you and your fellow policemen."

"We'll see when they open their pocketbooks," Harry said. "They haven't given any sign of relenting yet."

"Hopefully they'll come to their senses," Daniel said. "Then the next decision will be what kind of automobile to purchase for you police officers."

The professor sat up straight. "That's the beauty of commerce in our fine country. There are many choices."

"That's right," Daniel said. "You get to choose your strange diet, and I can eat delicious steaks as much as I want."

Benjamin shook a finger at Daniel. "It will kill you, boy. Stay away from that red meat. You'll never live to my age."

"Oh, I think I will and enjoy what I eat all the while. None of your horse oats and donkey straw for me."

Frederick returned to the compartment. "If you experts have finished spouting off regarding everything you both know nothing about, get out of the way so I can sit."

The professor stepped back toward his seat. "Of course. I don't want to inconvenience the returning war hero any more than necessary."

Daniel slid into his seat, and Frederick gave the professor an angry glare before sitting as well.

Once Harry was sure there would be no new bout of pugilism, he dropped into the seat next to Susan. The train shook and began to move forward.

"Ten minutes to Wall Street," Conductor Shultz shouted. "Our next stop."

Harry looked across the aisle at Frederick.

The young man stared straight ahead, eyes in cold concentration with fists once again clenched as if he expected to defend himself at any moment.

CHAPTER 13

The train built up speed, and Michael sent a few more shavings toward Frederick, who ignored the chips as they fell on his shoulder and lap.

Then Michael hunched over, stuck his tongue out the side of his mouth and concentrated on some detailed work with his knife. He seemed undisturbed by the motion of the passenger car as it sped along the tracks, gained altitude and headed up a valley between Sugarloaf and Gold Hill.

Finally, Michael arched his back, dusted some wood chips off his pants and handed the carved mountain lion to Allison. "Done."

Allison studied it carefully, and a smile broke across her face. "Why, Michael, this is wonderful."

"May I see his carving?" Susan asked.

"Is that all right with you?" Allison asked her brother.

Michael nodded and looked out the window. He appeared as engrossed in watching the hillside as he had been in carving.

Allison leaned forward and handed the completed mountain lion across the aisle to Harry, who inspected it and passed it on to Susan.

Lucille watched the carving change hands. "I once hired a carver to create an eagle on an old cottonwood tree that died in my backyard. Does Michael ever do large carvings?"

"No," Allison replied. "He only likes to work with pieces of wood small enough to carry with him. He prefers to hold the object he's working on. I tried to get him to carve on a log once, but it only made him nervous."

There was a lot more than getting nervous going on with that young man, Harry thought. Still, Michael exhibited a unique talent.

Susan turned the wooden mountain lion over in her hand. "This is remarkable. So intricate. Has he sold any of his work?"

"Not yet," Allison replied. "So far, he doesn't want to part with what he creates. He keeps most of his carvings on a shelf in his room. It's as if a whole zoo lives on that shelf. Even though he has carved the same kinds of animals numerous times, each carving is distinct. His other mountain lions aren't as wild-looking as the one he created today."

"This is the most lifelike image of a mountain lion I've ever seen." Susan handed it back to Harry, who took another look.

His wife was right. The figure came alive with a fierce expression on its face and appeared ready to leap on its prey. The teeth were sharp and similar to ones on a mountain lion killed by a sheriff's deputy last year. That animal had attacked a farmer's sheep. It was subsequently tracked down and shot. Harry wasted no love on mountain lions. They stalked deer but also attacked livestock and pets. Mountain lions made bad companions for a growing town, particularly with young children running loose.

Harry handed the carving back to Allison. "Much better than carvings I've seen for sale in Boulder."

Allison took it and put it in her carpetbag. "Do you hear that, Michael? Mr. and Mrs. McBride think you could sell your carvings."

Michael twitched, followed by arm flapping. "Not now." He started rocking.

Allison put her hand on his arm. "That's all right. We won't sell any of them until you want to. We'll keep them right where they are." She reached in her carpetbag and pulled out a fresh piece of wood. "I know you'll want to whittle some more. What will you make next?" She peered toward her brother. "A cat or dog?"

Michael continued rocking and said nothing.

"Maybe a cow or pig?"

No response.

"A crow or a hawk?"

Michael stopped rocking and grabbed the pine wood block. He put it to his nose and sniffed loudly. He tapped it with his right index finger and turned it over, inspecting all sides. "Fox." He began carving.

Harry watched this performance. What a strange young man with all his weird tics, but an incredible artist nonetheless.

The professor coughed, as if to catch everyone's attention. "Do any of you know the genesis of the name of our next stop, Wall Street?"

"Must have something to do with New York," Daniel answered. "That's the only other Wall Street I know."

"Very astute, young man. This town has gone by several names over the last forty years. It's been known as Delphi and Sugar Loaf, not to be confused with the Sugarloaf we'll stop at later on our journey today. The name Wall Street originated because Charles Caryl convinced financial backers from New York to invest five million dollars to build a giant mill to process gold from mined ore to finished product in this one location. After purchasing the nearby land in nineteen-oh-one, an assay office was built in Wall Street. The mill was unsuccessful, and after two years it closed. Its immense skeleton lines the hillside we'll pass in a few minutes."

"But there's a station at Wall Street," Lucille said.

"Yes, my dear. And gold mining continues to take place in the hills nearby, just not enough of it to justify a huge mill. At the turn of the century the station was a boxcar on a short section of rails off to the side of the main line."

Lucille groaned. "There you go again with the lecture."

"Please, my dear, you're interrupting pertinent information."

"That only you care about."

The professor ignored her and continued. "As I was getting ready to say, a permanent station replaced the baggage car. Too bad there isn't milled gold to be shipped down to Boulder from here."

"Like many who operate on the New York Wall Street, it sounds as though Caryl was a better promoter than businessman," Daniel said.

"Unfortunately so, young man. Like many entrepreneurs, Caryl had grand ideas that never met financial success. Gold has always brought out enthusiasm, and, in most cases, the reality of extracting the bits of useful material from the mass of rock has not made economic sense. Still, it hasn't kept thousands of men from trying."

"And will not keep others from trying in the future," Lucille said. "You men have your dreams that seldom are achieved."

The professor lowered his thick glasses and looked over his frames at Lucille. "My, my. You have become a cynic."

Frederick turned and set his gaze on Lucille. "She's always been that way. Never had much faith in people."

Lucille straightened her back. "Only for those who don't deserve it. People like you, Frederick Hammond."

Harry looked between Frederick and Lucille, wondering if he needed to prepare to separate a man and woman coming to blows. At that moment the car shook and slowed. Frederick reclenched his fists and stared straight ahead.

Lucille whispered something in the professor's ear that didn't carry to the other passengers through the hiss of steam escaping.

As the train rolled to a stop, Conductor Shultz announced, "Wall Street station. We'll only stop long enough to load and unload passengers." He headed toward the front of the car.

All eyes turned to watch two people step onto the platform from the passenger car ahead: a fat man who doffed his hat to Conductor Shultz, and his companion, a tall, thin, stern-looking woman who wore a prim blouse and black skirt. A large bag was unloaded and placed on the platform. Two men in overalls stepped aboard.

The whistle blew, and in a moment the train was on its way again. To the right they passed the abandoned mill. The large structure included a long horizontal building at the base, a stone wall that reached up thirty feet with another building on top, and two more levels of wooden buildings above that. At the base of the hill rested the remains of a steam-powered pump house. Along the side a tramway had carried coal and supplies. In its short operating career this mill had been fueled by coal brought up on the Switzerland Trail railroad. Now it lay abandoned, metal rusting, wood deteriorating and rocks collapsing. Altogether the mill covered a hundred vertical feet of hillside on the north side of the train. It was a tribute to dreams never realized—now a home to squirrels and mice and not even worth a second glance from Michael, who only carved animals but never people.

CHAPTER 14

The train continued west, climbing higher into the foothills. The passengers remained quiet for a few moments, absorbed in their own thoughts. Michael worked away on his new carving. The head of a fox seemed to spring magically from the block of wood. Chips flew, and Michael kept his full concentration on his creation.

Allison looked over at her brother. Anyone watching her recognized the pride reflected in her eyes.

Conductor Theodore Shultz had been at the rear of the car speaking with members of the climbing club. He made his way forward, stopped in front of Harry and Frederick, and scanned the compartment to check on his charges.

"Any stations before Sunset?" the professor called out.

Shultz leveled his gaze at the professor. "We're approaching Copper Rock. We only stop if the flag is out. We have no passengers getting off there." He regarded his watch. "We'll pass it in five minutes."

Lucille adjusted her bonnet. "All these colorful names of towns in the mountains. Why's it named Copper Rock?"

"There's a rock in the hillside with copper," Shultz replied. "You can see the greenish color as we pass by."

"But copper is reddish orange, not green," Lucille said.

The professor cleared his throat. "Corroded copper turns a light greenish shade. I've seen that color on copper plaques that have been left out in the elements for years. Copper is a most important element. Our telegraph and telephone wires make good use of it."

Frederick groaned. "Another cursed lecture."

Professor Sager harrumphed. "Pay attention, young man, and you may learn something useful."

"That will be the day."

Lucille nudged the professor. "I think we've heard enough on the subject of copper. Have some of your nuts."

"You know I have my strict regimen," the professor replied. "I'm not due for my next meal for an hour."

"Sounds like feeding horses in a stable," Frederick said.

"Watch what you say, young man. I'll have no more of your insolence or I'll request that our fine conductor throw you off the train."

Frederick gave a sardonic laugh. "I'd like to see him try."

Allison clicked her tongue. "Oh, Frederick, can't we have a pleasant day without all the threats?"

"Speaking of threats, there is a threat hanging over the whole future of the Switzerland Trail," the professor said. "As I mentioned earlier, this may be one of the last chances we have to travel this scenic route."

"And I'm sure you're going to tell us more why that is," Lucille said. "Go ahead and enlighten us."

"Of course, my dear. The inciting incident occurred in December of nineteen-seventeen, when the owners of the railroad filed to discontinue service."

"Why didn't they just stop?" Lucille asked. "If I want to close my boarding house, I do it. I don't have to file any fancy paperwork."

"It isn't that simple," the professor replied. "The Colorado Public Utilities Commission authorizes and, to some degree, controls the railroad. Before the owners of the Denver, Boulder and Western can make major changes, such as going out of business, they must submit an official document, and then the PUC must make a ruling. In fact the PUC turned down the request made by the railroad owners in nineteen-seventeen. The DB and W stated that it suffered from a funded debt of seven hundred thousand dollars at five percent interest, inability to pay dividends on the outstanding capital stock of three hundred thousand dollars, and operating expenses and taxes exceeding gross operating revenue for over four years."

"What does all that mean?" Allison leaned across the aisle.

Daniel joined the conversation. "It means that the owners milked the company dry."

"Not so, young man." The professor wagged an index finger at Daniel. "Please desist from your socialist propaganda. The facts were very clear. The railroad was struggling to support itself. The cost of railroad coal increased while the freight traffic decreased. The economic situation became quite gloomy." He waved his hand toward Lucille and Allison. "And not enough wildflower-picking women to support the passenger traffic, particularly because it's quite difficult to find wildflowers in the winter."

Harry pivoted to join the fray. "But obviously, the railroad survived."

"Quite right, Officer McBride." The professor adjusted his jacket. "At a hearing, all sides voiced their opinions. The railroad general manager described the declining revenue. The counsel for the railroad indicated liabilities now exceeded the assets. That's not a picture that encourages investors to keep a business going.

"On the opposing side, a state senator known for representing the interest of a local mining company argued that the owners were only trying to liquidate the railroad because scrap values were high. A number of other local businesses testified in regard to their dependence on the railroad. In the end, the commission allowed the railroad to increase its freight rates, but ruled it must continue to operate."

"But obviously the issue hasn't gone away," Harry said.

"That's correct. In spite of the insistence on the need for the railroad made on behalf of mining interests, with the end of war, the tungsten market completely dried up, and the DB and W laid off workers. Although Boulder businessmen attempted to support the railroad, other freight traffic also decreased. There wasn't enough business to sustain our dear Switzerland Trail. Additional expenses also hit the DB and W last year, when a dam broke in July and washed out a bridge in California Gulch, on the other leg of the railroad route. Amid all this bad economic news, there's no indication that business will pick up in the future."

Harry thought of the police chief's illness. "I'm sure the influenza epidemic didn't help either."

The professor cleared his throat. "No. With so many people sick, many businesses cut back. One more nail in the coffin, so to speak."

At that moment, Shultz called out, "Passing Copper Rock. We're not stopping."

Heads turned to see the sheer cliff overlooking the train.

"To continue," the professor said. "In spring of this year, the owners again requested the Colorado PUC to discontinue operations. This was met by a protest filing from mining interests. In April, the commission ruled that the railroad must continue to operate while additional hearings were conducted. In May, the PUC ordered the railroad owners to file a new petition, and earlier this month they told those who protested the closure they'd have until this coming Tuesday to file a brief outlining their arguments."

Lucille clutched the professor's sleeve. "So the railroad's fate will soon be decided. Everyone must be preparing their final arguments."

"Yes, my dear. All the mining interests, business owners and residents of mountain communities, through their lawyers, will be scrambling to get their viewpoints in front of the commission."

"Typical," Frederick groused. "Attorneys making money at the expense of all these people. Why fiddle around with this useless paperwork? The damned commission should just make a decision."

"It's called due process." Daniel sat erect. "All parties have an opportunity to express their views."

"Yeah, while you lawyers pick everyone's pocket."

"You certainly have a low opinion of the legal profession," Daniel said.

Frederick glared at his seat companion. "Only some of the people who practice."

Daniel snorted. "Coming from someone who does nothing."

"Now, gentlemen." The professor held his hand up as if blessing the poor. "We can argue all day over our legal and administrative systems, but that won't change anything. In July the PUC will reach a decision."

"And I assume you don't expect a positive outcome for the Switzerland Trail," Harry said.

The professor shook his head. "The owners of the DB and W have steadfastly communicated a single message over the last two years. They want to close down the railroad. Other interests have protested, but haven't been able to provide a compelling argument because the railroad business is declining. I don't know how much longer the PUC can force a reluctant ownership to keep this railroad running."

Allison put her hand to her mouth. "That means our conductor will be out of a job."

"No loss," Frederick said.

"I, for one, have a job at the moment and will find something new in the future." Shultz poked his finger in Frederick's chest. "What about you, loafing around?"

Frederick made a move to stand but dropped back in his seat.

The professor clapped his hands once. "Gentlemen, please cease and desist. To all of you, I say, enjoy your excursion in the mountains. It may be your last."

CHAPTER 15

As the train approached the Sunset station, the professor said, "This little community was once known as Pennsylvania Gulch. In the eighteen-eighties the railroad brought lumber down to Boulder from here."

"Not much of that left," Daniel said, pointing out the window.

"No. Like the hillsides we've passed along the way, these slopes were also denuded." The professor straightened his tie. "There were hopes at one time of running this railroad all the way to the Pacific from here. Unfortunately, never realized."

The switch was set for the left trestle leading to Eldora, and the train crossed and pulled to a stop at Sunset. The station resembled a smaller version of the depot in Boulder, with frame rather than stone and without the steep roof and steeple. To the right stood the two-story Columbine Hotel. A man in worn boots sat in a chair on the front porch, smoking. A mutt rested by his feet, eyes focused on the steaming metal monster, but not concerned enough with it to move more than one ear. A young girl skipped along a dirt road, her brown braids bouncing in the breeze.

"Five-minute stop," Shultz announced. "You can get off to stretch your legs but don't be late getting back on. We'll leave without you."

"Ah, yes," the professor said. "Death and the railroad wait for no man."

"I'm getting off," Frederick said, struggling to his feet. He limped through the door and lowered himself to the ground.

"I think I'll stretch as well," Harry said to Susan. "Care to join me for a pleasant five-minute excursion?"

"No, thanks. I'll stay here."

Harry stood, dusted off his pants and proceeded out onto the outside platform of the car. He lowered himself down the two steps, holding onto the handrail, and jumped to the ground. Strolling past the station's large waiting room and freight room, he continued through the town of Sunset with its smattering of wooden structures and sections of track forming a wye for locomotives to turn. This was one of the largest communities along the Switzerland Trail, resting in a valley between the two hillsides. From here, two lines of the railroad continued their separate routes over each hill and into the mountains.

He spotted Frederick looking toward the crumbling building at the entrance to the Sunset-Frances-Ward Tunnel. Harry had toured some of the mines here in his younger days. This particular mine was planned for high-grade gold ore, but it was abandoned after only fifty feet of digging. Like so many of the mountain endeavors, it bespoke high expectations but unrealized hopes.

A wistful expression crossed Frederick's face. He stood motionless, as if in another place, another time, or another reality.

Harry took a deep breath and exhaled loudly. "A beautiful mountain community, don't you think?"

Frederick gave a start and turned. He opened his mouth as if to say something but paused. Then his dark eyes registered recognition of who stood there. "I suppose."

Harry bowed slightly. "I'm sorry to hear of your troubles during the war and your influenza."

"Between the gunfire and the infection, it's been hell. I almost died twice."

"You're a strong young man to survive both."

Frederick eyed Harry warily. "Meaning?"

"Oh, I don't know. As you say, you've been through hell, but you're back in this beautiful country with a lovely young bride-to-be. In spite of all your troubles, you should have a fine future ahead."

Frederick's gaze returned to the hillside, and he remained silent.

Harry felt like he was interrogating an unwilling witness. "Where do you and your fiancée plan to live after you're married?"

"That's undecided. There are so many decisions to make before we get to that point, if we do."

Harry arched an eyebrow. "The wedding plans aren't firm?"

Frederick scuffed his boot in the dirt. "I may go to California."

"Does Miss Jacoby know of this?"

"No."

"Do you intend to take her with you?"

"I think I'll go by myself." Frederick pursed his lips. "I need some time by myself and don't want to be a bother to her. She'd be better off without me."

Harry regarded the young man and decided to be direct. "Although you seem to be doing everything possible to alienate her, she appears ready to stand by your side. She's a fine young woman."

"She is." Frederick reached in his jacket pocket, removed his flask and took a long swig. "She deserves better."

"That may be, but I sense she has resolved to be with you. At the risk of giving unwanted advice, I'd suggest having a long talk with the young lady. She should have a say in what your plans will be."

Frederick put the flask back in his pocket and gave a

dismissive flick of his hand. "As you said, unwanted advice." He turned and limped away.

Harry watched Frederick. What a shame that the Great War had so destroyed the life and vitality of this young man. Nothing Harry could do about it. It would be up to Allison, if anyone, to steer Frederick back onto a reasonable course. How difficult human relationships were with so many directions to go. Compared to this, the railroad was simple. Follow the tracks and go either forward or backward, with no other decisions necessary. Still, trains did derail. Right now Frederick had derailed with little sign of getting back on the tracks.

Harry checked his watch and realized he needed to get back to the passenger car. He climbed aboard as the whistle blew. He wondered if Frederick would make it back in time. The train started moving, and suddenly Frederick appeared, hobbling alongside. He grabbed the handrail and pulled himself up the steps. Another minute and he would have missed the train and been left to wait until they returned in the afternoon.

The engine picked up speed, passed over another trestle at the edge of town and made a turn to the left to head up the south slope above Sunset. The town stretched below outside the left windows.

"We're now on the newest leg of the Switzerland Trail," the professor announced. "The initial tracks laid ran only to Sunset. Then the Ward branch that we can see on the opposite hillside was added. Finally, the section we're on to Eldora was completed in nineteen-oh-five."

"Why did this part take longer?" Lucille asked.

"Money and business opportunity. Early mines dotted the hillsides between Boulder and Sunset, making it economically feasible to provide transportation to and from Sunset. Then with gold discovered near Ward, it justified adding that extension. With the tungsten boom and plans to build a reservoir near Nederland, the financial justification became clear to add this section of track. All a matter of timing."

"But you just lectured us on the financial problems of the railroad that may lead to its demise." Lucille graced him with her most pleasant smile.

"I'm glad you were paying attention, my dear. The railroad had some good years but then ran into financial difficulties. Unfortunately, as we discussed, I doubt it will survive the summer. Such a shame that future generations will not enjoy the sights we're seeing today."

"I'm sure the railroad owners will make out like bank robbers," Daniel said. "As you mentioned earlier, they'll sell all the equipment and walk off with the cash."

"Not as simple as that, young man. Dismantling a railroad is neither an easy nor an inexpensive task. And there are debts to pay off as well."

Daniel turned and squinted at the professor. "The owners will find a buyer who will undertake the debt in exchange for the scrap value. I'm sure they won't lose any money or sleep over the matter. The ones who will suffer will be folks like Theodore Shultz, who will be out of a job."

"I'm sure you can represent our good conductor in any legal proceedings to gain a final settlement."

"I'm getting tired of listening to the two of you." Frederick pounded his hand on the wood panel in front of him. "Can't you shut up?"

"Oh, Frederick," Allison said. "They're only having a healthy debate."

"They can debate all they want when we get to Eldora. I want some peace and quiet right now." Frederick closed his eyes and slumped into the seat.

Harry didn't think the young man would easily find peace and quiet.

CHAPTER 16

As the train progressed up the south hillside above Sunset, the professor pointed. "There's a train on the other route out of Sunset going to Ward."

All eyes in the front of the compartment, except for Michael's, turned to the left to view another train climbing the north wall above Four Mile Creek. Michael whittled, with no interest in anything around him. He had completed the head of the fox and was working on the body. More and more of his animal emerged from the block of wood as if it had been hiding there since the tree from which the wood came was cut down. He turned the wood block and began working on the front paws.

"I took that train up to Mount Alto once," Lucille said. "It must have been fifteen years ago. What a tremendous view. We danced and had a wonderful time. I vividly remember the fountain and pavilion."

"Unfortunately, that pavilion is no longer there," the professor said. "The railroad decided to move it to Glacier Lake. We'll see it when we make our stop there later this morning."

"Why was it relocated?" Lucille asked.

The professor tweaked his beard. "Probably because this route we're on became the preferred tourist destination as soon as this leg was added. The best view of the mountains and more chance for you ladies to collect wildflowers are along this section of track."

Harry leaned across Susan and watched an engine, billowing smoke, move up the opposing hillside. It pulled a tender and several gondola cars; not a tourist train like this one. "Looks like coal being taken to a mine."

"I'd imagine so," the professor said. "Mines need coal to burn to fuel their mining equipment, and a return trip of ore to the plains feeds the mills. Mining commerce trying to stay alive. With the current schedule, the passenger train to Ward is only running on Saturday."

"So if we had decided to take our excursion yesterday, we would have been on the other route," Lucille said.

"Precisely, my dear."

Lucille leaned toward Benjamin. "In that case, let's be thankful that we have this splendid view we're enjoying today."

"We have something else to be thankful for today," the professor added. "The Great War is over. I was most satisfied to read in the *Boulder Daily Camera* last evening the details of the signing of the peace treaty in Versailles."

"I don't know if the peace will last long," Daniel said. "That same newspaper article mentioned that the German press is already urging a war of revenge. I can't see the Teutonic people staying quiet. They rose up once to try to dominate Europe and will try it again. They're dangerous."

"That is a definite risk, my boy. For the time being Germany will be disarmed. We'll have to keep our eyes on the Huns to make sure they don't rearm. They seem to love their guns and other implements of war."

"And this debate over whether the Kaiser should face trial," Harry said. "After all the atrocities."

"Yes," the professor replied. "Now the old gentleman is threatening to commit suicide rather than be tried."

"Let him kill himself," Frederick groused. "Good riddance."

"Some may share your opinion," the professor said. "We're

seeing a lot of posturing. In any case, President Wilson is on his way home. He will also face huge obstacles. The isolationists in Congress don't share the president's strong support of the League of Nations. He will have a difficult battle to convince his fellow politicians of the benefit of a world organization. Wilson will need to have all his persuasive ability ready for a duel with our legislators."

"Common sense will prevail," Daniel said.

"This has never been a nation of common sense," the professor replied. "Just look at our insane prohibition law."

"I beg your pardon," Allison said.

The professor tipped his hat. "I've once again offended your delicate sensibilities, but prohibition is rubbish. It will never hold."

"It's necessary, and it will last." Allison gave a vigorous nod of her head.

"Time will tell, young lady. Time will tell. But the most important issue we face is preventing another war like the one we've been through."

"Look at all this beauty around us," Allison said. "Can't everyone forget the war?"

"I'm afraid not, Miss Jacoby," the professor replied. "If we forget, we run the risk of ending up in the same situation again. Much turbulence exists in Germany, and forces could rise again to try to take over Europe. We have a tenuous peace. It will be threatened by both the internal situation and external events surrounding Germany. China refused to sign the peace accord. They're concerned that the Shantung province remains in Japanese hands. In addition to future threats in Europe, we'll have to watch what happens in the Orient as well."

"That's why a worldwide organization such as the League of Nations is so important," Daniel said. "Somehow we need to get all nations to join."

Harry stroked his chin. "I doubt it will have much clout. We have enough trouble following laws in our own country. How can we expect anything to be put in place that will be enforced across national boundaries?"

"An astute observation from our police officer. Much like our nonsensical prohibition laws, which are unenforceable, an international dictate to keep peace will be difficult, if not impossible, to carry out. So for now, we can celebrate the signing of the peace treaty, but we must remain watchful over what next unfolds. Much like your duty, Officer McBride. You have laws to enforce and must be ever vigilant."

"It's because you men insist on fighting all the time," Lucille said. "If women ran the countries, the situation would be different."

"Possibly, but the men are often goaded by the women behind the scene. And think back to the time of the Trojan War, a battle fought over the honor of a woman. The feminine side of the equation is often complex and impacts the male psyche with disastrous results."

"Oh, you men." Lucille raised her chin. "Trying to slough off responsibility and blame someone else."

Conductor Shultz entered the compartment. "We will be stopping briefly at Sugarloaf, but not long enough to get off."

Susan pointed. "Look. There's Sugarloaf Mountain. I love looking up from Boulder at that cone-shaped hill."

"Yes, we do have our fair share of sights," the professor said. "With the Flatirons, Flagstaff Mountain and Sugarloaf. Conductor Shultz, will we stop between Sugarloaf and Glacier Lake?"

"We'll pass the town of Tungsten but won't stop there unless a signal is up, which I'm not expecting."

"Ah, the metal tungsten for which the town's named." The professor waved his hand toward the window. "Source of economic frenzy and frustration. During the war, prices soared and the mines went crazy. Then, with oversupply, prices crashed, and we have the potential demise of our beloved Switzerland Trail railroad. Mining has been boom or bust over the last fifty years in Boulder County. People get their hopes up, but, invariably, the prices of valuable minerals drop, jobs are lost and fortunes destroyed. That's why I prefer academia. None of this unwise speculation. Much more predictable."

"And you've never dealt with dangerous situations." Frederick turned and his eyes flared. "Tucked away in your safe office, pompous and self-satisfied."

"I . . . I beg your pardon." The professor sputtered.

"You heard me."

The professor ran his hand over his jacket as if to rid himself of soot. "I may not have fought in a war as you did, but I have learned the important lessons of history. I only hope your generation will do the same."

"We've learned the hard way." Frederick slammed his palm into the wood panel in front of him.

Allison jumped. "Frederick, be careful. Don't hurt yourself."

"As if anyone cares."

The train slowed before anyone delivered another insult. A bag was dropped on the ground ahead, and one person who had been waiting along the tracks entered the front passenger car. The whistle blew and the train started again. Two minutes later they passed Tungsten, and as predicted by Shultz, the train did not stop. Off to the left side of the car, the hillside dropped away to a valley.

Harry remained deep in thought. Peaks and valleys—the economy, the world situation, the mining trade, life, and the railroad itself. What lay ahead?

CHAPTER 17

The train rounded a bend and slowed as the view of a sparkling lake appeared on the right side. A few ripples were visible, and a breeze periodically ruffled the surface of the otherwise calm water. The background conversation from the hiking group filled the compartment.

"Glacier Lake," Conductor Shultz announced. "Not a regular stop but a destination today for the intrepid members of the climbers' group."

A great commotion arose in the back of the passenger car as people stood and gathered their gear. Several of them broke into a rousing rendition of "Rock-a-Bye Your Baby with a Dixie Melody," followed by foot stomping and cheering. Their festive mood bubbled over as they awaited their chance to hike and camp overnight.

"My goodness," Allison said. "It will be so quiet in here with all of them leaving. We'll practically have the car to ourselves. Michael, wouldn't you love coming on the train again and stopping here for a picnic?"

Michael ignored his sister and sent several wood chips in the direction of Frederick, who leaned toward the aisle to avoid the assault.

"As I said earlier," the professor announced, "this may be one of the last chances to travel on the Switzerland Trail. If you truly want to take a picnic here, Miss Jacoby, I'd suggest doing it in the next few weeks."

Allison pursed her lips. "We might just do that."

Lucille pointed across the aisle to the window beside Michael. "There's the pavilion I danced under when it was at Mount Alto. Imagine moving that whole structure all the way to this lake. What these railroad people can do."

Daniel raised his window and stuck his head outside. In a moment, he pulled himself back into the cabin. "By George, I remember this place. Look at those people out in canoes. I've paddled in the middle of this lake. A day I'll never forget. I came up here with my parents when I was a little tyke."

"You mean when you were a little brat," Frederick said.

"Let's refrain from insults," the professor's voice boomed out as the train came to a grinding halt. The climbers streamed out both ends of the car.

The man who earlier had handed out brochures stumbled by carrying a large rucksack and waved. "Come join us on one of our outings." He headed out the front door.

"Not likely," Frederick growled.

"Oh, Frederick," Allison said. "Don't spoil things. They seem like nice people, and, I'm sure, they would genuinely welcome any of us to join them. And they all look so chipper and healthy."

Frederick stomped violently as if trying to eliminate something stuck to the bottom of his boot. "Look at them off in their imaginary world of adventure. None of them would have survived a week in the trenches."

"And it's a good thing no one will ever have to do that again," Allison said. "We've had enough of the fighting."

"Until the next damned war." Frederick kicked his foot against the wood veneer in front of him.

"There's no assurance that we won't have another major war," the professor added. "Once the Germans lick their wounds, they may start a conflict again. I'm not sure they understand the meaning of the word 'peace.' "

"Why do you men insist on talking of war all the time?" Lucille nudged the professor. "Can't you give us one of your lectures on something else instead?"

"If you insist, my dear. Let me educate you on our current location. This lake was once called Pennsylvania Lake, but was renamed in nineteen-oh-four, during the construction of the Eldora branch of the railroad to give it a more vivid name. The natural lake has been enlarged by the addition of a dam on the far side, where you can see that distant canoe. In addition to being a spot of unsurpassed beauty, Glacier Lake also has economic value."

"Yes," Lucille said. "For tourists like that group of climbers. I'm almost tempted to stop here to gather wildflowers. Mrs. McBride and Miss Jacoby, wouldn't you like to start right now?"

Susan laughed. "I can wait until Eldora."

Allison said, "Michael would be disappointed if we didn't go to the terminus. Right, Michael?"

Michael made a grunting sound and kept whittling.

"I notice that none of you women is wearing gloves today," the professor said.

Susan smiled. "Of course not. It's warm, and the gloves would become soiled when we pick wildflowers."

The Rocky Mountain Climbers Club gathered by the small building that served as a lunchroom during the summer. They milled around, likely waiting for their leader to select the route for their first hike. A patch of sulfur-flower buckwheat grew amid the grass and dirt that lined the railroad tracks. To the west the Arapaho glacier shone in the morning sunlight.

The train began moving.

"Tourism has been one of the benefactors of this lovely lake," the professor said. "But there has been one other fruitful financial endeavor here. See that ramp that goes into the water? Winter ice is cut, brought up that ramp, loaded on trains and transported down the Switzerland Trail. From the Boulder depot, the ice is often taken into Denver, where there is much demand to replenish iceboxes."

Conductor Shultz stopped by, having finished helping the climbers disembark. "To add to what the distinguished professor says, this is often a major summer destination for our railroad. We have the small station, a building for the train crew to stay overnight when battling winter snow, a wye for engines to turn around, a water tank, telephone and telegraph. We're at the highest stopping point on the Eldora leg of the Switzerland Trail. Over nine thousand feet. Take a deep breath and notice the purity of the air." He breathed in and let out a long breath. "Ah, the aroma of pine."

"It smells like soot from your locomotive," Frederick said.

"Ever the cynic, young man," the professor said. "As our conductor has told us, we are fortunate to be up in these majestic climes. Think of all the poor souls down on the plains today, suffering through the sweltering heat, while we enjoy the refreshing coolness of the mountains. Do you often have large groups coming to this lake, Conductor Shultz?"

"Yes, indeed. The record was set in August, nineteen-oh-five, by the Denver Grocerymen's Association. We deployed eighteen fully loaded trains that day, transporting twelve hundred people. They enjoyed an excellent picnic, and the railroad crews worked from dawn to dusk that day. Quite an accomplishment."

"It probably kept another crew of people busy fishing drunken grocerymen out of the lake," Frederick groused.

Shultz chuckled. "Definitely the case. Being before state prohibition, there was no lack of beer brought along on that outing. And the grocerymen were in a position to procure as much liquid refreshment as they wanted."

"Another example of why prohibition is so necessary," Allison said.

"I don't know about that," Shultz said. "I imagine any large group will find a way to bring along something they prefer to drink."

"These men need to lean to curb their desire for whiskey and beer," Allison said. "I don't know why they're so insistent on getting drunk."

"Part of human nature, young lady. People work hard during the week and want to escape into the oblivion of alcohol on the weekend."

"I can't stand it much longer." Frederick smacked his hand onto the wood panel. "We have the professor boring us with nonstop facts, aided by the conductor, who is also an expert on all things mundane. With the noise in the back of the car taken care of, why can't we have the experts keep their drivel to themselves for the rest of the trip?"

"Only trying to keep the conversation going." Shultz stormed away and passed into the other passenger car.

The professor regarded his former student. "You certainly have developed a caustic tongue, young man."

"And you have turned into an old windbag," Frederick replied.

Harry's eyes met Susan's, and she gave an almost imperceptible nod. They had this way of silently communicating. He recognized she had the same thought as he did. Each of the seven people around them played his or her role in an ongoing drama. Allison, the prohibitionist. Daniel, representing the rights of the downtrodden and competitor to Frederick for Alison's hand. Michael, absorbed in his carving, living in his own isolated and silent world. The professor, the self-appointed expert on every imaginable subject. Lucille, goading the professor on while sharing her own antagonism. Shultz, stopping by to fuel the flames as he passed from car to car. Frederick—the naysayer in the group, the war survivor in body only. And Harry and his wife, the observers, taking in the dynamics of the other seven.

With no further lectures, observations or voicing of grudges, a deathly silence fell over the passenger car.

CHAPTER 18

The passengers remained quiet as they enjoyed the majestic view of the Rocky Mountains. To the left a ridge sloped up to intersect South Arapaho Peak, with a jagged corridor leading to North Arapaho Peak. Adventurous climbers scaled that section along a one-foot wide ledge that dropped off a thousand feet on either side.

To the right Mount Albion and Niwot Ridge commanded the view. Everyone looked out the windows, except for Michael, who was content to turn more of his wood block into a fox.

Conductor Schultz came into the compartment from the car ahead and broke the silence. "We're approaching Hill. No stop planned today."

Lucille patted her hair as if to make sure every strand was still in place. "Is that appropriately named because we're on a hill?"

"No, my dear. This spot was named for E. B. Hill, who built a sawmill in this location. He processed a good deal of pine wood here."

"This was once an important stop," Schultz added. "When the city of Boulder built a dam at Albion Lake, we unloaded workers and equipment here. Less than a mile past Hill there was also another siding at one time, for similar construction of a dam for Silver Lake. Both projects provided employment for a number of workers and kept our railroad quite busy."

"Ah, yes." The professor leaned back and put his thumbs on

the pockets of his vest. "Construction projects to provide a water supply for our fair city. Water is the lifeblood of the West. In our arid climate we must have good sources of the precious liquid, and our mountains with their winter snows provide an excellent source." The professor pointed to Frederick. "There's an occupation for you, young man. Follow your seat companion and get into law. Much money can be made arguing over water rights."

"As if I'd stoop so low," Frederick murmured.

"I heard you, young man. Don't be so high and mighty. Law is a fine profession, as Daniel can attest, even if he has gone too far in the radical direction."

"I have not," Daniel protested. "I'm helping those who have become exploited by society."

The professor chuckled. "You've made my point, boy."

The train turned south and headed along an east-facing hillside. To the left the passengers viewed the panorama of a sweeping valley. Harry imagined wild horses galloping through pastures covered with wildflowers—that is, if his wife hadn't been there first to pick all the flowers.

"Any of you looking for a good investment?" Shultz asked.

"On a policeman's salary, we don't have anything left to invest other than in food and clothes," Harry said.

Susan smiled. "Our big investment for the month was coming on this excursion. We'll have to be frugal for the rest of the summer."

"I'm sure our resident lawyer or the professor must be looking for something to invest in," Shultz said. "There's an amazing opportunity available. The Northern Gas and Drilling Company is offering shares at only fifteen cents each, requiring only five cents down. They're promising twenty-five cents a share when they complete drilling and begin selling gas. You won't find a better return on your money."

"I'd be careful of that, Shultz," the professor said. "No guarantee that they'll find usable gas resources."

"No, this is a sure thing." Shultz rubbed his hands together. "I've already put some money in. I thought I'd share the tip with you."

"For once I agree with the professor," Daniel said. "Here we have another example of rich men taking advantage of unsuspecting citizens. You're throwing away your money, Conductor, just as if you dropped it in the coal fire of your tender."

Shultz huffed. "We'll see. I've given you a chance to make some money. I won't waste my time again." He pivoted and stormed through the passageway into the other passenger car.

"I do believe you've insulted our conductor," Harry said.

"Maybe he can convince some unsuspecting people in that car," Daniel said. "Imagine anyone investing in such a scam."

"Many do," the professor said.

"I'm sure he was only trying to be helpful," Allison said.

"You have a good heart and are always willing to defend people," Daniel said.

"Like she does for her useless brother," Frederick said.

Allison reached forward and swatted Frederick with her hand. "Don't you dare insult Michael."

Frederick ducked to avoid a second blow. "So much for a good heart. I'd say we have a new contender to take on the reigning heavyweight champion."

"Speaking of which, there's the big bout coming up on July Fourth in Toledo, Ohio," Daniel said. "There will be lots of fireworks there. My money is on Jack Dempsey to unseat Jess Willard."

"I doubt it," the professor said. "The Great White Hope may be thirty-seven years old, but no one is strong enough to take down that six-foot-six, two-hundred-seventy-pound giant. The fight won't last two rounds."

"That might be, but I expect to see Willard on the mat." Daniel took out his billfold and held it up. "Care to place a wager, Professor?"

"No, thank you."

Daniel's eyes twinkled. "Won't put your money behind your convictions?"

"I'm not a betting man."

"We know our conductor is," Daniel replied. "Risking his money on outlandish investments in holes in the ground."

"Speaking of holes in the ground," the professor said, "we're heading into some of the most prolific mining country in our state. Mining first brought a large number of people to Colorado and Boulder, in particular. We had our share of hard-rock miners, digging into the hillsides to find precious metals. One of the first mines was established higher in the mountains at Caribou. Silver was found in the eighteen-seventies. With silver prices peaking in eighteen-seventy-four at a dollar twenty-seven per ounce, the town of Caribou exceeded two thousand souls. But with the overmining of silver, the eighteen-ninety-three repeal of the Sherman Act, which had sustained the price of silver, and the adoption of the gold standard in nineteen-hundred, the price of silver plummeted. Only a handful of residents remain in Caribou today.

"And concerning silver and railroads, in eighteen-ninety-six the Democratic Party in Denver staged a crash of two narrow-gauge locomotives as a fundraiser for candidates seeking to get the government to resume buying silver. They named the two locomotives Bill McKinley and Mark Hanna, respectively, after the Republican candidate and the party chairman. Thousands of people came to watch the two locomotives bash into each other."

Frederick groaned loudly. "We had to have an expert of all that no one wants to know on the train with us today."

"You didn't have to join us, young man."

"You did invite him, Professor Sager," Allison said.

"That I did, although I'm regretting that action at the moment." He patted Lucille's hand. "I can blame you, my dear, since you originally suggested this outing."

"Oh, you were talking about mining," Lucille said.

"Even if I only have an audience of one enthusiastic listener, I'll continue. Our mountains have been the source of silver, gold and tungsten, although as we discussed earlier, tungsten faced the same fate as silver after the peak during the war. The safest is gold. You can't go wrong when you find good gold ore."

Frederick gave a snort. "Right. As if you'd ever find anything other than your nagging voice."

"Frederick," Allison admonished. "Let's hear him out. The professor is sharing his knowledge with us, and I'm learning something."

"Which is quite amazing, given the source," Frederick shot back.

Shultz stuck his head back into the compartment. "We'll be stopping at another silver mine in a few minutes. Several passengers in the other car will be getting off at the flag stop." He stared right at Frederick. "Any of you care to lighten the load as well?"

"I do believe our conductor is encouraging one of the . . . uh . . . more obnoxious passengers to leave," the professor said.

"I'm staying," Frederick replied. "The yammering passenger behind is welcome to depart."

The professor glared for a moment at Frederick and said, "The Blue Bird mine that our conductor refers to is another tale of success and failure. It was reopened as late as nineteen-seventeen, but it succumbed to the influenza epidemic and closed again in November of last year. Several companies made money for a while and then went bust."

"But Blue Bird has been a good tourist attraction," Shultz said. "It's another excellent place to pick wildflowers. And for a number of years people stayed overnight at the boarding house."

"Very rustic, I'm sure," Lucille said. "Nothing like the service I provide at my boarding house."

"Nothing compares to your establishment, my dear."

Frederick gave a raucous laugh. "You've become a humorist in your old age, Professor. Mrs. Vickering's boarding house wouldn't compare even if the Blue Bird building had a ten-foot hole in the roof. And service . . . don't get me started on that."

"Watch your tongue, you evil war cripple," Lucille shouted.

Everyone sat in stunned silence as the train pulled to a stop at Blue Bird.

CHAPTER 19

With no siding at Blue Bird, the two passengers who disembarked climbed down onto dirt and proceeded across the grass toward the bunkhouse fifty yards up the slope from the train. The man carried a rucksack and the woman a parasol. Heads bobbing, they appeared eager to enjoy their day in the mountain sunshine and gentle breeze.

Harry stood to stretch his legs and regarded the fox Michael was carving, the body and legs taking shape. "Very lifelike. You certainly have an eye for details about animals."

"Oh, yes," Allison said. "Michael is very observant. He notices all kinds of things that most of us miss. That's why he's so good at carving animals."

"Shoes," Michael said.

Allison put her hand to her mouth to suppress a giggle. "That's another of his talents. He's an expert on shoes."

"Animals and shoes," Harry replied. "That's a surprising combination."

"Oh, Michael has many different areas of interest. Tell Officer McBride what kind of shoes he's wearing."

Without looking at Harry's shoes, Michael said, "Easy. Black Pershing boots like Frederick has on."

Harry looked toward Frederick and verified they wore similar boots. "Very good, Michael."

Allison smiled. "Michael notices all kinds of things that most of us miss. For example, he probably noticed something about the outside of the passenger car we're in. Michael, tell Officer McBride what you saw when we got on our car."

Without looking up, Michael said, "Dent in door five inches long."

Out of curiosity, Harry went to the door leading to the other passenger car. He opened it, stepped through and checked. Sure enough, he found an indentation that he estimated was five inches long. He returned to the compartment and said to Michael, "With your skills you could help our police work."

"Michael, would you enjoy helping Officer McBride?" Allison asked.

Michael didn't acknowledge the comment and kept on with his carving.

Allison looked up at Harry. "He'll only talk when he wants to. Don't take it as a rebuff, Officer McBride."

"Not a problem."

The whistle blew, and the train lurched forward. Harry caught his balance and looked out the window over Michael's shoulder as the man and woman who had left the train strolled toward the Blue Bird mine. Then he returned to his seat.

"Have you heard what some of the students at the University of Colorado want to do?" the professor asked. "They're seeking permission to construct a one-hundred-fifty-foot-high letter C on the side of Flagstaff Mountain. Can you image that? They think just because the Colorado School of Mines students have put an M on the side of Mount Zion in Golden that our students should be allowed to do the same in Boulder."

"I certainly hope the university administration squelches that plan," Lucille said. "I don't want our view desecrated with an obnoxious letter."

"Yes, my dear. And I will do everything in my power as a faculty member to prevent that from happening. They suggest painting white stones to form the letter. They think they can repaint them every year to keep the letter visible. I can't imagine Daniel or Frederick supporting such an idea."

"I agree with you, Professor," Daniel said. "I think student energy can be put to more productive use, such as assisting returning war veterans. I'm sure Frederick wouldn't mind a young female student helping him." He elbowed his seat companion. "Although come to think of it, Allison might not appreciate that."

"Quit goading him, Daniel." Allison's nostrils flared.

Daniel ducked his head. "My apologies."

"I have a suggestion for our young men in front," the professor said. "Instead of trying to kill each other, they should join the Boulder Rotary Club."

"I'm not familiar with it," Allison said.

The professor gave an indulgent smile. "It's a service organization, and the Boulder chapter received its national charter in April. A good use of a young man's time."

The train negotiated a lazy curve with a view out to the left of a large meadow. "Look at all the dry grass," Susan said. "This time of year it should still be green."

"The result of the drought, Mrs. McBride," the professor said. "With the low snowfall this last winter and the small amount of rain in May and earlier this month, things are parched."

"That's why people have been urged to save water." Daniel sniffed loudly. "I'm sure Frederick has taken that to heart and avoided taking baths."

Frederick reached for Daniel's throat but was interrupted by Allison banging on the back of their seat. "You two quit antagonizing each other."

Daniel gave a wry grin. "I was only stating a simple fact."

"Speaking of water," the professor said, "there's a fifty-thousand-dollar water bond being considered to extend the pipe above the current source of pollution for our city's water supply. You can't be too safe when it comes to drinking water."

Lucille crinkled her nose. "I've noticed the water tasting funny lately."

"That's probably because you need to replace the decrepit pipes in your boarding house," Frederick said.

"Why, of all the nerve." Lucille huffed.

At that moment Conductor Shultz stepped into the passenger car. "We're going past Anson."

"Not a regular stop?" Susan asked.

"No, ma'am. There's a passing track and a water tank fed from a spring, but we don't need to refill at the moment. Is everyone having a good trip so far?"

"Outside of frequent verbal and physical attacks, everyone has survived so far," the professor replied. "Much better than the unfortunate Miss Agnes Conville."

Lucille gasped. "Oh, dear. Was she the one mentioned in yesterday's newspaper?"

"The same, my dear. The poor woman who was visiting from Kansas City died in her bathroom at the Miles Hotel. Quite a tragedy."

"Foul play?" Daniel asked.

"Apparently not," the professor said. "The report indicated she died of acute indigestion."

"Much like I suffered at the Vickering boarding house," Frederick said.

"You are incorrigible," Lucille said. "Conductor Schultz, if there's an opportunity to send a passenger off the train at full speed, I can suggest a candidate."

"There will be no losing passengers today," Schultz chuckled. "I'm responsible to make sure everyone on the train returns safely." The train's whistle blew. "We're approaching Lakewood."

"Will we stop?" Allison asked.

"Probably not today. Lakewood was an important destination during the tungsten boom. We'll keep going unless someone signals to get on. After that, Wolfram, another flag stop, where coal and supplies were once delivered for the Conger mine. Again, we're not expecting to stop there."

The professor shook his head. "So many once productive mines sit idle."

"An idle mine is the devil's playground," Daniel said with a straight face.

The professor groaned. "Must you, Mr. Compton?"

A grin crossed Daniel's face.

Lucille nudged her seat companion. "Just ignore him, Benjamin. By groaning you're encouraging him."

"You're right once again, my dear. Now where was I? Oh. As I was saying, with the mines not being used, our Switzerland Trail railroad faces extinction. The only thing doing well right now is the motorcar. More and more of those every day. I read in yesterday's newspaper that because of all the motorcar traffic, city personnel have instigated a project to count automobiles on Arapahoe Street leaving the city yesterday, today and Tuesday. I guess they're trying to figure out if the road needs to be widened."

"The congestion is becoming more of a problem," Harry said. "Aided by inexperienced and impatient drivers."

"Must make more work for you, Officer McBride," Daniel said.

"That it does."

"Ah, yes," the professor said. "The motorcar is certainly a mixed blessing. Provides transportation but leads to a whole new set of problems."

"You men are so interested in automobiles," Lucille said. "I think celebrations are much more important." She leaned across the aisle toward Allison. "Miss Jacoby, did you attend the

118

Homecoming Day last Thursday?"

Allison brightened. "Yes. I enjoyed watching all the people marching. Afterwards, Frederick and I ate supper on the courthouse lawn. A' most enjoyable day. And we didn't have any unfortunate encounters with automobiles."

"There." Lucille gave a vigorous nod. "It proves that women have much more sensible interests than men."

"I don't know," the professor said. "Men have a very sensible interest. Women."

"Professor, I don't care what anyone says about how dry you are, you do have a sense of humor," Daniel said.

"Of course, young man, but I don't go in for the atrocious puns you tell."

"As they say, puns are a sign of an intelligent mind," Daniel replied.

"Or an idiot," Frederick said.

CHAPTER 20

The train lurched to a stop right before a trestle that crossed Coon Creek. "Regular stop at Cardinal," Conductor Shultz announced. An old man and woman exited from the car in front. They waited by the station as a young man offloaded boxes and stacked them by the couple. A horse-drawn wagon appeared, and the driver jumped down to reload the boxes in the back of the wagon.

"Ah, another historic stop on our mining tour," the professor announced. "Site of both mine and mill."

"Yes," Shultz agreed. "This station was extremely active in the past. It served as the terminus for supplies to both the Caribou mines farther up the mountain and for the town of Nederland down below. Nederland was the center of activity during the tungsten boom. We also transported ore away from both locations, at one time or another."

"Nederland is a fairly large town up here in the mountains," Lucille said. "Why doesn't the train stop there?"

"It's not on the railroad route." Shultz replied. "Supplies have to be taken by dirt road from here to Nederland. Back in the early part of the century, the railroad company built a spur to Nederland from Sulphide, our next flag stop. It was used to deliver material to build the dam for Barker Reservoir. After the completion of construction, the spur was pulled out, leaving only a dirt road."

"Why'd they do that?" Lucille asked.

"The railroad didn't think it made economic sense to maintain the spur," Shultz said. "The rails and ties were used to repair other parts of the route."

"There has been debate over the last three years about rebuilding that stretch of track," the professor said. "The railroad almost decided to make the investment, but after the bottom fell out of the tungsten market, economic justification to add the rail disappeared."

"Typical," Daniel said. "The people in the town of Nederland might have benefited, but the railroad owners didn't want to spend any of their precious cash."

"And rightfully so, young man. It would have been a waste of money with no tungsten to take to the mills. And speaking of mills, one of the largest in the county resides right at this Cardinal site. You can see it from the train."

All eyes turned to the windows on the right side of the passenger car. The horse cart loaded with boxes proceeded up a dirt road at a slow pace, with the old man, woman and young man walking behind it. The sunlight reflected off the silver handle of the cane the older man carried.

Daniel pointed. "That large building sloping down toward the creek?"

"That's the one. It's a concentration mill for both gold and tungsten. Compared to the Wall Street mill that attempted to process rock to final metal, this mill gets rid of the waste rock so that less material needs to be transported to the final processing step out on the plains. With transportation being the largest expense in mining, this is an important step."

"The expert spouts off again," Frederick said. "Too bad there isn't a way to concentrate all your words to a pithy few."

"And it's too bad you didn't listen to the advice I gave you as a student, Mr. Hammond. It's a shame my valuable words went to waste."

The train started moving, crossed the curved trestle and headed east along the south side of the creek through a stand of spruce. With the passenger car now in shade, the temperature seemed to drop ten degrees.

"A few trees have escaped the ax here," the professor noted.

"It certainly looks more appealing that the bare hills we've passed," Lucille said.

"I wonder how long it will take some of these hills to revegetate after all the destruction that's been done," the professor said.

"Longer than any of us will be alive, I'm sure," Lucille replied.

"You mentioned a mine as well as a mill at Cardinal, Professor?" Allison said.

"Why, yes, Miss Jacoby. You can find the Boulder County tunnel up the road to the right, where those people who got off were headed."

"On this side of the creek there's a spur that goes to the tunnel," Shultz added. "We still take supplies up there. If you'll excuse me, I must attend to the car ahead." He stepped through the door and disappeared.

"Why is it called a tunnel rather than a mine?" Lucille asked.

"Well, well. Don't we have the inquisitive female minds engaged?" The professor adjusted his bow tie. "Two types of mines exist in these hills: tunnel and shaft. The shaft is dug straight down and is less expensive to construct. But shafts are more expensive to maintain because they fill with water that must be drained. A tunnel mine is dug into the side of a hill. It takes more work to construct because beams are used to shore up the ceiling. But once in place, a tunnel doesn't face the drainage problems of a shaft and consequently is less expensive to maintain. As simple as that."

"Whereas the professor's mouth presents the worst of both shaft and tunnel," Frederick said.

Allison giggled. She caught herself and put her hand over her mouth as her cheeks reddened. "I'm sorry."

"Don't encourage the young knave," the professor said. "Apparently he never was taught manners and respect for his elders."

"Only when they deserve it," Frederick said.

Daniel regarded his seat companion. "How about that? I do believe our resident curmudgeon finally made a joke. And you're developing the debating skills of an attorney. If you ever decide to pursue my profession, you might excel at it. That is, if you'd be willing to actually work."

"Over my dead body," Frederick replied.

"I'm sure that can be arranged," Daniel said.

Frederick elbowed Daniel viciously.

Daniel let out a whoosh of air and shoved Frederick.

Harry jumped to his feet and separated the two men. "Gentlemen, let's refrain from the insults and fighting. I must remind you once again we have ladies present. We'd all welcome a pleasant day without further altercation."

Daniel dusted off his navy blue blazer. "Fine by me."

"Now that we have extra room, I suggest one of you should move." Harry waved toward the empty back of the car.

Daniel pushed past Frederick and Harry. "An excellent idea." He strode by the others and sat in the seat behind Allison and Michael. Once in place, Daniel leaned over the seat and gazed at Michael's carving. "Quite a fox you have there."

"Almost done," Michael mumbled.

"What are you going to carve next?" Allison asked.

Michael shrugged.

"When we get to Eldora, we'll find a whole new source of wood for you, Michael," Allison said.

Michael wrinkled his forehead. "Good wood."

"Michael has turned into a poet," Daniel said.

Allison smiled. "He likes to rhyme words. Michael, why don't

123

you come up with some other ones?"

Michael bit his lip, in deep concentration. Then his eyes grew wide. "Scary Harry."

"There you go," Daniel said. "Officer McBride has obviously put the fear of God into Michael."

"I wish some of the less-desirables in Boulder shared Michael's view," Harry said. "It would make my life much easier."

"What else, Michael?" Allison asked.

"Blue Sue," Michael said.

Susan patted her bonnet. "Why yes, Michael. That is appropriate. I'm not unhappy, but I am wearing a blue hat."

"Tan Dan," Michael said.

Daniel chuckled. "I have been out in the sun a lot lately. Good for you, Michael. Any other rhymes for us?"

Michael looked thoughtful but didn't respond.

"You can come up with one more," Daniel prodded. "What do you have for your sister's fiancé. I'm sure you have some meaningful words for him."

Michael raised his gaze for a moment and pointed toward Frederick with a shaky finger. "Dead Fred."

CHAPTER 21

There was stunned silence, and then Allison gasped. "Michael, using the words 'dead' and 'Fred' together! How could you say such a thing?"

Ignoring his sister, Michael went back to his carving as if nothing had happened. Everyone else in the passenger car remained quiet.

Shultz interrupted the stillness by returning to the car and announcing, "We're heading south. Next flag stop Sulphide, also known as Sulphide Flats."

The professor, not one to remain silent long, jumped in. "We're nearing the end of our journey."

"Good," Frederick said. "I hope you'll keep your comments to yourself on the way back."

"I wouldn't think of it, young man. You'll just have to get used to listening to advice from your elders."

The train slowed and came to a stop. A man came aboard and sat in the back of the car. He wore ragged brown trousers that had long lost their creases, scuffed boots, a shabby waistcoat and no hat. A foul smell that combined beer, vomit and body odor wafted through the compartment.

Allison swiveled and stared at the new passenger. "Oh, dear. I hope he's not having problems."

Lucille held her nose, leaned over and whispered to the professor, "I'm glad our new traveler isn't going far with us."

Shultz, standing between Lucille and Allison, chuckled.

"That's Old James. He lives in Eldora and walks down to Sulphide every morning or, should I say, stumbles down. If he indulged in too much liquid libation the night before, he'll put up the signal and catch the train back to Eldora."

By this time, Old James lay sprawled across the seat, head lolling against the window, feet dangling in the aisle. Periodic gagging snores sprang from his open mouth.

A water tank stood on the west side of the tracks. The fireman pulled a line to move a pipe to replenish the boiler water.

"There isn't much here at this stop," Lucille said.

"No, it doesn't compare to the heyday when Barker Dam was being built a decade ago," Shultz said. "But it has the wye for engines to turn around. The train backs down from Eldora, and here the engine can resume pulling the cars for the rest of the return trip to Boulder."

When the train started up again, it crossed a trestle over Middle Boulder Creek and headed west.

Michael looked up from his carving and shouted, "Deer!"

"Yes, Michael, that's a good idea." Allison patted her brother's arm. "Is that what you're going to carve next?"

Michael shrugged away from his sister, transforming into a banshee. He pounded on the window, his body racked with convulsions. "Deer!"

Daniel also pointed. "He's right. There's a deer down by the creek."

"You don't have to worry, Michael," Allison said. "The deer isn't going to get on the train."

Michael twitched, and his arms flapped wildly. His right hand struck the window, causing it to shake.

Allison grabbed his arms and brought them down to his side.

"What's wrong with him?" Daniel asked.

Allison sighed. "He was scared as a small boy when a deer came in our garden. Ever since, he becomes very agitated when he sees a deer."

The deer disappeared from sight, but Michael kept his face plastered to the window, his eyes wildly scanning the creek bed.

"One minute he's quietly carving and the next he's acting like a wild man," Daniel said. "Like a light switch turned on."

"Yes," Allison replied. "Certain things set him off. It may take him a while to calm down."

The train passed the next flag stop, where a steep dirt road headed up the hillside to the left, leading to Lake Eldora. A small square waiting room with a long bench stood by the tracks, no one inside.

"That looks like a forlorn place to wait for the train," Susan said.

"Yes, Mrs. McBride, it is," Shultz replied. "Particularly in winter. There's no heating in that little structure. Winter is difficult along here. On the really bad days when there's a blizzard, we have to leave the cars at Glacier Lake and make the run to Eldora with only the engine and tender."

"What happens to the passengers?" Lucille asked.

"The few winter passengers and mail have to be crowded into the cab. There have been a few times the engine couldn't get past Sulphide. On those occasions, one of the railroad crew hiked to Eldora with the mail."

Michael started to flap his arms again, whacking the seat in front of him.

Frederick turned and glared at Allison. "Can't you get him under control?"

"Now, Frederick. You know how Michael is."

"Yeah. And you coddle him too much. He needs to be taught how to act when he's out in public."

Allison pursed her lips and shook her right index finger. "You stay out of this, Frederick Hammond."

Frederick gave a disgusted grunt and turned back to stare at the wooden panel in front of him.

From the back of the train, Old James sputtered awake and gave a hacking cough.

Allison jumped up from her seat. "Oh, dear, I wonder if that man is all right." She dashed to the back of the car.

"There she goes again," Frederick muttered. "Kittens, dogs, people. Adopting another stray."

"Kind of like she did with you," Daniel said.

Frederick kicked the wood panel in front of him but didn't say anything else.

In a few minutes, Allison returned to her seat.

"What luncheon plans do people have when we arrive in Eldora?" the professor asked. "Lucille and I will be dining at the Gold Miner Hotel."

"Harry and I plan to do the same," Susan said.

"A wise choice, Mrs. McBride." The professor rubbed his stomach. "It's reputed to have a fine menu."

"I've brought a picnic lunch," Allison said. "James in the back mentioned a pleasant grassy spot surrounded by trees. He told me it's a five-minute walk from the station, west along the north side of the creek. It's one of the places where pine and aspen have grown back. I do like a meadow with woods nearby. Frederick, Michael and I will eat there."

"And don't forget the wildflowers," Susan said.

"Of course not," Allison replied. "We will picnic and pick flowers."

"And after our meal, I expect to pick wildflowers as well," Lucille said. "We have to be sure to leave enough time, Benjamin."

"We will, my dear. And your plans, Daniel?"

"I think I'll also enjoy a repast at the Gold Miner Hotel. I've worked up an appetite after fending off blows from Frederick for most of the trip."

"Typical lawyer," Frederick growled. "You start things, then pretend you have nothing to do with them and blame someone else."

Shultz looked over his charges. "All of you have an enjoyable stopover in Eldora. I'm taking a short break myself to see the sights."

"Did you know that Eldora was at one time called Eldorado?" the professor asked.

"No, but I'm sure you're going to bore us with a story," Frederick said.

Ignoring Frederick, the professor continued, "This area was first called Happy Valley and later Eldorado. Mail started coming to the wrong place as there was also an Eldorado in California. In eighteen-ninety-eight the name was changed to Eldora to eliminate the confusion. At that time, it was quite a town, with four stage lines, dance halls, nine saloons and over a thousand residents. A result of mining on the side of Spencer Mountain. There were also great hopes that the Mogul tunnel would be a major strike."

"But unfortunately it didn't pan out," Daniel said.

The professor groaned. "Oh, Daniel, you are incorrigible. But yes, the mine never produced much ore."

"I can't help noticing the lovely silver wristwatch you're wearing, Miss Jacoby." Lucille leaned across the aisle.

"Oh, this." Allison blushed slightly. "It was a present from Frederick."

"May I see it?" Lucille asked.

Allison removed it from her wrist and handed it to Lucille.

The train slowed and pulled into the Eldora station on the south side of Boulder Creek. Shultz looked at his watch. "Right on time. Exactly twelve-thirty. Remember, we'll be leaving at exactly two-fifteen. Everyone be back by then."

"And as you've told us before," the professor said, "the train

129

will wait for no one."

Lucille handed the wristwatch back to Allison. "A very attractive model. Benjamin, you'll have to buy me a wristwatch for my next present."

He winked at her. "Ah, yes. Something to adorn your lovely wrist."

Lucille put her hand to her cheek. "You say the nicest things."

"We have traveled thirty-three miles from Boulder," Conductor Shultz announced.

The professor gazed at Shultz. "It's interesting that we've traveled thirty-three miles. That number has many strange significances."

"That's also the number on the engine that pulled us here," Harry said.

The professor's eyes widened. "Quite a coincidence. That number is considered sacred or mystical or dangerous by some people. It was Jesus's age when he was crucified in thirty-three A.D. The human spine has thirty-three vertebrae. It's the periodic table number of arsenic. It's the highest degree in the Scottish Rite of Freemasonry. I'd call it a most auspicious—or inauspicious—number."

CHAPTER 22

The passengers left the train at the small, square stone station, no larger than nine outhouses. Windows and a door faced the train, revealing a stove inside for winter heat. Everyone took the bridge across Boulder Creek toward the center of Eldora. Allison, Frederick and Michael headed west along the creek for their picnic, and the other five continued their trek to the Gold Miner Hotel, a two-story wooden structure with log siding and a front porch supported by four white posts. They climbed the steps and walked through the doorway to the large dining room.

"Can you accommodate a party of five?" the professor asked.

The proprietor, a man with a handlebar moustache, directed them to a table near a window, which looked out toward a hillside dotted with pine, spruce and fir trees.

"What a lovely spot," Lucille said. "I can't wait to collect wildflowers after our meal."

"Definitely, my dear. I'll leave the flowers to you. I may sit on the porch of this fine hotel after our repast."

"You'll accompany me on my flower expedition, won't you, Harry?"

Harry smiled at his wife. "Of course. I'm sure I'll need a little exercise after eating a midday meal."

"I think I'll take a stroll on my own," Daniel said. "I want to enjoy the mountain air before our return trip."

The specialties of the day were roast turkey or pork chops; they ordered and soon were served a sizzling meal.

After taking his first bite of turkey, the professor announced, "As good as some of the best restaurants in Boulder. One of the few meats I eat. Much better for you than beef or pork."

"This is a special treat for me," Harry said. "I usually grab a quick bite this time of day when on patrol. It's a luxury to sit with no time commitment to get back on the street."

"Other than returning in time for the train's departure," Daniel said. "Conductor Shultz certainly threatened us with abandonment if we didn't get back to the passenger car in time."

"And I can't see the train waiting a minute even if one of us showed up dead," the professor said. He held up his glass. "Let me propose a toast to this fine day in the mountains and the good company here."

The others raised glasses as well.

"It must be quite an experience living in a town this far in the mountains," Susan said. "You'd have to be extremely self-sufficient."

The professor put his glass down. "That's very true, Mrs. McBride. This time of year it's quite mild, but in the middle of a winter the blizzard conditions would be daunting. I certainly don't enjoy having to shovel snow away from my door in Boulder. You can imagine what it's like up here with huge snowdrifts."

"I agree," Daniel said. "I wouldn't mind having a cottage up here during the summer, but I wouldn't like to reside here year round."

"To say nothing of not having much business, Mr. Compton." The professor wiped his mouth with a napkin. "I can't imagine an attorney supporting himself in this small town."

"No. It would be more for a summer retreat than a residence. Do you imagine the fishing is good around here?"

"I don't know if the fish bite in Boulder Creek," the professor replied, "but I've heard tales of good fishing in Eldora Lake."

"Tales of fish tails," Daniel said.

The professor groaned. "Stick with the law. Your sense of humor lacks both sense and humor."

"Listen to our clever professor." Daniel smirked. "He has become quite the humorist in spite of himself."

"I noticed a Stanley Steamer in the road on our walk to the hotel," Harry said. "Have any of you ridden in one of those contraptions?"

"Not yet," the professor answered. "They have become very popular in the mountains, navigating the wagon trails. They make a regular trip to Estes Park and have motored up from Boulder to Nederland and Eldora on the stagecoach road since nineteen-eleven."

Lucille's lips curled up slightly. "Our luncheon wouldn't be complete without a lecture on the illustrious automobile."

"Of course, my dear. The future of our country will be with those mechanical monsters."

The waiter asked for dessert orders, and Harry was pleased to find the hotel served vanilla ice cream. This made his day complete.

When they finished the meal and settled the bill, everyone left the hotel. The professor patted his stomach. "Ah, I think I will sit on the porch and watch the town go by." He plopped down in a rocking chair. Lucille and Daniel took off in opposite directions. Harry and Susan waited until everyone had taken their chosen routes and then walked back toward the main street through town.

"I take it you didn't want to pick flowers with Lucille," Harry said.

"No, I want to spend the time with you, Harry. It's not often I have you all to myself. Let's wander around town for a few minutes before we go look for flowers."

They made a pass through several blocks of wooden buildings, saw Daniel sitting on the porch of the general store, and then retraced their steps. As they passed the Gold Miner Hotel, Harry pointed. "The professor is no longer sitting on the porch. He must have decided to get some exercise."

"As will we," Susan replied. "Let's climb this hillside. I see some patches of yellow, red and blue above."

Susan lifted her skirt a few inches, and they headed up the incline. Within twenty yards they reached a spot with a smattering of flowers.

"Oh, look," Susan said. "Indian paintbrush. I must pick some." She reached over and snapped a stalk. She handed it to Harry.

"I'll be the beast of burden while you collect." He smiled at his wife.

Susan continued through a patch of flowers, identifying and picking anemone, prickly poppy and penstemon.

"I'm glad you know all the names," Harry said. "To me they're just flowers."

"Oh, you men. You never pay attention."

"As a policeman I'm an observer of people's behavior. I've never paid any attention to flowers."

"So give me your comments on the behavior of our companions on the train."

Harry paused, moved the flowers to his left hand and put his right index finger to his chin. "An interesting thought. We have a very strange collection of people."

"You make it sound like my bouquet of flowers."

"Just as you've found different colors and shapes of flowers, we have quite a composition of people. I'll start with Michael Jacoby. Quite a contrast within one person. Obviously, he suffers from developmental difficulties and emotional problems. A man in appearance, but not an adult in behavior. Amid the twitches and strange actions, however, is a unique creative talent."

"He is an amazing carver," Susan said.

"And very observant in his own strange way," Harry continued. "Noticing shoes, of all things."

"And his sister, Allison Jacoby?"

"Ah, the mother hen." Harry chuckled. "Herding Michael and trying to protect him at every turn. And I find her relationship with Frederick to be most unusual."

"How so?"

"They profess to be engaged, but I don't sense much affection between them. It's almost as if they're going through the motions. She has a lot of anger toward Frederick, particularly the way he treats Michael."

"Yes. The overprotective sister. And Frederick?"

Harry kicked a pebble. "A damaged soul. He was wounded in war and suffered through the influenza. Some people bounce back from adversity, but Frederick seems to have succumbed. He's full of anger. I'm afraid that young man doesn't have a bright future ahead of him. And he plans to break off his engagement with Allison Jacoby."

Susan came to an abrupt halt. "When did you hear that?"

"During my stroll in Sunset. Frederick hinted that he might pull up and go to California—without Allison."

Susan frowned. "And does Allison know of this pending change?"

"Apparently not."

"My, my," Susan said. "And what do you make of Professor Benjamin Sager and his companion, Lucille Vickering?"

"An interesting pair. The professor is certainly full of himself."

Susan giggled. "You can say that again. But he does share some interesting facts in his lectures."

"He is so tied to the role of professor that he can't get away from it, even on a Sunday trip on the railroad. I'm not sure why he invited Frederick and Daniel. It doesn't appear that he was very close to them. It's almost as if he wanted to have an audience on the trip. And Mrs. Vickering. She plays up to the professor as if manipulating him in some way. He indulges it because he seems taken with her. She certainly has an undercurrent of disgust, as when she lashed out at Frederick."

"Yes, a most unladylike response, although one can hardly blame her with Frederick insulting everyone. And, Mr. Police Officer, what about Daniel Compton?"

"Mrs. Police Officer, I'd say he's a typical young buck on the way up in his chosen profession. He detests Frederick and resents that Frederick and Allison are engaged. He's obviously still smitten with the young lady."

"Unrequited love."

"Something like that. He can't resist goading Frederick. I don't know if we'll get safely back to Boulder before they kill each other."

Susan picked another flower. "Oh, good. Here's a sandy lily." She handed it to Harry, who now had both hands full. "And what do you make of our conductor, Theodore Shultz?"

"Also another interesting link. It seems this group is all connected in odd ways. Shultz knew Frederick in the past, and there is lingering animosity between the two of them. Frederick doesn't seem to have many friends on the train today. There is no love lost between any of this crowd, except for Allison who is struggling to maintain a relationship with Frederick. But even in her, I sense contempt toward Frederick."

CHAPTER 23

Harry and Susan clambered aboard the Pullman car and discovered they were the first ones back. Harry checked his watch. Five minutes after two. He stashed the collection of wildflowers two rows back. "I don't know if you left any flowers in the hills around Eldora. Your bouquet fills up the whole seat. It's a good thing all those climbers aren't returning with us or there would be no room."

"Oh, Harry. I hardly took any at all. They smell so grand, and they'll look lovely in our living room."

"I don't know. There may not be enough room for you and me. We may have to move into a larger house to accommodate what you found."

Susan clucked her tongue. "Don't exaggerate."

Harry waved his hand toward the flower-strewn seat. "And the bees in Eldora are going to be very disappointed."

Susan rolled her eyes.

Allison and Michael came into the compartment. Michael appeared agitated, flapping his arms wildly.

Allison held a small bouquet of flowers in her left hand and her carpetbag in her right hand. She looked at Harry and Susan. "Have either of you seen Frederick? I thought he might be here already."

"He marched off with you and Michael," Harry said. "Haven't seen him since we left the train."

137

"Neither have I," Susan said. "Wasn't he with you and Michael?"

Allison bit her lip. "The three of us picnicked, but Frederick and I had a little . . . disagreement, and he stomped off into the woods by himself. We waited for him. Then Michael went off to carve by himself. I stayed by myself for a while before retrieving Michael, but I couldn't find Frederick. Finally, Michael and I came back to the train. I thought Frederick might have come directly here."

Michael tossed his head from side to side and waved his arms like a wounded crow, almost hitting the window.

"Michael, calm down." Allison stomped her foot. "I'm sure Frederick will be here any moment."

Michael dropped into his seat and began bashing his head against the window, causing it to quiver.

Allison put her bouquet of flowers on the seat behind her and grabbed Michael by the shoulders. "Stop that this moment."

He blinked rapidly, turned rigid and let out guttural sounds much like a cat growling.

"What's wrong, Michael?" Allison asked.

He shivered as if coming in from a winter blizzard and opened his mouth, but only managed a gurgling noise.

"He seems more upset than he's been all trip," Harry said.

Allison let out a deep sigh. "When he gets in a state like this, he won't even speak to me. I have to wait for him to calm down to find out what's wrong."

Michael pasted his face to the window as if searching for something outside. His breath fogged the window.

Allison sat next to her brother.

"How was your wildflower expedition?" Susan asked Allison.

"Between the picnic and looking for Frederick, I didn't pick very many. I did find some bluebells and columbines."

The car shook slightly and Benjamin came through the front doorway. "I almost tripped coming up those ladder steps," the professor announced. "They seem steeper than when I got off."

"It's all the food you ate." Lucille stopped behind him and scraped off mud from her shoes on the metal plate before coming into the car.

Benjamin and Lucille sat down.

Susan draped an elbow across the back of the seat and faced Lucille. "Didn't you pick any wildflowers?"

"I went off for a little stroll, and when I came back to find Benjamin, he was still on the porch of the Gold Miner Hotel. I woke him up, and he regaled me with the details of a dream. By then it was time to get back to the train."

"You must admit, my dear, I recounted to you a most unusual dream. I was an eagle soaring over the town of Eldora."

"I know. An eagle that ate too much turkey."

"That wasn't it at all, my dear. I experienced a most intriguing sensation of flying. I looked down, and all the people below looked like mice. I felt the strongest desire to swoop down and eat some of them."

"But fortunately, you were too full from your luncheon."

"Yes, my dear. And you, Mrs. McBride, did you rid the community of Eldora of your fair share of flowers?"

"Yes. They're right behind you."

Benjamin twisted around. "Egad. It looks like a flower store. You decimated the hillside."

Harry chuckled. "See, Susan. Professor Sager had the same impression I did."

Susan crossed her arms. "You men. Since Mrs. Vickering didn't get any flowers, I picked enough for both of us. She can have some of mine if she wishes."

"That's all right, Mrs. McBride. You deserve to keep what you found. I can get flowers around Boulder."

"By this time of summer there aren't that many wildflowers left in the lower elevations," the professor said. "But it's peak season up here at over nine thousand feet."

"Once again the last word from the learned professor," Lucille said.

The professor harrumphed. "I only thought a clarification was in order."

Conductor Shultz entered from the other passenger car. "We'll be departing shortly. All accounted for?"

Allison looked around the compartment. "Frederick isn't back yet. Have you seen him, Conductor Shultz?"

"Not since we arrived in Eldora."

"Daniel's not back, either," Harry added.

"In all the excitement, I didn't notice," Allison said. "Where could Frederick and Daniel be?"

As if hearing his name, Daniel came dashing through the door. "I'm here."

"Cutting it close," Shultz said.

"Sorry. I let the time slip away admiring the beauty of the mountain town. So many interesting old buildings to look at."

Shultz took out the watch on his gold fob and studied it. Then he snapped it shut. "We leave in one minute."

Daniel picked up Allison's flowers in the seat behind her, moved them toward the window and sat down.

"Oh, dear," Allison leaned across Michael to look out the window. Then she got up and dashed to the other side of the car to peer out. "Where is Frederick?" She returned to her seat, as agitated as Michael had been.

The whistle blew.

"Hopefully that will bring him running," Susan said.

"He'd better hurry," Shultz said.

Harry regarded Allison, who jerked her head from side to side, searching for her fiancé. Michael remained in the same position, as if glued to the window.

"I can't imagine what delayed him," Allison said. "He usually wants to be places early. This morning he made sure we arrived at the station with time to spare. Now this. It's not like him."

Harry remembered how close Frederick had timed his return to the train in Sunset. Was he going to try a last-minute dash again?

The train chugged forward with a hiss of steam and a clanking sound of the wheels engaging.

"We can't leave without him!" Allison shouted.

"We have our schedule to maintain," Shultz said.

A loud banging sound reverberated from the back of the car. All heads turned.

Frederick crawled through the doorway. He held a shaky hand up and pointed an index finger toward the front of the compartment. "You assassin!" Then he collapsed on the floor.

CHAPTER 24

At the sight of Frederick's limp body filling the aisle at the back of the passenger car, Susan gasped, and Allison screamed. Harry quickly scanned the people around him. Shultz stood at the front of the car with his mouth hanging wide open. Michael's face remained plastered to the window as if he didn't notice Frederick's dramatic entrance. The professor, Lucille and Daniel all swiveled to look at the body. The professor rotated his head, backward and forward and backward again. His face was a pasty white. Lucille held a hand over her mouth. Daniel wrinkled his forehead.

Harry realized he needed to take charge. "Everyone, remain right where you are!" he shouted. He stood, raced to the back of the car and bent over to examine Frederick. A knife handle stuck out of Frederick's back. It was ebony. Harry had seen that handle before, when Michael was carving.

Harry put his face close to Frederick's mouth. No breath. He felt for a pulse. None. Frederick's accusation had been his last act on this planet.

Harry slowly stood and paced back to where Conductor Shultz stood frozen in place. "What's the first stop with a telephone?"

Shultz remained in stunned silence as if he hadn't heard.

Harry reached out and shook the man's shoulders.

"I asked, where will we first be able to find a telephone?"

Shultz gasped. "Oh. At Cardinal. Do I need to signal to the

engineer to stop?"

Harry considered the question for a moment. He didn't think he would be able to find anything useful by hiking back to Eldora. Although technically they were in the Boulder County sheriff's jurisdiction, Harry didn't believe the sheriff would be able to marshal resources quickly on a Sunday. From Frederick's dying accusation, Harry knew the murderer was someone in the passenger car. No one would be getting off until Boulder. He would have to figure out who had killed Frederick in the next two and a half hours.

"No, we don't need to stop now, but I want to make a telephone call at Cardinal," Harry said.

"I'll notify the engineer when we stop at Sulphide," Shultz replied.

"Does someone have a blanket?" Harry asked.

Everyone remained motionless.

Harry repeated his question.

Finally, Allison pulled herself out of her shock and reached in her carpetbag. "Here . . . here's the one we used for our picnic."

Harry grabbed it and strode back to the body. He carefully draped the blanket over Frederick's lifeless form. He didn't want anyone, particularly the women, to have to keep seeing the body.

Harry took a deep breath to calm his own nerves. He, and he alone, was in a position to figure out what had happened. He had questioned witnesses and suspects numerous times, but this would require all his investigative skills. He would have to be very careful in speaking with his fellow passengers. Each might have important clues, but one was the murderer. Frederick had tried to point out the killer but died before revealing which of the six it might be. The only positive news—he had a contained list of suspects. He'd carefully question each of them and piece together exactly what had occurred.

Harry took out the notepad and pencil he always carried. He licked the tip of the pencil and began making notes.

He thought back to all that had transpired on the trip to Eldora. Every one of the six had a past relationship with Frederick, and each had a reason to dislike Frederick. So often, murders were committed by someone with a close relationship to the victim. Allison immediately came to mind. Although engaged to Frederick, she had argued with him, even admitting a final altercation during their picnic.

And Michael. Michael's knife in Frederick's back made him the prime suspect. But Harry faced a challenging interrogation with the disturbed young man. He would have to use all his wits to gain any useful information from someone who hardly spoke at all, and who, when he did speak, often didn't make much sense.

The professor had argued with Frederick on the way up, as they traded insults. Could he have become fed up with his former student and killed him?

Lucille and Frederick had also traded barbs. Frederick had been a resident in Lucille's boarding house, and obviously something had happened between them.

Daniel had a strong motive. He held affection for Allison, providing ample reason to want to get Frederick out of the way. With Frederick gone, Daniel would be in a position to renew his intention to woo Allison.

And even the conductor, Theodore Shultz. There had been a history of conflict with Frederick and they had almost come to blows earlier in the day.

Harry closed his eyes and tried to imagine what happened. Someone had taken Michael's knife, sneaked up behind Frederick and planted the knife in Frederick's back. He opened his eyes and surveyed his suspects. All the men were strong enough to do that. Lucille had the anger and apparent strength as well.

Allison was slight but possessed a toughness displayed by her handling of Michael.

Harry lifted the blanket and took a look at where the ebony protruded from Frederick's back. The handle was tilted upward. Someone had jabbed it with a downward stroke. All the suspects were tall enough to have made that motion. The knife was long and sharp, sharp enough to easily send chips of wood flying as Michael carved. Had the strange artist killed Frederick to protect his sister or had someone else gotten his or her hands on the knife? Michael would be the starting point for that line of inquiry, but would he say anything? Michael had been agitated ever since returning to the passenger car. Was that an indication of his guilt? Or had he seen the murder? Or was it something else that had disturbed him? Perhaps the loss of his knife, or the fact that it had been used to kill Frederick?

Frederick had been dealt a blow but had not died immediately. In his wounded condition, he had dragged himself back to the train, hoisted himself up the back ladder and crawled into the compartment before pointing, shouting and dying. Willpower had kept him alive for that last act, but then his body had given out.

Harry dropped the blanket over the body again and moved forward. He bent over Susan and said, "Please come to the back of the car with me."

"As long as I don't have to look at the body."

"It's covered."

She stood and followed her husband out of earshot of the others, where he stopped.

Harry whispered in her ear. "I want you to know that I'm going to be questioning each of the people in this car."

"Including me?"

"No. You have an alibi. I was with you all the time, so you couldn't have murdered Frederick."

"It's good to know I'm not a suspect."

Harry graced his wife with a half-grin and whispered to her. "But you can be very helpful in the investigation. You're very observant. I want you to keep your eyes and ears open. Watch the others and listen to what they say. You may pick up something useful while I'm conducting my interrogations."

"Are you making me a deputy?"

"Only the sheriff has deputies. You will be my extra eyes and ears."

Susan gave him a wry smile. "Will you put me on the police payroll?"

"I wish I could, but only Chief Bass can do that."

Susan pouted. "I guess I'll help you out of the kindness of my heart."

"I knew I could count on you."

"But I wouldn't do this for anyone else."

Harry gave his wife's shoulder an affectionate squeeze and bent over to her ear. "Now go back and be a good spy."

The train passed the small building at the Lake Eldora flag stop without slowing. No one except Harry seemed to notice.

Harry and Susan returned to the front of the car. Susan took her seat.

Harry cleared his throat. "I'd like your attention. Frederick has been murdered. I will need to speak with each of you individually. I ask for your cooperation so that we can get to the bottom of what happened."

"Before you covered him, I saw a knife in his back," Daniel said. "I assume that's what killed him."

"It appears so," Harry replied. "I will ask each of you, one at a time, to accompany me to a seat farther back in the compartment."

Allison shivered. "I don't want to see Frederick's body."

"I'll keep it covered with the blanket," Harry said.

Shultz signaled to Harry. "I'm sure you'll want to speak with me, but I must check on the passengers in the front car."

"Go ahead. Just don't leave the train."

Shultz did a double take. "You're kidding. I can't leave the train."

"I know. I'll want to speak with you later, but for now go about your business."

Shultz turned and disappeared through the passageway to the other Pullman car.

"We spoke of fingerprints earlier on the trip," the professor said. "Do you think there might be fingerprints on the murder weapon?"

"It's possible, if the murderer didn't have gloves on." Harry hoped he wouldn't have to resort to collecting fingerprints after they reached their destination. He wanted to find the culprit before they arrived at the Boulder train depot.

CHAPTER 25

Where to start? Harry surveyed his group of suspects. Each might have a piece of the puzzle. He would have to proceed carefully to put things together. He decided to begin with the murder weapon. "Michael, I need to speak with you."

Michael continued to stare out the window, his face pasted to the pane as the train headed toward Sulphide. The window was misted over and covered with drops, as if a dog had slobbered against it.

"Michael, Officer McBride needs to speak with you." Allison shook her brother's shoulder.

He gave a start as if awakened from a dream.

"This will only take a few minutes," Harry said. "I'd like you to accompany me to the middle of our passenger car, where we can speak in private."

Allison stood and pulled on Michael's arm to raise him. "Go on. It's fine."

He remained fixed in place.

"Michael, I insist you accompany Officer McBride."

Michael got up, furrowing his brow. His arms twitched as if he were trying to rid himself of a cloud of gnats.

Harry reached for Michael's elbow to steer him away from the others, but Michael snarled and violently pulled his arm away.

"He doesn't like to be touched by strangers." Allison turned toward her brother. "Michael, it's all right. Officer McBride won't touch you again."

"I'm sorry," Harry replied. "Michael, please follow me." He walked toward the back of the car, stopped and looked over his shoulder to make sure that Michael was following.

Michael shuffled along.

Harry pointed to a seat two-thirds of the way back. He wanted to be far enough away from the others but not too close to the body. "You can sit there."

Michael dropped into the indicated seat, and Harry sat across the aisle, leaning toward the fidgeting young man.

Harry wanted to touch him to reassure him but knew that would only cause further problems. He watched intently as the young man twitched as if infested with ants. "I need to ask you some questions."

Michael stared at the floor while his hands made washing motions. He acted unaware that Harry had spoken to him.

Harry straightened and tried again. "I will ask questions, and I need you to answer them. Do you understand?"

After a moment, still staring at the floor, Michael nodded.

Harry considered how he wanted to phrase his questions. He didn't want to increase the anxiety of this frail young man. He sought answers. He figured the best approach was to present a friendly demeanor and gain Michael's confidence. "I must say I was very impressed by your carving ability. How long have you been making animals?"

Michael's gaze rose as far as Harry's chest. "Five years."

"They're very realistic. You must study animals."

Michael tilted his head.

"Did you carve when you, Allison and Frederick went on your picnic in Eldora today?"

"Yes."

"You almost finished the fox earlier. Did you start whittling something else after you left the train in Eldora?"

149

Michael raised his gaze to Harry's throat level. He clasped his hands tightly. "Found wood and started a rabbit."

"That's right. Your sister said on the trip up that you wanted to find some more wood today. I'm sure the rabbit will be as good as the mountain lion and fox I saw earlier. You have a very unique knife with an ebony handle."

A tear appeared in the corner of Michael's eyes. "Gone."

"What do you mean, gone?"

For the first time Michael actually looked at Harry's face. He didn't exactly make eye contact, but seemed to be looking at Harry's chin. "Stolen."

Interesting. Harry thought for a moment and took a deep breath. "Let's start when you left the train in Eldora. What did you do?"

"Went with Allison on picnic."

"Was Frederick with you?"

His lips curled menacingly. "Yes."

"You don't like Frederick, do you?"

Michael's arms started flapping. "Not nice to Allison."

"Okay, okay." Harry held up his hands. "Just relax. Where did you go on your picnic?"

"Meadow by trees. Found good piece of wood." Michael dropped his arms.

"Did you eat?"

"Yes. Allison put down blanket. That one." Michael pointed to the blanket covering Frederick. "We ate."

"After your picnic, what happened?"

"Frederick shouted at Allison." Michael's arms started twitching again.

Harry wondered if Michael ever dislocated his shoulders with all his violent arm waving. "Then?"

"Frederick went into woods. Good riddance." He spat on the floor.

Harry moved his shoe. Fortunately, the spittle missed by inches. "And what did you do after Frederick left?"

"Went to the other side of the meadow and around bend. Found stump and sat to carve rabbit."

"Where was your sister?"

"She stayed on the blanket, crying."

Harry pictured the argument, Frederick going off in a sulk, Michael pursuing his own interest, and Allison left with the cleanup of both the picnic and her emotions. Not a pretty picture. He jotted a few notes on his pad.

"Did you carve long while sitting on the stump?"

"Finished rabbit's head. Had to relieve myself. Went farther into woods."

Harry needed to walk a fine line to get answers but not set off Michael into wild gesticulations. He posed his next question carefully. "Did you take your knife with you when you went to relieve yourself?"

Michael began twitching. "Left on stump. Stuck it in. When I came back, it was gone. Stolen."

"So someone took your knife?"

Michael rubbed his hands together vigorously. "Yes."

Harry decided to risk this one thing. It might shock Michael, but it was necessary. He stepped to the back of the car and lifted the blanket. "Is this your knife?"

Michael's eyes opened wide, and his arms flapped wildly. "Want it back."

Harry dropped the blanket over the body and stood in front of Michael. "The knife needs to stay there right now. You'll get it back after the investigation is completed. Did anything else happen when you went into the woods?"

Michael's eyes focused on the floor. "Only relieved myself."

"And then?"

"Went back to stump. Knife gone."

151

"Did you look for it?"

Michael shook his head. "Stolen. I left it stuck in stump." He made a sharp stabbing motion with his right hand. "Didn't fall. Someone took it."

"Did you tell Allison?"

"She got me. Said to go back to the train. I couldn't speak. No words came." His arms began flapping again.

Harry remained in place, watching Michael. "Did you kill Frederick?"

Surprisingly, his arm flapping stopped. "Deserved to die."

"Did you kill him, Michael?"

Michael squinted at Harry's stomach. "No. Wish I had."

CHAPTER 26

Harry walked Michael back to his seat. Michael's arms flapped, but not as dramatically as before.

Allison stood, and Michael scooted in next to the window. "Is everything all right?" she whispered in Harry's ear.

"For now," he replied.

Michael plastered his face against the window.

"Michael, if we can find another knife, do you want to carve?" Allison asked.

"No." Michael kept looking out the window.

"That's not like you," Allison said.

"Leave me alone," Michael said.

Allison looked up at Harry, who still stood in the aisle. "What did you do to him? He always wants to carve."

"We'll discuss that in a little while," Harry said.

The train pulled to a stop at Sulphide, and Harry grabbed the edge of a seat to keep his balance.

Conductor Shultz reappeared. "We'll be on our way again shortly. We're on the wye, so the engine can go forward from here to Boulder."

"Wye, oh wye," Daniel said.

The professor groaned. "Even in this serious time, Mr. Compton, you resort to your infantile remarks."

"Only trying to relieve the tension," Daniel replied.

Harry scrutinized the group of people in the front of the car. Who to question next? He wanted to corroborate with Allison what Michael had said, and discuss the knife, but he decided to first speak with Daniel, who had been the last person to get on the car—that is, the last before Frederick. Maybe he saw Frederick or noticed something on his way back to the train. Or maybe he was the murderer. "Mr. Compton, please accompany me to the back of the compartment."

Daniel looked up and gave a wry smile. "Do I need a lawyer?"

"I think you'll do at this point."

Daniel pulled himself up and followed Harry, who motioned to the seat Michael had vacated a few moments before. Daniel sat as Harry took his place across the aisle. The car jolted as they started forward. Harry wished it were only as easy as an engine changing direction for him to find the murderer.

"What did you do after we ate at the Gold Miner Hotel?" Harry asked.

"I'm usually the ones asking questions," Daniel replied.

"And right now I'm the one listening for answers," Harry said.

Daniel grinned. "Very good, Officer McBride. After our meal, I wandered around town by myself. As you might have noticed, I'm the only one in this illustrious group that doesn't have a traveling companion. I took the time to explore Eldora." He stopped and folded his arms.

The train gained speed before heading up the slope toward Cardinal. Harry needed to get some further information before that stop. There, he'd have a chance to place a telephone call to Boulder. "Please continue."

"After traipsing around for a while, I found the general store and purchased an apple and two oatmeal cookies to suffice if I became hungry on the return trip to Boulder. Please note those details."

Harry tapped his pad with the pencil but wrote nothing.

"I availed myself of a chair on the store's porch, an excellent vantage point to watch people pass by."

"Did you see any of your fellow passengers?"

"Only you and Mrs. McBride walking past. Mrs. Vickering had disappeared elsewhere, the professor was left resting on the porch of the Gold Miner Hotel, and the others were off on their picnic."

"And after that?"

"I relaxed there and watched the townspeople stroll by until a little past one-thirty. I saw several old men, two dogs, a cat and two children. Next, I meandered to the end of town, admiring all the wooden structures. Quite an eclectic collection of buildings in this mountain town. Does architecture interest you, Officer McBride?"

"Let's keep to the question at hand."

"Ah, the dedicated police officer. No time for hobbies or trivial discussions. Such a shame."

"Please continue with your account."

"There's nothing else. After wandering around, I made my way back to the train station. I didn't want to miss the train."

"Did you see any of the passengers at that time?"

Daniel opened his hands toward Harry. "The professor and Mrs. Vickering were climbing aboard the Pullman car when I came in sight of the train. I stopped to tie my shoe and boarded in the nick of time."

"Did you see Mr. Hammond?"

"No. The last I saw of him was when he left the train earlier, until he made his dramatic entrance." Daniel pointed toward the blanket. "He always was one to try to attract attention to himself."

Harry stared at Daniel. "Did you kill Mr. Hammond?"

Daniel flinched. "Good heavens, no. Why would you think that?"

"You and Mr. Hammond didn't get along very well. I sense

that you resented his engagement to Miss Jacoby."

Daniel gave a snort. "Those two didn't belong together. He treated her like dirt. I don't know what Allison saw in Frederick. Maybe she wanted to mother him back to health. I don't think that would have been possible. Frederick alienated himself from others. He had little chance of ever changing."

Harry continued to watch Daniel carefully. "Very convenient that your rival is out of the way."

Daniel sat ramrod straight. "What are you implying?"

"Only that Miss Jacoby is available again with her fiancé dead."

"I . . . I'd never resort to murder to gain her interest," Daniel sputtered. "What kind of person do you think I am?"

"That's what I'm trying to determine."

Daniel glared at Harry. "Just because I represent people who may disagree with you, Officer McBride, it doesn't mean I'd be involved in criminal activity. Yes, Frederick didn't deserve Allison, and I can't say I'm sad at his passing. You saw his behavior this morning. In spite of that, I had nothing to do with his death."

Harry kept his eyes glued on Daniel. Was he being truthful or protesting too much? The other passengers might lend some insight into that question. That gave him one more idea. "If you didn't kill Frederick, who do you think did?"

Daniel actually smiled. "Well, isn't this a switch? Trying to enlist my assistance in your investigation?"

Harry shrugged. "As an attorney you have to be an observant person. I'm curious to know if you have any opinions on the matter."

"Oh, I always have opinions." He put a finger to his cheek. "Let me do your work for you. Everyone in the compartment except you and Mrs. McBride argued with Frederick this morning. Professor Sager traded barbs with Frederick numerous times. Frederick insulted Mrs. Vickering on several occasions, and she lashed out at him. Michael obviously disliked Frederick, and even our conductor became angry with him. Allison, the supposed fiancée, also exchanged sharp words with Frederick. I can't imagine Allison killing him. The others are all possibilities."

"Any favorites?"

Daniel leaned toward Harry and in a soft voice said, "I'd go with the professor. After all, he arranged this strange trip. I wondered why he invited me, and then I find Frederick on the same journey. I must say I wasn't pleased at that development."

"Displeased enough to take action?"

Daniel gave a dismissive wave of his hand. "Let's not get back on that track of accusation."

"Anything else you'd like to add?" Harry poised his pencil, ready to write anything significant.

"No, I think you've drained this well dry."

Harry put his pad and pencil back in his jacket pocket. *We'll see.*

CHAPTER 27

Harry watched Daniel return to the seat in the right front where he had sat earlier on the trip.

As the train continued to climb, Harry approached Conductor Shultz. "Are things set for me to get off at the Cardinal station? I need to notify the authorities in Boulder as to what happened to Frederick Hammond."

Shultz regarded Harry thoughtfully. "I told the engineer. How long do you think it will take?"

"I have to reach the police chief and coroner. I should also get word to the sheriff, but the police chief can relay that message. Probably five minutes."

"We can make up that amount of time." Shultz disappeared through the passageway heading toward the front car.

Harry stepped toward Allison. "Miss Jacoby, who are Mr. Hammond's next of kin who should be informed?"

Allison bit her lip and looked up at Harry with tear-filled eyes. "His parents are dead. He had a sister who also died. He has a brother, Robert, in New York City, but they haven't kept in touch." She gulped. "No one else I can think of."

"Thank you. When we reach Boulder, I'll try to locate his brother. Do you have an address or telephone number?"

"There should be something in Frederick's room at the Jamison boarding house."

"Good. I'll check that out."

Allison placed her hand on Harry's arm. "You will find who

did this to Frederick, won't you?"

"I'm trying my best."

The train slowed as it crossed the trestle to Cardinal. Ominous clouds rolled over the peaks of the Continental Divide to the west. The sound of thunder rattled the windows.

"I think we're in for a storm," Susan said.

"Ah, the typical summer afternoon thundershowers in the mountains," the professor said. "I hope the climbers are safely encamped and not standing on the top of a hill. Do you realize how many people lightning kills? It's one of those tragedies that can be prevented. When you hear thunder, seek shelter and don't stay out in the open, particularly on an exposed mountain."

"You're full of good advice," Lucille said.

"Of course, my dear. And it pays off. I've never been struck by lightning."

Shultz entered the compartment. "Officer McBride, I'll also accompany you into the station to show you where the telephone is so you won't waste any time."

As soon as the train came to a complete stop, Harry and Shultz jumped down and strode into the station.

Shultz pointed to the box on an interior wall. "Right there."

Harry stepped over and picked up the receiver. Shultz followed him.

Harry swung around and stared at Shultz. "I need to make this call in private, if you don't mind."

"Oh, sorry." Shultz flushed red, matching his nose. "I'll meet you back in your Pullman car." He spun on his heels and hurried out of the station building.

Harry thought for a moment and decided to call the police chief first. He gave the handle a full crank and waited for the operator to pick up. Sometimes it took a while on Sundays. Finally, a nasal woman's voice answered. Harry leaned over and spoke into the transmitter, giving his instructions and waiting to be connected. Fortunately, the chief had a telephone in his home, a necessity for the department. Harry wasn't sure how much the chief could accomplish, given that he was suffering from a relapse of the influenza, but he might be able to make a further telephone call or two. It had been a tough year for the chief, who had been ordered to bed in January. In February, Chief Bass struggled out of bed to investigate the burglary of two stores, catching the culprits with stolen goods. Unfortunately, the exertion had not helped the chief, who returned to bed sicker than ever. He seemed on the mend, but in June he had come down with a bad cough he couldn't shake.

After a minute, the chief's wife picked up. She had a pleasant voice with a touch of a Southern accent.

Harry identified himself and indicated he was calling from Cardinal in the mountains above Boulder.

"What are you doing up there?"

"Susan and I went for a day's excursion on the Switzerland Trail railroad. There's been a murder, and I need to speak with your husband."

"Oh, dear. He's not feeling very well today, but I'll get him for you since you have urgent business."

Harry heard a banging sound. He waited.

It took another minute before Police Chief Bass's gravelly voice came on the line. "What's this about a murder, McBride?" He went into a coughing fit, and Harry waited until the coughing subsided.

"When we reboarded the train in Eldora one of the passengers, Frederick Hammond, staggered into the Pullman car and collapsed with a knife in his back. Before dying, Mr. Hammond shouted at someone in the car, accusing the murderer."

"Have you arrested that person?" More coughing.

"It's not that simple. Frederick pointed but didn't call out a name. Besides Susan and me, there were only six other people in the direction he indicated. Consequently I have six suspects and have begun interviewing them." Harry adjusted the receiver to his ear in order to hear more clearly.

After the next coughing jag, the chief said, "I'll notify George Savage to meet you at the Boulder station."

Harry was gratified to hear that his fellow police officer would be enlisted to assist. "Tell him we're in the last Pullman and to enter at the door between the two passenger cars."

"What time do you expect to arrive?" Chief Bass asked.

"Arrival is scheduled for four-forty. We may be a little late as they're holding the train so I can make this call."

"Give me a quick rundown on what you've learned so far."

Harry hesitated. He didn't want to go into too much detail yet, nor did he intend to keep the chief on his feet when he should be in bed. "The murder weapon belonged to one of the suspects. Each of the suspects had one or more arguments with the victim on the trip into the mountains. I'm in the process of figuring out where everyone was right before the train left the Eldora station."

"Do you know where the stabbing took place?"

Good question. "The victim was assaulted somewhere in or around Eldora. Apparently, he stumbled or crawled to the train and died in the back of our passenger compartment."

"I doubt whether Savage will be able to notify anyone in Eldora today to take a look around—" The chief's speech was interrupted by another hacking cough. He didn't sound well at all.

"Chief, I don't want to keep you. If you have a chance, call the coroner, or I can do it on the next stop that has a telephone, but I don't want to hold up the train any longer. If you could reach the sheriff, I'd appreciate it. Do you think he will have

161

any concern over jurisdiction?"

"Nah. He'll be glad that someone is taking care of it for him. He's as strapped for people as we are. We can get the appropriate parties together when you return to Boulder. What about the body?"

"It's covered with a blanket in the back of the passenger car."

The chief coughed again. "Go find who did this."

"Yes, sir."

"I assume you're not armed."

"Correct. I'm off duty."

"Be careful. Interview the suspects, check all the facts, pay attention to your intuition, but don't make assumptions. Got it?"

"Yes, sir."

Harry rang off and replaced the receiver. He needed to get back so as not to delay the train any longer. As he strode out of the station, he thought about the next step in the investigation. He would speak with Allison. She might be a key witness or even the person who committed the murder, given her tenuous relationship with the victim. After Allison, he would decide on the next person to interrogate. Fortunately, he had the ideal place to question people, and no one would be leaving until they reached Boulder. He knew what he needed to do.

Harry climbed aboard to the sound of a thunder clap accompanied by large drops of rain striking the car. He waved to Schultz. The conductor dashed past Harry, then leaned out the side between the two cars and signaled the engineer. In response, the whistle tooted. In seconds, there was a hiss of steam, and the wheels began moving.

When Schultz stepped back in the compartment, Harry asked him, "What's the next stop with a telephone?"

"Not until Glacier Lake."

"I may need to make another call there."

Shultz took his watch from his vest pocket and peered at it. "Your other call caused a delay. We're five minutes behind schedule."

"I understand," Harry said, "but police business is more important right now. I don't know if I need to call again, but I'll let you know as we get closer."

"I don't expect that we'll have many flag stops on the way back to Boulder. I'm hoping we can make up some of the time on the downhill from Glacier Lake to Tungsten. That doesn't have many turns, so we can pick up some speed."

"If we do have any additional passengers joining us, put them on the car ahead. I don't want anyone else in this car until we reach Boulder."

Shultz frowned. "We only have four open seats in the car in front. As long as we don't have too many additional passengers, I'll accommodate your request."

"Even if there are more, you'll need to find a way to put them somewhere else," Harry said. "We don't need anyone else in the middle of this mess."

CHAPTER 28

Harry had done what he could to get things going in Boulder with the call to Police Chief Bass, but here on the train it was up to him to move this investigation forward. The next important link involved Allison's testimony.

"Miss Jacoby, please accompany me to the back of the car."

She looked up at Harry with large, pleading eyes. "I don't know if I should leave Michael alone."

"He seems occupied looking out the window at the moment. I'm sure he'll be fine. We'll only be half a dozen seats away, so if there is any problem, you can return."

Allison let out a deep sigh. "I guess. Michael, I'll be right back." She stood and followed Harry to the seats used for questioning.

Once they settled in, Harry said, "First, I'd like you to tell me everything that happened after you left the train when we arrived in Eldora."

Allison twiddled the hem of her dress. "I took my carpetbag with all the picnic supplies and went with Frederick and Michael to a meadow surrounded by trees."

Harry ventured a peek out the window. The rain fell hard amid flashes of lightning. A good mountain storm. "How did you find that particular spot?"

"It was the one Old James mentioned. I followed his directions. It's over the bridge and along the creek in a stand of trees."

Harry nodded. "Describe the meadow."

Allison wrinkled her brow. "It's shaped like a curvy Y. We came in on one leg and another leg leads out toward town. Then there is the curvy part that disappears behind trees. We ate in the meadow where the three legs intersect. I spread the blanket . . ." Allison's eyes turned to the blanket covering Frederick's body. She gasped.

"Take your time, Miss Jacoby."

She covered her eyes for a moment before returning her gaze to Harry. "This is difficult."

Harry looked out the window, and the train sailed through Wolfram without a flag stop. "I know. But what you have to tell me may be crucial in finding who killed Mr. Hammond. Please continue your account of the picnic."

Allison clenched her fists as if steeling herself and took a deep breath. "After placing the blanket on the grass, I set out the food. Michael was hungry and started to eat immediately. Frederick paced for a few minutes and finally sat down. He was in one of his moods and didn't talk much. I tried to keep a conversation going, but it was pretty much one way.

"When we finished, I put everything back in the carpet bag, except for the . . . the blanket. Michael went to look for wood, and I picked flowers. Frederick stayed on the blanket, moping. Later, I returned with a small bouquet, and Michael came back, having found several good pieces of pine."

"Do you know what time that was?"

Allison shook her head. "I hardly ever look at my watch. I wear it because I like how it looks, but I'm not that interested in checking the time like some people."

At a thumping sound, Harry jerked his head toward the front of the compartment to see Michael bashing his head against the window.

Allison jumped up. "I need to go see what's happening with

my brother."

"All right. But come right back. I'll wait here."

Allison dashed forward and leaned toward Michael. He waved his arms in the air for a moment, and she put her hand on his shoulder and whispered in his ear. He put his face back against the window.

Harry waited as the train passed Lakewood, again not stopping. He regarded the desolate surroundings that once supported thriving mines.

Allison spoke in a low tone to Michael and then returned to her seat across from Harry.

"Is everything taken care of?" Harry asked.

"For the time being. Michael saw some deer again and became agitated. He's settled down now, though."

"You were telling me about after you picked wildflowers."

"Oh, yes. I came back, put my flowers on the blanket and sat next to Frederick. He was still in his mood. I told him to quit sulking. He shouted at me to leave him alone. Michael started shaking and in his usual halting voice told Frederick to stop shouting at me. Frederick stomped off into the woods."

"What direction did he go?"

Allison put her hand to her mouth and looked toward the ceiling as if trying to picture the scene. "There was a muddy spot where some water seeped up from an underground spring. He headed that direction. It was between the two openings where we came in and the one from town."

"And Michael?"

"He got up and said he'd found a stump around the bend where he wanted to carve. This was in the opposite direction from where Frederick had gone. In a moment, I was by myself. I arranged my flowers, lay on the blanket and closed my eyes for a little quiet time to myself until Mrs. Vickering appeared."

Harry raised an eyebrow. "Mrs. Vickering?"

"Yes. I didn't see her arrive, but I heard footsteps and sat up. She said she had been taking a walk while the professor rested on the porch of the hotel."

"Did Mr. Hammond or Michael see Mrs. Vickering arrive?"

Allison clenched her teeth for a moment and then relaxed. "No. Michael was out of sight around a stand of trees, and Frederick was off in the other part of the woods."

"How do you know they were still there?"

"Michael wanted to work on his carving, so he was at the stump he found earlier. While Mrs. Vickering was there, I heard Frederick curse once, so I knew he was still sulking in the woods."

"Did Mrs. Vickering stay long?"

"No. She asked what time it was. I checked my watch, and to my surprise, it was already two o'clock. I showed Mrs. Vickering the time. She acted surprised as well and said she needed to get back to the hotel to retrieve the professor if they were going to make it back to the train on time. I realized I needed to gather Michael and Frederick as well. I dashed around the bend to get Michael. He was in one of his states, flapping his arms and twirling wildly. I had to calm him down. I asked what was wrong, but he only stammered and couldn't speak. He went rigid and refused to move. It took forever, but I finally led him back to our picnic spot, put the blanket in the carpetbag and shouted for Frederick. He didn't answer."

"What did you do then?"

"We had to get back to the train. I shouted one more time, telling Frederick that Michael and I were going back. I figured he must have decided to return to the train by himself, so I picked up the carpetbag and flowers, and we headed to the station. I dragged Michael the whole way, concerned we might not get there in time."

"Did you see any of the other passengers along the way?"

"No. I was so intent on moving Michael along that I didn't notice anyone else. When we entered the car, I saw you and Mrs. McBride." Tears welled in Allison's eyes. "The others arrived, and then that awful thing happened."

"Bear with me, Miss Jacoby. I have to ask you this question." Harry took a breath. "Did you kill Mr. Hammond?"

Allison gasped. "Of course not. How could you ask such a thing?" Then, as if a railroad switch in her mind had been changed to another line of track, her teary eyes dried and bore in on Harry. "I was mad at Frederick, but I wouldn't have done anything to hurt him, much less kill him. He had enough problems as it was." She straightened her shoulders. "Now, Officer McBride, I expect you to find who did kill Frederick."

"That's my purpose in asking these questions. Do you know why your brother was so upset?"

"No. He hasn't told me yet."

Harry pointed to the blanket-clad body. "Michael is unhappy because he doesn't have his knife. It was the weapon used to kill Mr. Hammond."

Allison let out a gasp. "No. Michael didn't do it. Not Michael."

Harry grabbed her hands. "Please stay calm. I don't know that Michael committed the murder. I only know his knife was the weapon used."

Allison put her hands to her temples. "I don't understand how this could have happened. Michael's knife. How?"

"I will be speaking with everyone here to find out." Harry leaned closer and spoke in a quiet voice. "Do you have any idea who killed Frederick Hammond?"

Allison frowned. "I can't imagine anyone doing such a horrid thing."

Harry spent a moment writing notes on his pad. Some of the

pieces were starting to fall into place, but much was left uncertain.

They passed Anson without a flag stop. Harry considered all he had learned. He had to find out if anyone else had seen Daniel wandering around by himself. Harry also needed to interview Lucille Vickering very carefully. She and Allison provided an alibi for each other, if she corroborated Allison's account. They had parted with very few minutes to spare. Allison only had enough time to collect Michael and get back to the train. Lucille had to return to the hotel, get the professor and trek to the station, a trip that would have allowed only enough time for Lucille and the professor to arrive precisely when they did—not enough time for either Lucille or Allison to find Frederick in the woods and stab him.

CHAPTER 29

After excusing Allison to return to her seat next to Michael, Harry looked out the window to see that the rain had stopped and blue sky had appeared to the west. Mountain storms—intense, and then they blew past. He was caught in his own storm, but saw no possibility of it quickly dissipating.

He needed to think through the best approach with the rest of the suspects. Somewhere in this compartment was the answer to what had happened to Frederick Hammond. Who to question next? It was a toss-up between the professor and Lucille. Harry made his decision and strolled to the front of the passenger car.

"Mrs. Vickering, may I have a few minutes of your time?"

Lucille smiled. "Why, of course, Officer McBride." She slid out of her seat and accompanied him to the designated interview location as the train slowed. They both grasped the tops of the seats to keep from falling.

"Flag stop at Blue Bird," Conductor Shultz announced.

As Harry sat, he noticed two men waiting to get on the train. They wore shabby trousers, wrinkled shirts and dusty caps. Probably miners returning to Boulder. He watched to make sure Shultz followed his directions and placed these passengers in the car in front, and then he turned to Lucille. "I need your assistance in understanding what might have happened to Frederick Hammond. Kindly recount everything you did after our meal at the Gold Miner Hotel."

"Let me see." Lucille crinkled her nose. "Benjamin chose to stay on the porch, and I wanted to take a walk, so I left him there. It was such a beautiful day that I couldn't resist a pleasant breath of air. The view of the mountains, the smell of fresh pine, the stream. Do you enjoy hiking through the hills, Officer McBride?"

Harry thought again of his usual sore feet at the end of a day on patrol. "Not as much as the members of the hiking club that were in our car until Glacier Lake, but my wife and I go into the foothills on occasion. Did you see any of the other passengers after you left the Gold Miner Hotel?"

"Not immediately. I thought of picking wildflowers as we discussed earlier, but I got caught up in admiring the scenery. Eldora is quite a beautiful little town. Did you notice all the quaint houses? And that lovely Gold Miner Hotel we dined at. I circled it to take in its full splendor. For a mountain structure, it's built solidly, but the owners maintain an attractive combination of the rustic and the elegant."

Harry tapped his fingers on his leg. "Please continue with what you did after our meal."

Lucille gave an embarrassed laugh and put her hand to her cheek. "I'm sorry. I do carry on. Next, I wandered through several side streets and out through the meadows and trees. I once again considered picking flowers but decided I didn't want to bother carrying them back with me to the train. It was fine just to admire them in place. Do you ever pick wildflowers? Oh, probably not, but I know your wife does."

With the passengers safely accommodated in the car ahead, the train began moving again. The sound of the wheels reverberated as they crossed the trestle over North Boulder Creek heading north. Shultz came into the compartment and gave Harry an "all clear" hand wave. Harry waved back and returned his gaze to Lucille. "But you must have seen some of the other passengers during the afternoon."

"Shortly before the time to reboard the train, I came across Miss Jacoby sitting on a blanket in a small meadow. It's that very blanket." She pointed to the covered body. "I appreciate good blankets. In my line of business, it's useful to have a good eye for that sort of thing. My boarders must have the best linens and blankets for their beds. I speculate that Mrs. McBride has a similar eye. She probably keeps your house immaculate."

Harry leaned toward Lucille. "This is important. I want you to tell me in as much detail as you can about what transpired when you encountered Miss Jacoby in the meadow."

A commotion in front interrupted their conversation. All eyes turned toward Michael, who flapped his hands and struck the window.

Allison grabbed his arms and tried to constrain him.

Michael flailed again, almost striking Allison in the face.

Harry thought for a moment he might have to go forward to help her, but Allison secured her brother, and he calmed down.

"I don't know about that young man," Lucille said. "Miss Jacoby has her hands full taking care of him. One of my boarders acted like that. He once knocked over a chair with his wild gesticulations. Quite a problem."

"Yes. Please continue."

Lucille gave a dismissive wave of her hand. "You men. So single-focused. The meadow. I came through an opening in the trees to find Miss Jacoby lying down. I thought she might be hurt so I approached her. She sat up, startled by my arrival. Has that ever happened to you, Officer McBride? You're resting and someone appears. It can be quite unsettling. I didn't mean to surprise her. It's not good for one's health to be frightened like that. I had an uncle who was literally scared to death. He died on the spot."

Harry resisted the urge to roll his eyes. "Did you see Michael

Jacoby or Frederick Hammond in the meadow?"

Lucille concentrated for a moment. "No. Only Miss Jacoby. She seemed upset. I noticed from the red around her eyes that she had been crying. She is a most attractive young woman and those blue eyes. Very striking. Well, except when she's been crying. Have you observed her eyes, Officer McBride?"

"Yes. You were saying."

"Miss Jacoby certainly had a difficult time between her brother and the despicable behavior of Frederick Hammond." Lucille clenched her jaw. "Men can be such a bother. That's why I enjoy the company of Benjamin. He's easygoing. Oh, he lectures all the time, but once one gets used to that character flaw, he can be quite entertaining. Have you listened to some of his stories on this trip?"

Harry felt as though he was trying to corral a runaway steer in keeping Lucille focused. "You were mentioning Miss Jacoby in the meadow."

"Oh, yes. Don't mind me. My mind has a tendency to wander. So there was Miss Jacoby. She stood, and we spoke for a few minutes. That was a lovely spot she selected for a picnic. The next time I plan a picnic in Eldora, I'll choose the same location. Do you go on picnics with Mrs. McBride?"

"Once in a while. Back to you and Miss Jacoby."

"Oh, yes. I asked her what time it was, and she showed me her watch. I was surprised to learn that it was already two o'clock. I realized I needed to return to the Gold Miner Hotel to retrieve Benjamin. Did you notice the hotel has a new coat of paint? I like when people take good care of their buildings. I'm careful to keep my boarding house freshly painted. Every two years."

"Did you hear anyone shout while you were in the meadow with Miss Jacoby?"

Lucille put her finger to her chin. "Hmm. There was

something. I couldn't tell if it was human or an animal or maybe the wind going through the trees. Have you ever been up in the mountains when the wind is howling? It can be most distracting. I remember a time—"

"I hate to be curt, but I need you to answer my questions, and I have other people to speak with."

"I understand. What else can I do for you, Officer McBride?"

"After you found out it was two o'clock, what did you do?"

"Miss Jacoby went to retrieve her brother, and I raced out of the meadow toward the Gold Miner Hotel as fast as my legs could take me. Well, I didn't actually race, since that isn't easy in a skirt, but I hurried. I made it back and found Benjamin ensconced on the porch. He yammered about a dream before I yanked him to his feet and propelled him toward the railroad station. We practically dashed the whole way. It's a good thing it was downhill. I'm sure you're used to running, but Benjamin isn't that fit, and it certainly isn't ladylike to be running in a skirt. In spite of everything, we made it in time. Barely."

"Did you see anyone else along the way?"

"I saw Miss Jacoby and her brother ahead of us crossing the bridge and heading toward the station. She didn't have as far to go, since I needed to return first to the hotel to fetch Benjamin."

"Was the professor at the hotel the whole time you explored around Eldora?"

Lucille shrugged. "I suppose so. I didn't ask him. He was in the same spot I left him, so I assume he stayed there the whole time."

Harry knew that Professor Sager had left for a period of time, a subject to explore in his next interview.

Lucille prattled on. "Of course, Benjamin can be unpredictable. He once said he'd meet me at a restaurant, but he became distracted with his reading and stood me up. Can you imagine that? I was most perturbed."

Harry had listened carefully. Lucille's answers fit with what Allison had related. The two women definitely corroborated their respective alibis. One more item to explore. "Tell me this, Mrs. Vickering. You and Frederick Hammond exchanged several acrimonious accusations on the ride up. What caused the hard feelings?"

"You heard what he said. He insulted me on several occasions. I won't put up with that kind of behavior." Lucille held her chin high.

"Yes, but there seemed to be some rancor going back to when he lived in your boarding house."

"He was a most unpleasant man, even then. Not as bad as he became after the Great War, but still insufferable. I was glad when he moved out of my establishment."

"I sense there was something more between you and Frederick Hammond."

"No. Only his beastly behavior."

Harry watched her carefully and spotted a little twitch at the side of her mouth and a subtle furrow of her brow, but he realized for once she wasn't going to say more. He needed to pose his final question. Making sure that their eyes met, he asked, "Did you kill Frederick Hammond?"

She smiled demurely. "Of course not, Office McBride. He may have deserved such an end with his atrocious behavior, but a lady doesn't do such things."

CHAPTER 30

When Mrs. Vickering returned with him to the front of the passenger car, Harry asked the professor to slide out before Lucille took her seat.

"So I'm to be your next victim, Officer McBride." Benjamin scooted across the seat and stood.

"No, we only have one victim." Harry suppressed a smile.

"Give the professor a good grilling, Officer McBride," Daniel said. "It's only fair after all the questions he asked us as students."

"I'll do my best," Harry replied.

"Ah, yes. I must now be interrogated." Benjamin patted Lucille's hand. "Was it painful, my dear?"

Lucille adjusted her hat and slid in toward the window. "He was a gentleman. I guess I'll look out the window while you're gone, Benjamin."

Harry led the professor to the same place used with the others and pointed for his subject to sit.

"Now, what can I do to assist your investigation, Officer McBride?"

Harry decided to start as with his other interviews. "First, tell me everything you did after our meal together at the Gold Miner Hotel."

"Ah, yes. That was a fine luncheon. As far as my subsequent actions, it was pretty simple. I sat on the porch until Lucille retrieved me."

Harry's eyes bore in on Benjamin. "No, it wasn't as simple as that. After we left you on the porch, Susan and I took a stroll. Later, when we passed the Gold Miner Hotel, you were no longer sitting there."

The professor snapped his fingers. "Oh, yes. I forgot. I did take a short constitutional, probably for ten minutes or so."

"And where did you go?"

"Nothing more than stretching my legs. That must have been when you and your wife walked past. After my promenade, I returned and resumed my position in the rocking chair, dozing until Lucille came back. The time slipped by. I found that porch a most comfortable place to sit."

"Did you see any of the other passengers while you took your walk?"

The professor ran his fingers through his beard. "No one."

"And after you returned to the porch of the hotel?"

"Since I shut my eyes, I didn't see anyone until Lucille arrived. Then we headed back to the station and boarded the train."

"Did you see anyone along the way?"

"I noticed two people ahead of us, but with my poor distance vision I couldn't identify them. Once on the train I saw you, Mrs. McBride, Miss Jacoby and her brother."

For all the professor's earlier pontification, he was certainly giving short answers. Harry decided to try a different tack. "You and Frederick Hammond exchanged some heated words during our trip to Eldora. Tell me more about your relationship with him."

The professor gave a little snort. "That young man was quite a dichotomy. One of my best students at times and an inattentive dunce on other occasions. Very inconsistent. He showed great promise but didn't seem to be able to stay focused on his schoolwork. Then, of course, he encountered his problems with the Great War and the influenza. A shame. A shame."

"Why did you invite him to come on this trip?"

"Hmm. A good question. Lucille insisted that we take an excursion into the mountains. We picked today as a convenient day for such a journey. The idea came up of having some traveling companions. I proposed several friends, but she indicated she didn't like them very much. She asked if any of my former students might want to join us. I went through a list of several names, including Frederick's, and ended up with him and Daniel."

"I'm still curious about the barbs you traded with Mr. Hammond."

The professor let out a sigh. "I think that's a function of our respective personalities. He can be most obstreperous, and I like challenging him—you know, make him stand up for what he believes. I have to admit that he made my emotions boil with some of his comments today, and I'm prone to attack verbally when that happens."

"Did your emotions boil enough that you killed him, Professor?"

His mouth dropped open. "Are . . . are you accusing me of murdering the young man?"

"Only asking a question."

"Good heavens, no. I wouldn't do such a thing. I don't resort to violence. Only healthy debate."

"Whatever happened wasn't healthy for Mr. Hammond. Do you have any suspicion of who killed him?"

The professor paused for a moment with a blank look on his face. Then he pursed his lips. "From the altercations I witnessed this morning, two individuals come to mind—Daniel Compton and our conductor, Theodore Shultz. They both came to physical blows with Frederick. As I say, I'm not a violent man. One of those two might have taken an argument one step too far."

"What about Michael Jacoby, Allison Jacoby or Lucille Vickering as suspects?"

Benjamin chuckled. "No, I don't consider any of them viable candidates for you, Officer McBride. Michael Jacoby has developmental problems. He lacks the foresight to commit a murder."

"It was his knife that killed Frederick Hammond."

The professor's eyes shot open. "Good heavens." He shook his head. "No, I can't imagine him sticking it in Frederick's back. And you can rule out the fiancée. She acts too protective of both Michael and Frederick to commit such a crime. And Lucille. There's not a harmful bone in her body."

"But all three of those people exchanged harsh words with Mr. Hammond during the morning's trip. Especially Mrs. Vickering."

The professor flicked his wrist. "Oh, that. Of course, she became angry. Frederick insulted her and her establishment. She's very protective of her boarding house."

Harry thought for a moment about how he wanted to word his next question, since it covered sensitive territory. "I sense there was something more than a boarding house owner to boarder relationship between Mrs. Vickering and Mr. Hammond. Care to comment?" Harry sat back and waited.

The professor blinked rapidly several times but remained mute.

Harry stared at him without saying anything.

Finally, the professor flinched. He leaned close to Harry and whispered, "Why . . . ah . . . yes. There was a short romantic entanglement between them. It didn't last long and was a thing of the past for both of them."

"And yet when you suggested inviting Mr. Hammond to join you for the trip today, Mrs. Vickering didn't object."

"Of course not. As I said, the relationship was insignificant.

For her, gone and forgotten."

"And you didn't feel threatened in any way to have Mr. Hammond here with Mrs. Vickering?"

"Egad, no. She may have had a little fling with a younger man, but she's now interested in a more mature relationship."

"Passing Hill but not stopping," Conductor Shultz shouted from the front of the car. "Next stop Glacier Lake."

Harry cupped his hands and called out, "Conductor, may I have a word with you back here?"

Shultz strode to where Harry stood.

"I need to make a telephone call at Glacier Lake. Please notify the engineer to hold the train for me."

"I'll pull the cord to signal a stop at Glacier Lake. When we get there, I'll step off the train and let him know to wait until you're done." Shultz tipped his cap, turned on his heels and marched forward and out of the passenger car.

The professor raised an eyebrow. "Talking to the authorities?"

"Yes. I have to follow up with Police Chief Bass in Boulder."

"Ah, the busy police officer. It's a shame all this happened. You can't even enjoy a day off with your wife."

Harry shrugged. "It's part of the life of a policeman."

"I'm sure it is. May I return to my seat?"

Harry thought for a moment. Something was still bothering him, but he couldn't put his finger on it. He watched the professor for a moment. What was it? Oh, well, he'd have an opportunity for another interview when he figured out what had concerned him. "Yes. We're done for the time being."

"I guess you know where to find me if you have additional questions." The professor stood and sauntered forward to rejoin Lucille. She got up and let him take the window seat.

Harry continued to watch them for a moment. A most unusual relationship. And the little slip the professor made during the questioning—the convenient oversight of not mentioning right away that he disappeared for a time from the porch. He glibly recovered from forgetting that, but it was still interesting he had not volunteered this information at the outset. Did Professor Sager disappear long enough to kill Frederick? A possibility.

And Lucille Vickering not mentioning a previous relationship with Frederick Hammond. Another "little" oversight.

Harry spent a moment reviewing his suspects. Michael was implicated because of his knife being the murder weapon. Allison was in the meadow close to Frederick, although she had an alibi—that Lucille had seen her right before she needed to depart for the train station. Lucille had the same alibi. Daniel had no alibi and had been wandering around at the time of the murder. Professor Sager also had left his place on the porch to wander around. And Harry had Theodore Schultz to interview. Something else still nagged at Harry. He'd come up with it.

CHAPTER 31

Harry stood in the middle of the passenger car between Frederick's lifeless body and the group of people gathered in the front.

Michael's face remained plastered to the window. He twitched slightly, but he no longer flapped his arms.

Allison sat with her hands folded in her lap, and she remained as rigid as if in a coffin, staring straight ahead. What must she be thinking, with her fiancé dead and her brother's knife the murder weapon?

Daniel sat in the seat in front of Allison, fidgeting. Where had he been when the murder happened?

The professor stared out his window. For once he seemed content to watch and not speak.

Lucille also rested her hands in her lap. She looked once at Allison and then turned her head toward the professor, before she returned her gaze to the front of the compartment.

Conductor Shultz stood in the front facing the passengers as he reached into his vest pocket, pulled out his watch and studied it.

Susan sat quietly. Harry admired her composed demeanor. No matter what the circumstance, she stayed above the fray. A calm in the storm of suspects. He also respected her power of observation. Yes, that would be of help to him. He'd have to make time to take her aside and ask for her thoughts. A grin crept across his face. His own spy in the land of suspicious individuals.

Harry took a moment to review his notes. He wanted everything organized in his mind before he made his telephone call.

He came up with no further insights as the train slowed, approaching Glacier Lake. Looking out the window, he saw no signs of the climbers' group—obviously they had headed farther into the mountains. His gaze rested on the blue water of the lake, and he considered what lay in its depths—fish, lost hooks and line, probably discarded beer containers. Somewhere in the different depths he was dredging, he must find the answer to what happened to Frederick. There was an answer here. He could feel it nibbling like a trout exploring the bait, cautious but ready to strike. He needed to plant the hook and reel in the murderer.

When the train bumped to a complete stop, Harry signaled to the conductor and dashed off the train to use the telephone.

"I'll notify the engineer to wait," Theodore shouted to his back. "Please don't take more than five minutes."

"I'll try my best," Harry called over his shoulder. He descended the ladder between the two Pullman cars, strode into the station and located the telephone on the wall. After picking up the receiver and giving the handle a thorough crank, he waited for the operator to answer. He really needed to speak to several people, but given the time constraint, he decided to start with Chief Bass.

Once again the chief's wife answered, and after her admonition to not keep him out of bed too long, Harry heard his boss's greeting accompanied by a racking cough.

"Chief Bass, a quick update," Harry said. "I've interviewed five suspects. I may have eliminated two, but still need to speak with the conductor. I haven't found evidence to confirm who committed the crime."

"Keep at it. I spoke with the sheriff, and, as I suspected, he has no problem with you taking charge of the investigation." The chief gave a hacking laugh. "He has no one who can get involved right now given his caseload."

"I think I made the right decision to continue with the train and interview the suspects," Harry said, "but because of that, I never investigated the actual crime scene."

"I reached Officer Savage. There's no way to get anyone to do that today. You may need to catch the train back to Eldora tomorrow morning to check it out. You can line up John Penrod to go with you to take photographs."

Another whole day would be consumed with the murder. Penrod was an excellent photographer, used under contract when the police needed pictures of a crime scene and didn't mind a full day billing his hourly rates. Even with the tight budget, Chief Bass seemed willing to cover that additional expense. Penrod was a good traveling companion, full of stories and jokes. And for Harry, a return trip would give his feet a rest, except for having to traipse through the woods to the scene of the knife attack. "I'll make arrangements when I get back to Boulder."

"Good." The chief paused for another coughing jag. "Damned influenza. I can't seem to kick it."

"I'll let you get back to bed."

"Not yet, McBride. I want a full account of what you've learned." The chief blew his nose.

Harry recounted his interviews, with an emphasis on the testimony of Allison and Lucille regarding their encounter in the meadow.

"And you don't think the owner of the knife killed the victim?"

"I haven't ruled it out completely, but I don't think he did it.

I believe his statement that someone took his knife. He's a disturbed young man, but I don't sense he's capable of lying. I could be wrong, but I feel I'm close to figuring out something important. I just can't put my finger on it yet."

"That happens. Keep a close eye out for reactions from the people you're speaking with. Find the facts but don't dismiss your gut feelings, either."

Harry smiled to himself. Chief Bass possessed outstanding investigative skills and had taught him much. Harry had learned to pay attention to any advice the chief gave. "Yes, sir."

"Finish with the conductor and go back and interview everyone again. With what you've learned along the way, you'll gain some new insights. See if the stories change during the second questioning. Look for nervous tics and discomfort."

"I agree." Harry remembered something. "Did you have a chance to notify the coroner?"

"Damnation. I'm afraid not. After speaking to the sheriff, I felt too weak and didn't get around to it."

Harry looked at his watch. "Don't worry. I have enough time to make one more telephone call."

"Keep after it." The chief hacked, and it sounded to Harry like he spat before the line went dead.

Harry hung up the receiver and cranked again. When the operator came on the line he requested to be connected to the coroner, A. E. Howe. This took a few minutes, but finally a distinguished-sounding voice answered. "Yes?"

"Mr. Howe, this is Officer Harry McBride. I'm calling from Glacier Lake."

"What takes you up in the mountains, Officer McBride?"

"An outing with my wife, but as we boarded the train in Eldora to return to Boulder, one of the passengers stumbled into the car with a knife in his back and died on the floor. I need to make arrangements with you to have someone meet the train in

Boulder to take responsibility for the body."

"What time do you expect to arrive?"

Harry looked at his watch again, which showed 3:10. "It's scheduled for four-forty. We may be five to ten minutes later than that."

"Given the seriousness of this, I'll be there myself," Howe said. "We'll also need to schedule an inquest."

"Yes. I'm in the process of questioning a group of suspects. The murderer is one of six people on the train with me. I've spoken with the chief, and he wants me to return to Eldora tomorrow to collect more evidence."

"Has anyone touched the body?"

"After the victim collapsed on the floor, I checked for a pulse, and when I determined he was dead, I covered the body with a blanket. No one has been allowed near it since. I also made arrangements with the conductor to not allow anyone besides the suspects, my wife and me into the passenger car."

"Good. Is there anything else I should know?"

Harry thought for a moment. He felt comfortable sharing his nagging concern with the chief but not with the coroner. "Not at this time. I'll be happy to give you an update upon our return to Boulder. You can also speak to the chief before I get back to Boulder, if you need to."

"I know your chief has been ill, so I won't bother him at this time. It's a shame what this influenza has done to our community. Keep me informed."

They rang off.

After Harry replaced the receiver, he stepped outside and regarded the train, poised to continue its journey. The two green Pullman cars rested behind the black steaming locomotive and tender. Somewhere in the second car was the answer to this puzzle. He needed to find that answer.

CHAPTER 32

Officer Harry McBride took one last look at Glacier Lake, shimmering in the afternoon sun. Only one rowboat out on the water. Harry remembered how his father had taken him fishing in Boulder Creek and taught him the difference between lake and stream fishing. Sitting in the middle of a calm body of water versus finding the holes below rocks and casting so his line drifted naturally into the hole, with the fly attracting the unwary fish. Attract, strike, hook and reel in.

He needed to do some stream fishing in regards to Frederick's murder. He stood at a pool with a group of trout, one of which he needed to lure into striking. But how was he going to do it? He needed to learn more concerning the whereabouts of a number of the suspects. Six people on the loose in Eldora, each of whom had a reason to kill Frederick Hammond.

He built a mental picture of a meadow with a blanket, surrounded by woods. Michael had disappeared around a bend to work on his carving and later gone to relieve himself. If he wasn't the murderer, someone took his knife and waited for the opportune time to kill Frederick. Meanwhile, back in the meadow, Lucille Vickering showed up and spoke with Allison Jacoby. Allison claimed she heard Frederick cussing in the woods, an indication he was very much alive. He hadn't shouted for help, so he hadn't been stabbed at that time. Lucille heard a noise but said she couldn't tell if it was caused by a human. Possibly sometime during the conversation between Allison and

Lucille, Frederick had been stabbed. Had Michael circled around to do it? Had Daniel Compton, Benjamin Sager or Theodore Schultz snuck into the woods to dispatch Frederick? And then with a few minutes to spare before the train departed, Lucille dashed off to retrieve Benjamin while Allison gathered her picnic things and went to find Michael.

The sight of Susan descending the stairs of the passenger car interrupted Harry's thoughts. He was pleased to see her smiling face, but wondered why she had gotten off the train. "You checking up on me?" he asked.

"I wanted to speak with you for a moment in private before the train started again. As you asked, I've been watching the people in our car. I have several thoughts for you."

Harry put his arm around Susan and pulled her close. "I'll take all the help I can get. What's on your mind?"

"I've been watching Michael Jacoby. I don't think he's capable of killing anyone."

"Oh?"

"He exhibits very strange behavior but nothing indicating a tendency for violence. And I don't believe Allison is capable of killing."

"Do you have a favorite suspect at this time?" Harry asked.

Susan bit her lip. "I don't think it's the conductor. That leaves Professor Benjamin Sager, Mrs. Lucille Vickering and Daniel Compton."

Harry gave his wife a hug and led her to the stairs. "I have a lot of questioning to do, so keep watching. I'll want to sit down with you later for more of your observations."

They climbed aboard, Susan took her seat and Harry spoke to Shultz. "You can signal the engineer, and then I need to talk with you."

The conductor arched an eyebrow but stepped to the space

between the two passenger cars, leaned out and waved to the engineer.

Without hesitation, the train began to move. Harry wondered when he would next see this placid lake. Then he remembered he'd be taking the train again tomorrow to find the scene of the stabbing. A photographer rather than Susan would accompany him.

When Shultz returned from signaling the engineer, Harry led him to the designated spot, and they both sat.

"I need your assistance to determine who killed Frederick Hammond," Harry said.

"I'll help you any way I can."

"Good. I'm trying to trace the movements of everyone after we disembarked in Eldora. I've spoken with all the passengers." Harry waved his hand toward the front of the compartment. "You're the only other person who was with us on our arrival. As a conductor, I'm sure you notice things, so I'd be interested in your observations. Please recount what you did after we pulled into the Eldora station."

Shultz adjusted his tie. "Our railroad crew always has work during the stopover in Eldora. I first go through the passenger cars to make sure everything is stowed and to do some cleanup." He snickered. "Some of our passengers aren't very neat, and I don't want the cars smelling like a saloon or trash bin for our return trip to Boulder."

"Our car didn't look too bad from what I remember," Harry said.

"No, the Rocky Mountain Climbers are sticklers about picking up trash, and the rest of you kept your seating area in the car neat. People in the other car caused a problem. I found pieces of salami on one seat, paper wrappers strewn everywhere and some foul-smelling cheese littering the floor. I took care of that and met with the engineer and fireman. After they checked their equipment, we discussed the schedule. We sat in the station and made sure our watches showed the same time. We also discussed the next week's runs. We'll be coming to Eldora every day except Saturday, when we'll go to Ward instead."

"Don't you get any days off?" Harry asked.

"I'm fortunate and get Friday off—the Fourth of July. It will be the first time in three years that I haven't worked that day."

"I may even join you tomorrow for this same trip," Harry said.

Shultz chuckled. "Having so much fun that you want to do it again, eh?"

"Unfortunately, it will be a working trip rather than pleasure. Please continue with what you did after our arrival in Eldora."

"We chewed the fat for half an hour, and then we pulled out the food we brought and ate. While you folks dined at the Gold Miner Hotel, I enjoyed a lighter meal—beef jerky, cheese and an apple."

"Anyone else there besides the three of you?"

"No, we had the station to ourselves. Everyone else went into town. This is usually a good time for the railroad crew to relax. In fact, the engineer and fireman stretched out on the grass outside the station for a little snooze, but I decided to wander around and stretch my legs. If I sit too long I get stiff."

"I know what you mean. In both of our occupations we're on our feet a lot. I try not to walk too much when I'm not on duty, but I do need some exercise. Did you see any of the passengers from our car?"

"Not at first. I wandered up toward the Gold Miner Hotel and went to buy some tobacco. Only one place in town open, but I did manage to replenish my stash. I thought of the women off picking wildflowers but had no desire to wander into the hills. I'm a city person, and staying around the streets suits me fine. I found a place to sit and watched the town go by. Not that many people, maybe a dozen or so passed me. I did spot Professor Sager at one point. He seemed to be wandering around aimlessly. He disappeared into a stand of trees. I also saw Daniel Compton. He was strolling by himself, shortly after I spotted the professor. He was looking over his shoulder as if to make sure no one was following him. He also ducked into the woods."

Interesting. "Did either of them see you?"

"I can't say for sure. I didn't wave or shout out. I didn't think anything of their actions at the time."

"And what did you do next?"

"I returned to the station. I like to get there fifteen minutes before departure in case anyone needs assistance. I made one more pass through the two passenger cars and waited in the other one, since there would be more returning passengers on that than yours."

Harry reviewed the timeline in his head. It all seemed to fit except for the fact that neither Daniel nor the professor mentioned going into the woods. He'd explore that on his next round of interrogation. "Tell me one other thing. I noticed some animosity between you and Frederick Hammond."

Shultz's eyes grew dark. "I didn't much care for him. You heard how he insulted everyone. He has always made demeaning comments. He was one of those kids in our neighborhood whose neck you wanted to wring . . . I . . . I mean I wouldn't actually do something like that but . . . you know what I mean."

"Did you hate Frederick Hammond enough to kill him, Mr. Shultz?"

Theodore gaped. "N—no, Officer. I'd never do such a thing."

Harry watched the conductor carefully. He acted nervous but not necessarily guilty. Hard to tell. "You witnessed a number of the verbal exchanges between Mr. Hammond and the other passengers. Who do you suspect killed him?"

"I don't know. Each person except you and Mrs. McBride had a reason to dislike Frederick. If pressed, I'd have to say Daniel Compton. There is nothing like a romantic conflict to cause serious problems." Shultz took out his watch and regarded it as if studying a timetable. "I better go check the other car. We'll stop in Tungsten in five minutes."

"I thought it was a flag stop," Harry said.

"On the way up, Sugarloaf is a regular stop, and Tungsten is a flag stop. On the way down, it's the opposite. Do you have any other questions?"

"Not for now."

Theodore jumped up and dashed forward.

Awfully anxious to get away from me. Harry watched as the conductor disappeared through the front door of the car. As Police Chief Bass had suggested, Harry needed to interview everyone one more time and look for discrepancies. And follow his intuition. At the moment, his intuition was in a quandary. There continued to be something he couldn't put his finger on. Something that was important for the investigation. He had several lines of questioning he intended to pursue with the professor and Daniel.

CHAPTER 33

Harry remained in his interrogation seat after Theodore Shultz left. He faced quite a challenge conducting a murder investigation. Much different from his previous cases. He had been involved in numerous assaults, robberies and thefts, but this was the first time working a murder.

In the town of Boulder, homicides were rarer than fist-sized gold nuggets. His biggest previous case had been in December of 1917, when he and fellow patrolman George Savage came across a robbery in progress at the Keeler Brothers store. Harry noticed the door ajar and heard banging inside. Upon entering the store, they found a man helping himself to money in the cash register while another pointed a knife at a frightened clerk. After a tussle that left Harry with a gash on his right forearm, the patrolmen apprehended the two robbers and took them to jail.

Susan tended to his arm that night. It became infected and took two weeks to heal. Harry chuckled to himself at the final outcome. The store owner had been so grateful that the robbery had been stopped and no money or supplies taken that he wrote checks for twenty dollars apiece to Harry and George. When the chief received the checks, he proudly handed the money to the two patrolmen. Not every day that a citizen thanked the police that way.

But that had been simple. Harry had witnessed the culprits ransacking the store and had caught them in the act. This current circumstance was much different. He hadn't witnessed the event, only the aftermath when Frederick Hammond staggered onto the train and died with a knife in his back. It was up to Harry to figure out who and why.

The train stopped in Tungsten. One man got off the other Pullman car and stood at the side of the train as the locomotive whistled and moved forward. As the second car passed this lone individual, he doffed his worn hat as if to thank the railroad for his passage.

Harry continued to watch until the stranger disappeared from sight before he lifted himself out of the seat to head to the front of the compartment.

"Mr. Compton, I'd like another word with you."

Daniel looked up. "Is the interrogation going to continue?"

"I have a few more questions if you'd accompany me."

Daniel gave a resigned sigh, stood and followed Harry to the "reserved" seats. Once ensconced, he asked, "What's on your mind, Officer McBride?"

"I'm still trying to piece together what happened in Eldora. You gave me an account of your whereabouts, but one thing puzzles me." Harry paused.

"Yes?"

"Conductor Shultz also wandered around town and spotted you. Did you happen to notice him?"

"No, I can't say as I did."

"Mr. Shultz told me that he saw you go into the woods. You never mentioned that in our previous conversation."

Daniel shrugged. "I didn't think it was worth mentioning. If you must know, I found a patch of trees and went into the woods to relieve myself. It is over a two-hour trip back to Boulder."

"I understand." Harry stared intently at Daniel. "It's disconcerting that no one saw you after Mr. Shultz's sighting and before you returned to the train. During that period of time, Mr. Hammond was stabbed."

Daniel gave a disgusted grunt. "Here we go again. You're not back to suspecting me, are you?"

"You're one of the few people here who disappeared during the time of the knifing. I have to take that seriously."

"I can assure you I didn't kill Frederick." He crossed his arms. "And you have no evidence to indicate I did."

Harry sat back. That was the darned problem. He might try to intimidate Daniel as much as he wanted, but the man was right. He had nothing other than a period of time unaccounted for. Sure, Daniel had a motive and could no doubt handle a knife, but Harry had nothing specific to link Daniel to the crime. He decided to take another tack. "Mr. Shultz also said he saw Professor Sager go into the woods. Did you happen to notice that?"

Daniel uncrossed his arms and rested them in his lap, tapping his fingers on his knees. "Come to think of it, I did see someone disappear into a stand of trees. I wasn't paying attention that closely. It might have been the professor, but I can't say for sure."

"Try to think back. This could be important."

Daniel closed his eyes. After a moment he said, "I can picture a man going into the woods but only saw the back of a jacket and a hat. Might have been the professor."

From the front of the car, Conductor Shultz shouted, "Passing Sugarloaf, not stopping."

The train made a wide turn to the left and headed down the slope toward Sunset, with a wide view off to the valley on the right side. The train was definitely moving faster than on the way up. The engineer was trying to make up time without endangering the passengers.

"You told me before that you saw Professor Sager and Mrs.

Vickering getting on the train as you approached. Did you see which direction they came from?"

"No. I didn't spot them until they were going up the stairs."

Harry tried to picture the scene. People converging on the station. Lucille and Benjamin walking south down the street from the Gold Miner Hotel. Allison and Michael returning from their picnic spot, which Allison described as being five minutes to the west. Conductor Shultz returning to greet his passengers. And Daniel wandering around town and showing up at the last minute. And finally, as the train left, Frederick staggering aboard. As if bits of iron had been drawn to a magnet.

"Do you have any more questions for me, Officer McBride?" Daniel asked.

Harry wished he knew the probing question that would break this case open. Nothing came to him. "Is there anything else you noticed pertinent to this investigation?"

"Nothing that I can think of. But I have one question for you, Officer McBride."

Harry jerked upright. "What's that?"

"It seems to me you have two hours to figure out what happened. Then we all scatter in Boulder. Right now, you have a captive audience on the train. After we get to Boulder, anything can happen. What are you going to do?"

"That's why I'm speaking with each of you again. I feel I'm close to solving this puzzle."

"Fine. Just remember I didn't kill Frederick. Are you through with me?"

"That will be all for now."

Daniel returned to the front of the compartment. Harry remained deep in thought. He needed a diagram. He took out his notepad and pencil and drew a line across a sheet. He put an arrow to the left indicating west. Next, he intersected this horizontal line with a vertical line with north at the top. He put an X along the top of the vertical line for the Gold Miner Hotel. Along the horizontal line he put another X to the left for the picnic spot. At the bottom of the vertical line he put an X for the train depot. He noted earlier that it took two minutes to walk from the station to the Gold Miner Hotel. Below he wrote the names of suspects. For Michael and Allison he wrote five, the time it took to return from the picnic spot. For Lucille he wrote ten; five minutes from the picnic spot, two minutes to go to the Gold Miner Hotel to collect Benjamin, one minute to hear his dream, two minutes to return to the station. Beside Benjamin, Daniel and Theodore's names, he wrote a question mark.

Had he any new gut feeling? He looked over the list of names. Not one jumped out at him to shout, *It's me.* He raised his gaze to watch the people in front of him. Conductor Shultz was leaning over, speaking with Lucille. Michael's face remained pressed to the window. Everyone else looked forward. He ran his eyes over all six of his suspects. No, he couldn't sense anything.

His eyes rested on the back of Susan's blue bonnet, and warmth surged through his chest. In the midst of all the chaos, one bright spot. Too bad this couldn't have been a relaxing day in the mountains. He owed Susan a respite from life's usual frantic pace, and then this unforeseen death occurred. But it couldn't be helped in his profession. What if he had been a plumber or watch repairman or a dentist? No, he would be bored out of his mind. He loved his work, although at times, like now, it became frustrating.

Harry tapped the pad with the eraser end of his pencil. How to solve this case? The discouraging part was that any one of the suspects might have been near Frederick. Allison, Michael and Lucille were already seen by one or more witnesses at the picnic spot. Daniel and Benjamin were seen going into the woods.

Could that have been near the picnic spot? And Theodore Shultz had also been wandering around. Then another insight struck him. Everyone heard Allison describe where she planned to have her picnic. If someone wanted to find Frederick, that person knew right where to go.

CHAPTER 34

With resigned, heavy steps, Harry returned to the front of the passenger car to invite Professor Benjamin Sager to join him.

"Ah, yes, the interrogation continues." The professor stood and dusted off his pants. "This reminds me of the faculty inquisitions we hold periodically at the university. With the American Association of University Professors' declaration of principles in nineteen-fifteen, the university administration can't bend to the desire of a donor to dismiss a professor, but assistant professors are subject to review by their peers. Unless you're a full professor, you can face discipline at any time. The younger professors are concerned that they may make a misstep and run afoul of the academic committees." He prattled on. Harry resisted the urge to yawn. "I, myself, am past that indignity, but others are afraid that any miscue may lead to an investigation. I've served on several of those disciplinary review boards, and it's not a pleasant experience for the recipient of intense questioning." Benjamin held his wrists out in front of him. "So take me away to your dungeon for whatever you have in mind."

Harry smiled in spite of himself. "Very dramatic, Professor. Are you sure you're not in the theater department rather than history?"

Benjamin blew air loudly through his lips. "Teachers must be dramatic. If you have students like Frederick and Daniel, you have to exhibit a flair to catch their attention. Students these days are much more easily distracted than when I went through college. You have to put on quite a show; otherwise they will sit there in a comatose state."

Harry flinched, realizing Frederick rested in more than a comatose state. "Let's go talk, Professor."

They walked toward the back of the car and took their seats facing each other. The train continued its descent toward the town of Sunset. Afternoon shade already covered the valley. Harry wasn't sure he'd like living there, where, particularly in winter, the sun didn't peek above the south hill for much of the day. Winter sunset for the town of Sunset must have occurred by two in the afternoon.

The professor adjusted his jacket. "You mentioned earlier on our journey, Officer McBride, that your police department faced financial challenges and hadn't yet bought a motorcar. We face some of the same problems at the university. If you look back at the history of our fine institution, we received a mandate from the public. Citizens of Boulder lobbied the state legislature to have the university located in our fair city, provided land and even accumulated donations. That started our institution, but now that the university is ensconced in Boulder, the legislature is being miserly on funding any expansion. You'd think they'd have more interest in the enhancement of young minds. It is, after all, the university educated who will become the future leaders of our state."

"Maybe the legislators don't want the competition from smart young people," Harry said.

"A most astute observation, Officer McBride. I hadn't considered that possibility, but you could be right. Politics is strange. Your statement makes more sense than many explanations I've heard regarding legislative behavior."

"Be that as it may, I have some questions for you," Harry said.

The professor gave a resigned sigh. "Yes. I guess I'm not going to be able to distract you from what's on your mind. You must get on with your investigation. What do you want to know?"

"I thought you might be able to lend some insight into the animosity between Frederick Hammond and Daniel Compton."

"Ah, yes, let's see." He paused and tapped his cheek before continuing. "That goes back a long while. There was obviously tension between the two of them over the lovely Miss Jacoby. But even before she entered the picture, those two had their conflicts. When they were my students, they got on each other's nerves, mixing as well as oil and water. Daniel was a prankster, and Frederick was very serious, not one who appreciated jokes. Daniel once arranged for a . . . uh . . . lady of the night to make an appearance during one of my classes and call out to Frederick that she was with his child. Frederick turned as white as a sheet, and Daniel burst out laughing and took credit for the practical joke. I can't say I approve of such behavior, but the class and I did have a good chuckle at the time."

From the experience this morning, Harry understood how this animosity between Frederick and Daniel continued to the present time.

Another thought stuck him. "When we spoke before, you told me you remained on the porch of the Gold Miner Hotel after our meal."

"That's correct. I relaxed and enjoyed the view of the street, passersby and the occasional wandering dog. Do you know that dogs have been domesticated by humans for over ten thousand years?"

Harry rolled his eyes. After the curt answers given by the professor in the last interview, he was back to pontificating. Harry periodically experienced trouble with dogs while on patrol. He thought it might be the uniform, because he never had problems with them when in civilian clothes. "An interesting fact, but I'd like to hear about you on the porch after lunch, Professor."

Benjamin yawned and stretched his arms. "Given how comfortable it was, I must admit I nodded off for a few minutes while I sat there. Too much to eat, the pleasant mountain air and a touch of summer sunshine."

"But you didn't stay on the porch the whole time before returning to the train. I pointed out to you in our last conversation that my wife and I noticed you missing from the porch for a period of time—"

"And you rightfully jogged my memory that I took a stroll for a few minutes, nothing more."

"It turns out that you were seen going into the woods by our conductor and also possibly by Daniel Compton. You told me before you didn't see anyone from the train while on your walk."

The professor looked thoughtful. "No, I didn't see either of those two gentlemen during my promenade. But I'm not surprised they saw me going into the woods." He winked. "Taking care of some bodily functions."

It seemed that there was a lot of that going on with the passengers. Why didn't they use the outhouse next to the station?

"Where exactly did you go into the woods?" Harry asked.

"I noticed a small stand of trees towards the west and in the direction of the stream from the hotel. A brief respite before I returned to the porch and settled in. The porch rockers are very comfortable, did you know that?"

Harry stared at him without acknowledging the question, hoping he wouldn't go off on a discourse about the history of porch rockers.

Not waiting for a response, the professor continued. "Then after my short nap, Lucille retrieved me for our jaunt back to the station."

Could have been the right direction and time frame, Harry thought. Somehow the professor might be at the hub of this puzzle.

"I asked you before if you killed Frederick Hammond. Have you reconsidered your answer, Professor?"

Benjamin bit his lip for a moment. "Oh, I killed him, all right."

CHAPTER 35

At the professor's admission, Harry's heart beat rapidly. His mouth went dry, and he forced himself to look carefully at Professor Sager, who remained motionless, his lips set.

Had Harry forced a confession? Had it been this easy to find the killer? He now only needed to take the professor down to Boulder and off to jail. Yet, something didn't feel right. The nagging sensation in the back of his mind hadn't been relieved. "Please clarify your statement, Professor Sager."

"I didn't physically kill Frederick, Officer McBride, but I might as well have. I feel responsible for his death. Without me insisting that he join this cursed outing, he wouldn't have been murdered. He wasn't that interested in attending, but I cajoled him until he agreed to come. I will never be able to forgive myself for that."

Harry took a deep breath to calm his thumping heart. So much for an easy conclusion to the case. "You had me going there for a moment. I thought you put the knife in Mr. Hammond's back."

"No, I didn't do that. But it pains me to think that I organized this ghastly expedition and it resulted in Frederick's death. The young man certainly had a chip on his shoulder larger than one of the wood blocks Michael Jacoby carves, but he had been through some trying times and didn't deserve to end up this way." He waved toward the covered body. "If only I hadn't invited him to join us today."

"You can't take responsibility for that, Professor. You can't predict what will happen on any day. People are struck by automobiles crossing the street, choke on a piece of steak, or trip and hit their heads on walls."

"That's true. We can't predict bad luck and fatalities. Still, I wish this unfortunate situation hadn't occurred. If only I hadn't listened to Lucille."

Harry paused for a moment. "I'm not following you. What does Mrs. Vickering have to do with it?"

"I guess she kind of planted the idea of inviting some of my old students on a trip into the mountains." He coughed. "As a married man, you know how women are. They hem and haw and broach an idea. You don't think anything of it, but then it pops back again, and you know it can't be ignored. That's how it was with Lucille."

Harry perked up. "Tell me more."

"For a number of months we have been discussing taking a trip on the Switzerland Trail. We wanted to wait for good weather, but with the uncertainty of the railroad's future, it wasn't clear that passenger service would continue. I put the whole idea aside until an article appeared in the *Daily Camera* in early June announcing the resumption of the summer passenger schedule. She suggested it might be fun to invite some of my old students. I didn't care one way or the other, but I decided to humor her request. We went through a list of names and came up with three. One couldn't make it, but Frederick and Daniel accepted."

"That's interesting. As you told me before, Mrs. Vickering knew Mr. Hammond from when he stayed in her boarding house, and you implied there might have been a romantic connection. I'm still surprised you selected Mr. Hammond."

Benjamin shrugged. "He had suffered through the war and influenza. I'm not threatened by his being an old beau of

Lucille's. It made perfect sense to include him on the trip. Although inconsistent, he was at times an outstanding student."

"But now you're regretting that you invited him."

The train slowed as it pulled into the Sunset station. The south side of town was in shadows, but light played brightly on the north hillside.

The professor's eyes darted to the blanket-covered body. "Yes. In hindsight it was an unfortunate decision—you might say a disastrous one."

CHAPTER 36

After completing the interview with Professor Sager, Harry's shoulders drooped. The surge of excitement at thinking he had induced a confession was replaced by an aching sense of disappointment. He hoped his lack of experience in conducting a murder investigation wasn't obvious to the suspects.

On second thought, he figured no one would question his ability. After all, they probably had never been suspects before so wouldn't know what to expect anyway. He had collected their testimony, but of all he had heard, what was relevant in helping to identify the killer? He had gained a good sense of where people were during the stopover in Eldora, but he hadn't yet found the clue to crack this nut. Would he be able to solve the murder? Should he give up and wait to turn it over to the police chief and sheriff?

He clenched his fist. No. He remembered what the man from the climbers group said earlier in the morning. Persistence and perseverance. He couldn't quit.

The train pulled away from the Sunset station. Not too many stops before they'd be back in Boulder.

With renewed determination, he strode forward to find some answers. He needed to speak with Lucille again. "Mrs. Vickering, please accompany me to the back of the car."

She looked up at him and then waved a limp wrist toward the covered figure. "As long as we don't have to go too far back."

"Right where we sat before."

She reached over and patted the professor's arm. "In that case, Benjamin, if you'll excuse me, I'll join Officer McBride."

"Go ahead, my dear."

Lucille stood, arranged her dress and joined Harry to walk back and take their respective seats.

"This questioning is quite a bother," Lucille said. "I expect you'll be speaking with various people in this compartment until we reach Boulder. You must get tired of it, too, Officer McBride."

Harry realized that some of this was bothersome, but other parts intrigued him. "It's all part of the job."

"I know, you men and your jobs. Benjamin gets so wrapped up in his university responsibilities sometimes it's astounding. As you know, that man can run on for hours at the drop of a hat. And he's so consumed with his research, writing and teaching. You appear to me to be the same way in regards to your police work. I'm sure Mrs. McBride would like to see more of you around the house."

"I don't know. She's always complaining that when I come home I track mud inside. Now I have a few questions for you."

Lucille adjusted her hat. "Go right ahead."

"One item intrigues me. When we talked earlier, I asked you about Frederick Hammond, and you indicated only that he once resided at your boarding house. You gave no indication of knowing him very well. Professor Sager implied you and Mr. Hammond were romantically involved at one time."

Her nostrils flared momentarily, then she regained her composure. "Oh, that. It was such a minor thing I didn't even bother to mention it. A few stolen kisses here and there. He reminded me of my late husband, but nothing became of it. He was too young, and I had my business to run." She gave a piercing stare in the professor's direction. "I'm surprised that Benjamin even mentioned it."

"I don't think he meant to say anything behind your back. It just came out during our conversation."

"Nothing serious transpired."

"It does provide an interesting link—with your past relationship, the two of you ended up on the train together today."

"A mere coincidence."

Harry watched Lucille carefully. "I don't consider it a coincidence. Professor Sager did invite Mr. Hammond."

"Oh, that." Lucille flicked her wrist. "Frederick was one of Benjamin's students. Benjamin invited him, nothing more."

Harry tapped his fingers on the armrest. "That's the other point I find interesting. In my discussion with Professor Sager, he mentioned something that surprised me. I was under the impression that he had instigated the plans for this outing that included the two of you, Frederick Hammond and Daniel Compton. He indicated that you actually suggested the original idea."

Lucille gave a dismissive wave of her hand. "Oh, who can say about those things? We were talking, and the idea of who to invite sprang up like daffodils in the spring. His idea, my idea, it just happened."

"In either case, you were involved in the decision. You obviously approved of the plan, whoever came up with it."

She shrugged. "Why not? A beautiful day in the mountains. Nothing wrong with inviting other companions along."

"But given your past history with Mr. Hammond, that doesn't sound like such a good idea."

Lucille gave a derisive laugh. "I'm not one to harp on the past. Benjamin invited some of his previous students, and that seemed like a fine thing to do."

Harry realized he had little chance to get more from Lucille on this subject. He decided to pursue another train of questioning. He took out his notepad and pencil. "I'm trying to build a timeline of exactly when things happened in Eldora. I thought you might be able to help me with that. Let's start from the point you left Professor Sager on the porch of the Gold Miner Hotel. What time was that?"

"I'm sorry. I'm not sure exactly what time I left the hotel."

Harry tapped the eraser end of his pencil on the pad. "Okay. Do you have any idea how long you walked until you came upon Miss Jacoby on her picnic blanket?"

Lucille shrugged. "Maybe thirty minutes. I didn't pay close attention. The only time I'm sure about is when I asked Miss Jacoby, she told me it was two o'clock, and we both realized we needed to hurry back to the train. Conductor Schultz was very explicit that we not be late. Can you imagine if we had been left in Eldora? We would have needed to find a place to stay overnight and not been able to return until Monday. I couldn't leave my boarding house unattended for that length of time."

"It's fortunate that all of you made it back in time. Miss Jacoby had the same reaction you did. She realized she needed to gather her small group and get back quickly. Did you see anyone else from the train before you encountered Miss Jacoby?"

"No. As I told you before, she was the only one until I retrieved Benjamin on the porch of the Gold Miner Hotel."

Harry shuffled his right shoe. There was something he couldn't quite piece together. He felt he should have some penetrating question to ask, but nothing occurred to him. Maybe if he kept her talking, something might occur to him. "What route did you take back after speaking with Miss Jacoby?"

"I headed back into Eldora. Then I turned left to go to the Gold Miner Hotel."

Harry jotted a note. "And obviously you had no trouble finding the picnic spot in the first place."

"I wasn't exactly looking for it, but Miss Jacoby had described the location from her conversation with that old smelly man who got on the train at Sulphide. I happened upon it. There aren't that many places with trees."

Harry would have to retrace Frederick's route on Monday when he returned. From the description, it should be easy to find. There might even be remnants of blood along the way. "There have been other statements that people from our passenger car were seen going into a wooded area. Please think carefully. Did you see anyone else?"

"No. I heard some noises, but those might have been squirrels or raccoons. I can't say for sure if anyone else was nearby or not."

"You mentioned earlier that Miss Jacoby appeared to have been crying. Did she tell you what upset her?"

"No, we never discussed it. At that moment we discovered our time in Eldora had run out. I needed to get back to the train."

Harry remembered a question he asked some of the other passengers but not Lucille during their previous conversation. "Who do you think killed Frederick Hammond?"

Lucille put her hand to her cheek. "My goodness, you're asking me? I wouldn't know."

"Just venture a guess."

"It couldn't be Benjamin." She leaned closer and whispered. "Daniel Compton might be a good suspect for you. Or that erratic Michael Jacoby."

From the front of the car Conductor Shultz shouted, "Passing Copper Rock. No flag stop this afternoon."

Another question occurred to Harry. "Before encountering Frederick Hammond on the train, had you seen him recently?"

She flicked her wrist. "It's possible. I run a lot of errands."

Harry looked out the window at the jagged rock formation on the left side of the train across Four Mile Creek. He hadn't noticed it on the way up, but he now saw a definite green stain, as if it had leached out of the rock, halfway up the peak. Like someone trying to scale a steep slope, Harry, too, was grasping for a handhold to get him closer to reaching the top, but he had reached a dead end with Lucille. He racked his brain but came up with a blank. "Is there anything else helpful you've thought of?"

She graced him with a full smile. "Not at this time."

CHAPTER 37

Lucille Vickering returned to her seat next to Professor Benjamin Sager, and Harry strolled forward to accost Theodore Shultz. He found him speaking with Daniel Compton. "May I have a word with you, Conductor?"

Shultz pulled out his watch from his pocket and regarded it. "We'll be in Wall Street in eight minutes and making a flag stop for a man in the other car who needs to get off. I can spend a few minutes with you."

They walked back to the "private" section of the car and sat.

"While we make the stop in Wall Street, I'd like to speak with the engineer and fireman," Harry said.

"That should be fine as long as you don't take too long. You can get off and go alongside the locomotive to signal that you want to talk with them. I'll be busy helping a passenger off. He's an old man and needs assistance with several parcels he brought on board in Eldora."

That worked perfectly for what Harry had in mind. "I'll also need to make another telephone call before we reach Boulder."

Shultz rolled his eyes. "You're determined to make us arrive late in Boulder."

"This will be a brief conversation. Where can I next find a telephone to use?"

"The only one before we get back to town is in the Salina station. Mention it to the engineer when you speak with him in Wall Street. After Salina we only have one more scheduled stop, which is Chrisman, and a flag stop in Orodell, although I'm not expecting anyone to get on or off there."

Harry had his actions mapped out in order to accomplish his main task—find the murderer. He looked at Shultz. "I'm trying to piece together where everyone was at specific points in time in Eldora. You mentioned seeing Daniel Compton and Professor Sager go into a wooded area. Help me reconstruct the time-frame."

Shultz removed his cap and scratched his head. "Let me see if I can re-create what happened. As I told you, I ate my food and wandered around town. I'd venture a guess that I saw the professor at approximately one-forty-five and Daniel Compton . . . um . . . maybe at one-fifty. Then I returned to the station."

"And when did you get back to the train?"

"That I know precisely. I checked my watch and returned at exactly two."

"Did anyone see you arrive at the station?"

"The engineer and fireman were waiting. We all headed back to the train at the same time, them to the locomotive and me to prepare the two passenger cars."

Harry recalled everyone comparing time on their watches earlier on the trip and having their various timepieces showing nearly the same time. If Allison Jacoby checked her watch at two o'clock, Shultz would have been back at the train by then. That eliminated him as a suspect for killing Frederick. It left Daniel and Benjamin as viable suspects, given their disappearance into a wooded area earlier. Which of the two could have stabbed Frederick? But what if Shultz was lying and actually returned to the station later? Harry would be able to verify that with the engineer and fireman.

Harry pointed to Shultz. "Any other helpful recollections?"

"Nothing comes to mind."

The train began to slow.

Shultz jumped up. "We're arriving in Wall Street. Come with me and you can exit in the front of the other passenger car."

Harry followed Shultz through the door, across the two metal plates and into the other Pullman car.

Shultz shouted, "Wall Street!"

As Harry continued through the car, he noticed that all the seats were taken. Shultz had certainly done his part to keep strangers out of the "inquisition" car. A man wrestled with two packages, preparing to get off. Harry slipped past and went to the front of the car and out the door. Ahead he saw the tender. As the wheels ground to a halt, Harry jumped to the ground and ran to the locomotive. The engineer leaned out of the cab, and Harry waved. "Hello up there. I'm Officer McBride of the Boulder police department. I need to speak with you and your fireman for a moment."

"I'm Bill Tipps," the engineer shouted back. "My fireman will be with us in a moment. What can I do for you?"

"I'm gathering some information about what happened during our stopover in Eldora. Could you tell me what you did after the train reached the station?"

Tipps patted the side of the locomotive. "I shut things down and went into the station for a bite to eat."

"And who was with you?"

"Only my fireman, Oscar Bernsten, and conductor, Theodore Shultz."

"And did you notice what Conductor Shultz did after eating."

"He went off for a walk while I rested."

"Did you or your fireman leave the station?"

"Nah, we stuck around until it was time to get up a good head of steam."

"And did you notice when Conductor Shultz returned to the station after his walk?"

"At two o'clock." He stuck his head back inside the locomotive. "Hey, Oscar, come here. This policeman wants to talk to you."

A man covered in coal soot stuck his head out the window of the cab. "Ya want something?"

"My name's Harry McBride. I'm verifying times and events in Eldora today. Tell me who you saw after you ate by the station."

Oscar Bernsten ran his hands through his dirty black hair. "I was with Mr. Tipps and Mr. Shultz. After we finished eating I stretched out on the grass. Shultz went to wander around town."

"And when did he return?"

Bernsten scratched his darkened chin. "Right around two. Then we started getting ready for leaving at two-fifteen."

Harry had the corroboration he needed. "Engineer Tipps, I need to make a telephone call in Salina."

"Hope you won't take too long. I've made up most of the time from your two earlier telephone calls." Tipps chuckled. "I've had snow delays, a bear on the tracks, but never a murder causing us to fall behind schedule."

"I'll be quick in Salina. Thanks for your assistance, and I won't hold you here any longer." Harry headed back, climbed up the steps and into the first passenger car. The train immediately began moving. Conductor Shultz stood in the compartment speaking to a woman wearing a large black hat decorated with daisies.

Harry interrupted them. "Conductor Shultz, may we continue our discussion?"

"Sure. I have seven minutes before we reach Salina."

They passed through the car, into the second Pullman and took their seats toward the back.

"The engineer and fireman were very helpful," Harry said. "All the times mentioned line up with what I've previously heard. I'd appreciate one other observation from you. Between Daniel Compton and Professor Benjamin Sager, have you noticed anything else to lead you to suspect one or the other?"

Shultz crinkled his brow. "Mr. Compton acted the most furtive when I saw him going into the woods. Other than that I can't give you any other impression."

"Thanks, I'll let you resume your duties. I told the engineer I'd be making a telephone call in Salina."

Shultz stood and strode forward, pausing to announce to the passengers, "We'll be stopping shortly in Salina." Then he headed into the other car.

Harry sat, thinking. He took out his pad and pencil. He began listing a number of times:

1:45 – Sager goes into woods

1:50 – Compton goes into woods

2:00 – Shultz returns to station

Right before 2:00 – Miss Jacoby hears Frederick swear in woods

2:00 – Miss Jacoby notices time when asked by Mrs. Vickering

Sometime around 2:00 – Frederick stabbed

Order of passengers returning:

Susan and me

Allison and Michael

Benjamin and Lucille

Daniel

2:15 – all passengers back, train leaves and Frederick dies

Based on the testimony of the engineer and fireman, Shultz was no longer a suspect. Allison Jacoby and Lucille Vickering had barely enough time to get back to the train. This didn't allow either to go into the woods, find Frederick and put a knife in his back.

Michael Jacoby had been rounded up immediately by Miss Jacoby, so it seemed unlikely he could have killed Frederick.

That left Daniel Compton or Benjamin Sager. One of them had time to stab Frederick, right after Allison heard him swear, probably by the time Allison and Lucille parted. The professor would have needed to beat Lucille back to the hotel in time to be seated on the porch, an unlikely scenario. The most suspicious—Daniel. He had been the last to reach the passenger car before Frederick stumbled aboard. He was the only one who appeared to have had time to kill Frederick before returning to the train.

CHAPTER 38

As the train pulled into the Salina station, Harry dashed forward and stood on the metal platform outside the car, ready to jump off the moment the wheels came to a stop. The railroad crew had been cooperative, and he didn't want to take advantage of their willingness to wait for him. He would complete his errand as fast as possible.

His gaze focused on the barren hillside. So many trees gone. And in Eldora one stand of trees that had hidden a knife attack. If those trees in Eldora hadn't grown back, would Frederick Hammond still be alive, thereby not necessitating Harry having to pursue this murder?

He was certainly becoming familiar with stations along the Switzerland Trail, a side effect of his investigation and telephone calls to Boulder. The wooden building here in Salina had experienced lots of use—paint was scraped off where people leaned against the side of the structure, a few boards on the porch needed to be replaced, and the threshold of the doorway into the station contained scuff marks from many boots.

A man in a gray coat and black bowler sat on a cracker barrel off to the side of the station, whittling. Another artist, like Michael Jacoby. Wood chips fell onto the dirt. Harry discerned a face appearing in the wood. Was this a present for a child? Something he'd put on his shelf at home? Or simply an occupation to while away the time?

The train jolted to a stop. Harry hopped to the ground, raced

219

into the station and located the telephone. After lifting the receiver, he gave the stiff crank a vigorous tug. No sound on the line. *Uh-oh.* Was the telephone broken or the line disconnected? Would Harry have to wait until he reached Boulder to communicate with the chief?

He cranked again and this time heard a crackling sound. He waited a moment, and an operator answered.

"Please connect me with Police Chief Lawrence Bass in Boulder."

Within a minute, his boss picked up.

"I hope you're feeling better," Harry said.

"Damned cough. It does seem to improve in the afternoon. After struggling all winter, it's mighty disconcerting to suffer a relapse and have to limit my activities."

Harry smiled to himself. He knew the difficulties the chief's wife faced trying to keep Bass resting and not off traipsing through Boulder chasing some law offender.

"What's the status of your investigation, McBride?"

"I'm making progress." *Yeah, but not enough.* "I have a main suspect. By a process of elimination, the evidence is pointing to him, but I don't have definitive proof yet."

"What makes you suspect this one person?"

"He held a grudge against the victim, was seen in the area of the crime soon before it occurred and was the last person to return to the train."

"But you haven't wrested a confession out of him yet?"

Harry clenched his free hand. "No confession."

"Why have you eliminated the others?"

How much to tell? "It gets down to a matter of time and location—who could have been in the vicinity of the stabbing site and who could have committed the act and returned to the train in time."

Chief Bass cleared his throat. "I have one piece of advice for you."

Harry pushed the receiver closer to his ear. "I'm always open to suggestions. Let's hear it."

"As I told you before, don't make any assumptions. Even though you think you've eliminated others, be careful that you haven't done so with a false set of information. It's easy to get wrapped up in a piece of evidence, decide it's solid and miss another clue. Keep your eyes and ears open."

"I'm trying to do that. The evidence isn't conclusive, and that's why I can't say for sure I've identified the right person yet."

The chief made a spitting sound. "I've come across some shifty criminals in my day who lie convincingly, change evidence and paint a picture that appears credible at first blush but turns out to be a sham. Pay close attention."

"Yes, sir." Harry thought of who might have deceived him. Michael Jacoby in his strange universe. Was that all an act? He didn't think so, but it merited another round of questioning when Harry got back to the train.

Lucille Vickering having to get back to the professor in time. Was there something he had missed here?

The professor seen in the woods before the knife attack but then back on the porch of the Gold Miner Hotel. Something in the timing he had overlooked?

Allison Jacoby? Appearing to be the caring sister and fiancée but secretly resenting Frederick? Harry winced. Had he made a bad assumption, not heeding the chief's warning? Allison claimed to have heard Frederick swearing. Lucille said she heard a noise but not necessarily Frederick. Had Allison lied and already put the knife in Frederick before Lucille appeared? Maybe Allison had fooled him. He needed to speak with her again.

"Are you there?" the chief shouted.

"Sorry, I was thinking about the suspects."

"I thought we lost the connection. Did you contact the coroner?"

Harry pushed aside his ruminations. "Yeah. I spoke with Mr. Howe after our last conversation, and he'll be at the station to claim the body."

"That's good. It will keep you from having to get into the mortuary business." Bass gave a hacking laugh.

Harry moved the receiver away from his ear. A strange thought jumped into his mind of contagion coursing through the telephone wire like electricity. He obviously had been concentrating too hard on this murder case.

"And you indicated George Savage would be at the station to meet me. That will be very helpful." Harry hoped he'd have the case solved so George could lead the right culprit away to jail. Otherwise, George would wonder why he'd been called on a Sunday afternoon to report to the railroad station.

"Oh, George will be there with his handcuffs ready. Make sure you have someone for him to arrest."

Harry pulled out his watch with his free hand. He had thirty-five, maybe forty minutes, before the train pulled into the Boulder depot. Could he put the puzzle pieces together by then? A drop of sweat trickled down his forehead. He had damned well better figure this out. "I'll see to it, sir."

"I hope your wife hasn't been disappointed in this outing because of your involvement in this investigation."

Harry twitched, the chief's words digging into him like a dagger. "Well . . . uh . . . we had a good time on the way up and in Eldora. It's unfortunate a murder interfered with her otherwise pleasant day."

"At least you both had some chance to enjoy the mountain air. Maybe that's what my lungs need." Chief Bass coughed.

"Susan even collected wildflowers."

"These women." The chief chortled, which turned into a hack. "They love to collect flowers. Say hello to Susan for me and get back to work." The chief clicked off.

Harry stared at the telephone for a moment and dropped the receiver in the cradle. What a situation. As soon as he returned to the train, it would be heading to Boulder with no delays other than stopping in Chrisman and a possible flag stop in Orodell. The chief could do nothing further to help him. It was in Harry's hands, and his alone.

A thought occurred to him. He wasn't completely alone. He had his one observer, Susan. She had been his "spy" on this return trip. Maybe, just maybe, she had picked up something to help his investigation.

With renewed vigor in his step, he returned to the platform. After one last glance at the Salina station, he signaled to the engineer, hopped aboard and entered the car. Susan looked up at him, and her lips curled slightly in a smile.

Professor Benjamin Sager and Allison Jacoby regarded him with blank expressions, which reminded him of a time he'd testified before a jury. The same expressions on the faces of the people in the jury box, waiting for something to happen. It seemed to communicate, "What do you have to offer? Tell me something interesting and don't leave me sitting here with nothing to do."

Lucille Vickering and Daniel Compton glared at him, and he cringed at their disapproval. Were they tired of being questioned, or did they resent that he had delayed the train, or was it something else?

Harry turned his eyes toward Michael Jacoby, off in his own world with his face pasted to the window. The strange young man was unaware of the activity in the passenger compartment. Had he forgotten about the body in the back? Did he not care?

What a group. Harry needed to bring this to a conclusion.

He waved to his wife. "Susan, please join me for a moment in the back."

"Is she a suspect as well?" the professor asked.

"Oh, she may have done many things, but she's not a murderess," Harry said.

Susan gave him a wary look but stood to join him.

CHAPTER 39

Susan walked behind Harry toward the back of the passenger car, put her hands on his shoulders and leaned close to his left ear. "Not only am I a spy, but now I'm facing an inquisition."

They took their seats and Harry regarded his wife thoughtfully. They had known each other almost thirty-three years, and he still couldn't predict what she would say. He looked into her intelligent eyes, which gave him a twinkle.

"What can I do for you, Officer McBride?"

Harry rolled his eyes. "Merely a few simple questions, Mrs. McBride. We're far enough back that the others can't hear us. I'd be interested in any further observations you have from watching the six suspects."

Susan gave Harry a pert smile. "Let's go through the list." She held up her index finger. "First, Allison Jacoby. She continues to be the mother hen, watching over her disturbed brother. She was definitely upset by Frederick's death. I sense her concern was at the loss and not because he showed up after she plunged a knife in his back."

"So you don't think she committed the murder."

Susan shook her head. "No, my intuition says she didn't."

The chief had said to pay attention to intuition, and Harry certainly respected Susan's insights.

Susan held up a second finger. "Michael Jacoby. He has been distraught ever since he returned from Eldora. It could be that he killed Frederick, but more likely he's upset over the loss of his knife. He was certainly obsessed with his carving on the way up, and now he can't whittle."

"That makes sense." Harry admired the way Susan got right to the point. Not like some people, the professor in particular, who became overly enamored with their words.

She held up three fingers. "Our conductor, Theodore Shultz. Although there was bad blood between him and Frederick, I don't think there was enough to cause him to commit a murder. He would have also had the most difficulty getting away and back in time, given his responsibilities on the train."

Susan put up four fingers. "Professor Benjamin Sager, our own hot air machine."

Harry chuckled.

Susan acknowledged Harry with a tilt of her head. "He doesn't strike me as the type of person to take decisive action. He might assassinate someone with words, but he doesn't have the gumption to actually put a real knife in someone's back."

Harry tried to picture the professor sneaking up on Frederick and plunging the blade into the young man. Susan was right. That didn't seem realistic.

Susan extended all five fingers on her right hand. "Lucille Vickering." She paused for a moment. "She's a different case. Something about her concerns me."

Harry perked up. "Say more."

"She comes across as an astute businesswoman, running her own boarding house and plays the coy femme fatale with the professor. I detect a streak of the theatrical in her. She isn't all that she appears to be. That makes me suspicious."

"Anything specific you can put your finger on?" Harry asked.

"That's the problem. It's only a sense I have, no real evidence." Susan held her right hand up and extended the index finger on her left hand. "And sixth, Daniel Compton. He comes across as the class jester at times, but there's intelligence behind his dark eyes. He's calculating. Notice how he baited Frederick earlier in the trip. He has the lawyer's skill of getting someone to react. It's obvious that he's not at all concerned over the demise of Frederick. He benefits from it in his pursuit of Allison Jacoby. As they say, all is fair in love and war."

"He's my main suspect," Harry said.

"Definitely possible," Susan replied. "I can't say for sure I know yet who committed the crime. That's my up-to-the-minute summary."

"Thank you. I want to show you some notes I've made." Harry took out his pad and showed Susan the diagram he'd drawn. "This is an important piece of what I've discovered so far. The crucial event probably took place in the woods near the picnic spot where Allison, Frederick and Michael ate. You remember Allison mentioned their destination based on the conversation she had with Old James before we reached Eldora."

"Yes. She came back and described how it was a five-minute walk west from the train station along the creek."

"Exactly. And everyone on the car heard that, so anyone who wanted to find them would have known where to look. So here's the diagram that shows the walking time to the picnic spot and to and from the Gold Miner Hotel. I've listed the estimated transit times that people needed to get back to the train." He flipped to another page and showed Susan the names of each of the suspects with the times of each entering and leaving the woods, along with the list of the order of people returning to the train.

Susan studied the list intently. She tapped the pad with a finger. "How do you know Benjamin and Daniel went into the woods at one forty-five and one fifty respectively?"

"That was based on the statement of Theodore Shultz."

"He might have been lying."

Harry nodded. "True, but he would have no reason to do so."

"Unless he was trying to implicate someone else."

"But he returned to the station at two, and the murder took place at approximately that time."

Susan tapped the pad. "How do you know Theodore was back?"

"I received independent verification from the engineer and fireman."

She arched an eyebrow. "Maybe they're in cahoots."

"I don't see any reason that the engineer and fireman would be involved in any of this."

"Probably right. How do you know exactly when the stabbing was committed? Tell me more about Miss Jacoby hearing Frederick swear in woods and noticing the time when asked by Lucille."

"This is a key event," Harry said. "Allison testified that she heard Frederick swear in the woods after Lucille arrived."

"Did Lucille hear it as well?"

"She said she heard a noise but couldn't confirm it was human."

"So either Lucille wasn't that familiar with Frederick's voice, or she pretended not to recognize it, or Allison made up hearing the voice."

Harry marveled at the insight from his wife. "I had the same thought, that Allison made it up. If so, she could have already stabbed Frederick before Lucille appeared."

Susan wrinkled her brow. "How do you know Allison and Lucille both saw each other?"

"Again, they independently verified the conversation."

"And how do you know it was two o'clock?"

Harry smiled. "That's easy. Lucille asked Allison for the time. They both corroborated that when Allison looked at her watch it was two o'clock."

"The watch could have been incorrect," Susan said.

"True, but do you remember earlier in the trip when several people compared the time on their watches?"

"Yes."

"Allison's watch showed the same time as Conductor Shultz's, the official railroad time. So when she noticed the time at the picnic spot, it would have been the same time as on Shultz's watch, meaning Shultz was already back at the station." Harry turned back to his diagram and notes. "And Lucille and Allison had a short time to return to the train, and the order people arrived made sense, given that Lucille had a longer trip to retrieve the professor at the Gold Miner Hotel. Everyone appears accounted for except Daniel Compton. Since he was seen going into the woods and was the last to return to the train, he could have taken Michael's knife from the stump, found Frederick, stuck the knife in his back, and headed back to the train. He's the only one who can't be accounted for and doesn't have an alibi, given the times involved."

Susan pursed her lips. "You may have found the murderer, but I'm not sure."

Harry realized he had the same feeling. "That's the problem. I'm running out of time before we reach Boulder, and I can't definitively say Daniel is the murderer. Something is nagging at the back of my mind, but I can't put my finger on it."

Susan patted his hand. "I'm sure you'll come up with it."

Harry hoped that was the case, but he had his doubts. He looked out the window and saw Black Swan. He remembered the account of the wreck on this treacherous turn. He hoped the engineer wasn't going too fast in trying to make up time for the delays Harry had caused. He held onto the seat tightly as the car jostled through the turn. When they exited safely,

Harry let out a breath of air. They were safe for the moment, but he had precious little time to find a murderer.

CHAPTER 40

After his discussion with Susan, Harry escorted her back to her seat. He looked through the window at the rugged treeless hillside and thought about how miners had struggled through the gullies and around the outcrops looking for gold. He was a miner in his own right, searching among six people to find the nugget to solve this case.

"Have you completed your inquisition, Officer McBride?" Professor Sager asked.

"Not yet. I have a few more people to speak with on my second round of questioning."

The professor tweaked his beard. "You keep at it and find out what happened."

"I'll try my best." Harry leaned toward Allison. "Miss Jacoby, I need you to join me again."

Allison gazed over her shoulder at her brother. "Oh, dear. I'm not sure I should leave Michael alone. He's still in such a state."

Harry regarded Michael, who kept his face plastered to the window. "As we discussed before, you'll be close by."

With one final worried glance toward Michael, she stood and followed Harry toward the back of the car.

Once they both sat, Harry asked, "How is your brother doing?"

Allison bit her lip. "He's very upset. He can stay sullen for such a long time. I'm worried about him."

"Has he said anything to you regarding what happened in El-dora?"

"No. He's keeping to himself. He can go days without saying much when he's in one of his moods."

"Given how much he likes carving, he should have mentioned his missing knife."

"No. He's too distressed to speak of it."

Harry imagined the difficulties of living in the same house with someone like Michael. All the idiosyncrasies and strange types of behavior. It would take some getting used to. He was glad his children hadn't been this extreme. Sure, they had their sullen and uncommunicative times, but they snapped out of it quickly. He remembered the time his son, Tom, at age nine, wanted a new baseball after he lost his. He had pouted, thrown himself on his bed and covered his head with a pillow saying he'd never come out of his room. Harry almost smiled at the memory. That tantrum had lasted an hour until Susan had baked a batch of oatmeal cookies. Suddenly, Tom appeared in the kitchen with a huge grin on his face, volunteering to sample the cookies. Much different than dealing with a young man in his twenties who acted like a little boy.

"Miss Jacoby, I'm trying to re-create the events that took place at your picnic spot in Eldora. I'd like you to go through in detail everything that happened after Frederick went off by himself into the woods."

Her nostrils flared. "I've already told you everything."

"Humor me. Sometimes when you recount an event a second time, you remember something you might have missed the first time. This could be extremely important in finding who killed Frederick Hammond."

Allison let out a deep sigh. "All right. After Frederick left, Michael also went off on his own in the opposite direction. I passed the time by myself until Mrs. Vickering appeared."

"Why do you think she showed up right then?"

Allison looked puzzled. "I don't know. I hadn't thought about it. I suppose she was out walking and saw me."

Harry gave her a reassuring smile. "Continue with your account."

"I was on the blanket. I stood to speak with Mrs. Vickering, and that's when I heard Frederick cussing in the woods."

"Mrs. Vickering said she heard a noise but didn't know if it was a person or an animal or the wind. Are you sure it was Frederick?"

Allison clenched her fists as if preparing to defend herself. "Absolutely. I know his voice. There was no mistaking it."

"It couldn't have been an animal or the wind?"

"Certainly not. It was Frederick."

Harry watched her carefully to see if he could detect a lie. "Yet, Mrs. Vickering didn't recognize the sound as coming from Frederick."

Allison crinkled her brow. "She doesn't know him as well as I do, and maybe her hearing isn't as good as mine. I heard Frederick."

A banging noise caught his attention, and Harry jerked his head away from Allison to see Michael Jacoby flapping his arms, his right hand striking the window.

"I need to go help Michael." Allison started to rise.

Harry reached across the aisle and put a hand on her wrist. "Give him a moment. Don't rush off yet."

Allison tensed at being constrained but sat down. In a moment Michael stopped flapping and put his face back to the window.

Harry removed his hand from her wrist. "There. I think things are under control with Michael. Continue telling me what happened at the picnic spot after you heard Mr. Hammond swearing in the woods."

"Then Mrs. Vickering asked to see my watch, and we discovered it was two o'clock. We didn't have much time. She left and I went to retrieve Michael."

"Were you absolutely sure of the time?"

"Yes. I looked at the dial and showed it to Mrs. Vickering. It was two o'clock, no question."

The train slowed, and Conductor Shultz appeared at the front of the car to announce, "We're at Chrisman." The car shook as it came to a jerky stop in front of the station, which appeared abandoned.

Harry had a thought. What if Allison had committed the crime? What would happen to Michael if she went to prison? The young man would end up in an institution. No, he didn't think she would risk that, given how protective she was of her brother. "How long did it take you to gather your belongings and retrieve Michael?"

"I didn't check my watch again, but it must have been five to ten minutes, including time I spent calling for Frederick. When I didn't think I could wait any longer, Michael and I went back to the station."

The whistle blew and the train began moving again.

Harry pulled out his notepad and did the calculations. Checked the watch at two. Five to ten minutes to prepare to leave. Five minutes to walk to the train. That checked out with his previous notes on when they boarded the train. "Do you think Mr. Compton hated Mr. Hammond enough to kill him?"

Allison winced and put her hand to her mouth. "I . . . I don't think so."

"So here's my quandary, Miss Jacoby. Someone sitting in this compartment stuck a knife in Frederick Hammond's back." He waved his hand toward the other passengers and Conductor Shultz, who was speaking with Susan. "It's not my wife or me, which leaves six of you, including our conductor. All of you argued with Mr. Hammond on the trip to Eldora. One of you took the argument a step too far."

She met his eyes with unflinching intensity. "One thing I can say for sure, Officer McBride. It wasn't Michael or me."

Harry attempted to stare her down, but she didn't avert her eyes. He tried to read what she was thinking. Was she protecting Michael or herself? He had seen how she tried to shelter her brother. If Michael committed the crime and she knew it, Harry didn't expect she would admit what happened. And as with his earlier thought, she wouldn't want to be incarcerated and leave her brother unattended. He remembered the revelation made by Frederick during the stopover in Sunset about planning to break the engagement and go to California. Had Allison found out about this plan and seized her brother's knife to dispatch Frederick?

"Miss Jacoby, did Mr. Hammond ever mention any plan to break off the engagement?"

She stared at him with wide eyes. "Why would you even ask such a question? Of course not."

Harry had no direct evidence that either Allison or Michael had stuck the knife in Frederick's back, and the time frame didn't allow a chance to accomplish it anyway. "If neither you nor Michael committed the crime, which of the four do you suspect?"

Now she focused her eyes toward the front of the car. "I . . . I don't know. I can't imagine Mrs. Vickering, or Professor Sager, or Conductor Shultz or . . ." She paused. Her hand went to her mouth again. "I don't think it was Daniel . . . I . . . I just don't know."

Harry watched her reaction. She was having second thoughts concerning Daniel. In accord with his own thinking.

Allison closed her eyes and sat motionless for a moment. When she opened her eyes, she met Harry's gaze and replied in a soft voice, "Daniel might have done it."

"Why Daniel?"

"When Daniel and I were seeing each other, he was very possessive. I broke off the relationship. Later, he resented that Frederick and I became engaged. I don't think he could stand that Frederick and I were going to be married."

"That's a possible motive," Harry said. "Did you see Mr. Compton anywhere near the meadow where you had your picnic?"

"No, but he's devious. He might have sneaked up."

"Anything else you'd like to tell me, Miss Jacoby?"

"No, I better get back to Michael."

"I need to speak with him again as well."

Allison straightened her back as if resting against a board. "Must you? He's not in any condition to be bothered again."

"I can assure you I'll be gentle with him. It's imperative that I ask him a few more questions. He's very observant. He may have noticed something that will shed light on catching the murderer."

Allison's eyes darted toward Michael.

Harry could tell she was torn between protecting her brother and helping uncover what had happened.

Finally, Allison turned toward Harry. "All right. Just find out who did this awful thing to Frederick."

CHAPTER 41

Harry and Allison walked forward in the passenger car to retrieve Michael Jacoby.

"Officer McBride needs to speak with you again, Michael," Allison said.

Michael kept his face pressed to the window. "Don't want to."

Allison reached over and gently placed her hand on his shoulder. "Please cooperate."

Michael shrugged his shoulder as if trying to remove an irritating fly. Finally he looked toward Allison, although not meeting her eyes. "Why?"

"Officer McBride is trying to find out what happened to Frederick. He thinks you might be able to help."

Michael wrinkled his brow. "Help?"

Harry stepped closer. "This won't take long. You notice things the rest of us don't. I thought you might be able to assist."

Michael's eyes widened but still didn't meet Harry's. "Like solving a puzzle?"

Harry watched the young man. "Exactly. Like solving a puzzle."

"Michael loves puzzles," Allison said. "He's very good at them."

"Will you come speak with me?" Harry asked.

Michael focused on Harry's chest, never looking toward his face. "Okay." He scooted out of his seat and followed Harry away from the others.

Once they were seated, Harry said, "When we spoke before, you told me that you went off on your own after your picnic. I'd like you to tell me everything that happened after you found the spot with the stump."

Michael turned his eyes toward the floor. "Already told you."

"I know you did. As I mentioned to your sister, it's very useful to go over your memories a second time. Sometimes you'll recall something you missed at first."

"Won't change. I see pictures of what happened."

Harry stared more intently at Michael. "What do you mean?"

"I remember things . . . just like watching a moving picture show. I can see everything happening."

"Really? Tell me about the pictures you see of when you left the picnic to go off by yourself."

Michael crunched his eyes closed. "Trees around me. Aspen and pine. Walked around a bend. Saw a stump. Found a piece of wood on a pile of leaves. Took out my knife. Stripped off the bark. Smoothed off the edges. Someone watched from the woods."

Harry's heart thumped. "You didn't mention this when we talked before."

"I didn't watch the pictures that time."

"How could you tell someone was watching?" Harry asked.

"Branches moved. Not a squirrel. Bigger. Not a bear. Too quiet. A person."

"And who was it?"

Michael scratched the side of his head like a dog with fleas. "Don't know."

"Man or woman?"

"Don't know."

"Keep your pictures going," Harry said.

"Had to go relieve myself. Put knife in stump. Stuck it one

inch in wood. Went far enough so no one saw me. Place with leaves and pine needles. Ducked under branch. Relieved myself. Came back. Knife was gone."

Harry thought it all over. "So if someone had been watching you, that person could have taken your knife."

Michael looked toward the blanket-shrouded body. "Want it back."

"You'll get your knife back later. Right now it's evidence in the murder investigation."

"Want it back now." Michael started flapping his arms.

Harry tried to try to calm Michael by touching his shoulder, but the young man jerked away and screamed.

Allison raced up the aisle. "What are you doing to him?" she shouted at Harry.

"I'm trying to calm him down."

"Don't touch him. That only makes him worse." She leaned over. "Michael, it's all right."

Michael let out a sob and covered his face.

"Take a deep breath. Officer McBride won't touch you again."

Harry pulled away as if he had put his hand on a hot stove. Never again would he touch Michael. But what if Michael was lying and had killed Frederick? He would need to be handcuffed and arrested. That would lead to quite a scene.

Michael finally settled down.

"Are you through with him, Officer McBride?" Allison asked.

"Not quite. I'll be more careful with him."

Allison looked at Michael one more time and returned to her seat.

Harry waited until she was out of earshot. "Michael, tell me what you see in your pictures after you discovered your knife was missing."

"I sat on the ground and cried. Dry leaves. I picked one up. Three holes in it."

"Did you see the person in the woods again?"

"No. Gone."

"Describe the stump after the knife was gone."

Michael closed his eyes. "Two feet off the ground. Jagged like a tree blown over in the wind. Ants crawling on top. Twenty-two ants. One carrying a piece of bark. No knife in it anymore. Nuts on the ground."

Harry leaned closer to Michael. "What kind of nuts?"

Michael bit his lips and scrunched his eyes shut tighter. "Walnuts, almonds and hazelnuts."

Ah-ha, Harry thought. *Now we're getting somewhere.* "And how long did you sit there?"

"Until Allison came."

"How much time was that?"

"Don't know."

"And then?" Harry realized he was speaking in short statements just like Michael did.

"Said we needed to get back to train. I didn't want to leave. Wanted knife. She said we'd miss train. We walked back. Sun shining. Followed creek. Saw fish jump. Stepped over red rock in path. Broken branch on one tree. Came out on dirt road. Crossed bridge. Train station. Got on train."

"How long did that take?"

"We walked whole time. Didn't stop."

From everything Harry had heard, that took approximately five minutes. It seemed to fit. But the new piece of information—someone in the woods had watched Michael. That person had waited until Michael went off, took the knife and used it to kill Frederick. And then Michael had seen nuts near the stump that had once held the knife. One person had those kinds of nuts. He now had another significant clue.

"Did you see anyone before you reached the train?" Harry asked.

Michael scrunched up his nose. "Two squirrels. One chipmunk. No people."

"We talked earlier about solving a puzzle," Harry said. "Will you help me solve this puzzle?"

Michael opened his eyes and ventured a look that almost met Harry's chin. "Yes."

"Think back to anything you noticed today. Anything to help me find out who killed Frederick?"

Michael closed his eyes again.

Harry waited for what seemed like minutes.

Suddenly, Michael opened his eyes wide. "Shoes. Mud."

"Huh?" Harry was caught by surprise.

Michael's arms started flapping. "Shoes! Mud!"

Harry started to reach out and caught himself. "Stay calm. Tell me more about shoes and mud."

Michael stopped flapping and let out a gasp. He pointed toward the blanket-covered body. "Shoes. Mud."

Harry looked where Michael pointed. He stood and went over to look at Frederick's boots, extending beyond the blanket. Mud covered the heels.

Harry remembered his earlier comment in regards to tracking mud into his house after a long day on patrol. Then it clicked. Harry slapped his forehead. Of course. How could he have missed it? Assumptions. He had made a number of bad assumptions along the way. Now he thought he knew who killed Frederick. But one problem remained. He couldn't resolve the timing.

Harry stepped back to where Michael sat. "You can return to your seat next to your sister. You've helped me solve the puzzle."

Michael stood, said, "Puzzle," and loped back to rejoin Allison.

Conductor Shultz stuck his head in the compartment. "Passing Orodell. Not stopping."

Harry walked slowly to the front of the compartment. He stopped in front of each seat and looked at the feet of the passengers. He continued to the front and regarded Shultz's shoes.

"Mr. Shultz, please stay with us for a moment before returning to your duties," Harry said.

Shultz took out his watch and checked it. "For a short time. We'll be to the station in twelve minutes."

Harry turned to face the passengers. He was getting close. He needed to figure out one last piece of the puzzle.

CHAPTER 42

Harry took a moment to compose his thoughts as he stood in the front of the compartment facing the passengers. Before he could say anything, Lucille Vickering leaned across the aisle toward Allison. "Miss Jacoby, may I see your watch again?"

"Of course." Allison removed it from her wrist and held it out to Lucille.

This action caught Harry's attention. Several things passed through his mind. First, was the admonition from Chief Bass not to make assumptions. The second was the question from Susan of how he knew the discussion between Allison and Lucille had taken place at two o'clock. "Wait," he shouted. He reached out and grabbed the watch before it reached Lucille's hand.

"What time do you have, Conductor Shultz?" Harry asked.

Shultz removed his watch. "Four-thirty-one. We're almost on time." He glared at Harry. "We'd be exactly on time without the stops for telephone calls."

Harry looked at Allison's watch. It read four-thirty-six. The last piece clicked into place. A sense of excitement and dread coursed through Harry's chest. He held Allison's watch out for Shultz to see. "Conductor, please look at the time on this watch."

Shultz leaned over and stared. "It's five minutes fast."

"Exactly," Harry said. "And does everyone remember earlier in the trip when a number of you looked at your watches?"

"Yeah," Daniel said. "The conductor's, the professor's, Allison's and mine all had the same time—that is, after I adjusted mine to be the same as the others."

"But now Allison's watch is five minutes fast," Harry said.

"I didn't change it," Allison said.

Harry nodded. "I know, but someone else did."

"Why would someone do such a silly thing?" Allison asked.

"To provide an alibi." Harry pulled out his notepad and tapped it. "All six of the people in this compartment, except my wife and I are suspects. Allison and Michael Jacoby were picnicking with Frederick Hammond right before he was stabbed, so they are under suspicion."

"I can assure you that neither Michael nor I did it," Allison huffed.

Harry held up a hand. "I'm not accusing you or your brother, Miss Jacoby. I'm stating the facts. Please just listen."

Allison breathed loudly through her nose like a horse snorting.

"To continue," Harry said, "Frederick Hammond was stabbed with Michael Jacoby's knife. That made him a suspect at the outset. But it appears that Michael left the knife in a stump when he went off into the woods. Someone took the knife and used it to dispatch Mr. Hammond."

Michael started flapping his arms. "My knife."

"Shhh." Allison whispered.

Harry waited until Michael calmed. "Conductor Shultz arrived back at the train at two o'clock, and this was corroborated by the engineer and fireman. He did have an interesting set of information though. He had seen Professor Sager and Mr. Compton go into the woods at approximately one-forty-five to one-fifty." Daniel turned around and gawked at the professor.

"If you are accusing one of us." The professor spat out the words. "I can assure you it was Daniel and not me."

Harry held up both hands. "Everyone bear with me for a moment. I'm not at the point of accusing anyone. I'm stating the facts."

"You better watch what you say, Officer McBride," Daniel said through clenched teeth. "Even though you're a policeman, you can be held accountable for slander."

"I can assure you I'm not slandering anyone, Mr. Compton. Now, we come to a very interesting part of the story. Miss Jacoby heard Mr. Hammond swearing in the woods after he stormed away from their picnic. That was right after Mrs. Vickering appeared. Mrs. Vickering asked Miss Jacoby for the time and what did you do, Miss Jacoby?"

"I checked my watch, which showed two o'clock."

Harry smiled. "But from what we just learned, Miss Jacoby's watch was five minutes fast. So that conversation actually took place at one-fifty-five."

Lucille clutched the seat in front of her. "So Conductor Shultz's alibi wasn't so solid after all."

"Wait a minute. I had nothing to do with Frederick's death." Shultz lunged toward Lucille.

Harry put out an arm to constrain Theodore Shultz. "Everyone, please listen until I finish what I have to say. This time discrepancy could have made it possible for Mr. Shultz to have committed the stabbing and raced back to the train, but he wasn't the one who changed Miss Jacoby's watch."

"I haven't taken it off since we arrived in Eldora," Allison said. "And I certainly didn't change it."

"But there was one time you took it off on the trip into the mountains," Harry said. "You handed it to Mrs. Vickering as we pulled into the Eldora station."

"And all I did was admire it and return it to her," Lucille said.

Harry's gaze bore in on Lucille. "No, that's not what happened. You set it forward five minutes. And a few moments ago you asked to see it again so you could change the time back to what it should have been."

Lucille gave off a forced laugh. "How could you think such a thing?"

"I'll get to that shortly." Harry realized how close he had come to missing this vital clue. If he had allowed Lucille to take the watch or if Lucille had possessed the foresight to ask for the watch earlier in the return trip, he would never have made the connection. "Another relevant piece of information. Michael Jacoby remembered seeing nuts on the ground by the stump where he had left his knife. They were specifically almonds, walnuts and hazelnuts—the type that Professor Sager ate earlier on our journey."

"Are you accusing me?" the professor shouted. "I didn't go near any stump in the woods."

Harry held up his hand. "I'm not saying you did. Someone else had a handful of your nuts as well. Now, another important piece of evidence. At the edge of the clearing where the picnic took place, Miss Jacoby mentioned seeing a muddy spot. Michael Jacoby, who is very observant, pointed out to me that Frederick Hammond had mud on his shoes." Harry pointed to the body at the back of the compartment. "When he left the picnic, Mr. Hammond went into a muddy part of the woods. Whoever stuck the knife in his back also went through mud. I've checked your shoes. I remember one person wiping mud off when returning to the passenger car. That person still has mud."

Everyone looked at their shoes.

Harry waited a beat. "I can see you weren't able to wipe all the mud off when you tried right before our departure from Eldora, Mrs. Vickering."

Lucille lunged to her feet. "Of all the gall! How can you accuse me? I'm an upstanding citizen, and resent what you're implying."

"There, there, my dear," the professor said. "Let's hear what Officer McBride has to say."

Harry stepped next to Lucille. "I can clearly see some of the mud right now."

"I had no reason to kill Frederick," Lucille thrust out her chin.

The train came to a stop.

"This doesn't look like the station," Allison said staring out the window.

"We're stopping at the water tank," Shultz said. "It will only take a minute or so. Please continue, Officer McBride."

"Although all six of you had arguments with Frederick, there was history between Mrs. Vickering and Mr. Hammond. A romance gone bad." Harry pointed directly at Lucille. "You sought your revenge. While on the train, you listened to Miss Jacoby describe the picnic spot mentioned to her by Old James, asked to see her watch and changed the time. After your meal at the Gold Miner Hotel, you left Professor Sager on the porch and went off on your own. After speaking so fondly of collecting wildflowers, you never actually collected any because you had a different mission in mind. You found the picnic spot, stood in the woods watching, noticed Michael Jacoby disappear after leaving his knife in a stump, collected the knife, dropped a few of Professor Sager's nuts that you had taken from his sack earlier on the trip, and spoke with Miss Jacoby to set up your alibi about the time. Miss Jacoby heard Frederick cuss, but you professed to not hear his voice, even though you really did. When Miss Jacoby rushed off to collect Michael, you went into the woods where you had heard Frederick swearing, put the knife in his back and hightailed it back to the train in time. I assumed that neither you nor Miss Jacoby could have stabbed

Frederick because there wasn't enough time to accomplish that between two o'clock and your return to the train. But it turns out you had an additional five minutes, adequate time to stab Frederick. I briefly thought Professor Sager had committed the crime because of the nuts found by Michael Jacoby near the stump, but those were deliberately left to throw suspicion onto the wrong person. Lucille Vickering stuck the knife in Frederick Hammond's back."

As the train started moving again, all eyes turned to Lucille. She reached in her bag and pulled out a handgun, which she pointed at Harry.

"What are you doing, my dear?" Benjamin Sager asked.

"Oh, shut up, you old buffoon. Officer McBride and Conductor Shultz, please be kind enough to sit down."

Harry recognized the handgun as a Baby Hammerless .22-caliber six-shot revolver. "I bet you intended to use this gun on Frederick. When the knife presented itself, you had a different and quieter alternative."

"Enough of your babbling," Lucille brandished the gun again. "Sit down!"

Harry took his seat next to Susan, and Shultz dropped into the seat next to Daniel.

Lucille stepped to the front of the car. She turned to face the passengers. "All of you remain right here until I get off the train."

The train slowed as it passed through the train yard. Harry looked out the window at the rolling stock lined up. He spotted one engine resting along a siding. He knew Officer George Savage would be waiting at the station. He had to find some way to get a message to him.

CHAPTER 43

An idea occurred to Harry. He scanned around the compartment and verified that Susan was out of direct line of sight of Lucille. Keeping his eyes on Lucille at the exit to the passenger car as she brandished her handgun, he waited until her attention was distracted. He quickly removed his notepad and pencil and kept the pad in his lap out of view of Lucille. He jotted a note: "Help! Armed suspect."

Quietly, he tore the page out and handed it to Susan.

Susan glanced at the note and squeezed Harry's hand in acknowledgment.

Harry knew he could count on her.

The station appeared ahead and to the left. Half a dozen people milled around on the platform, waiting to meet passengers or merely admiring the arrival of locomotive number thirty-three and its two green Pullman cars.

Harry nudged Susan, and she leaned over and put the note up to the window with her hand covering it. Craning his neck to peer out the window, Harry spotted the dark blue uniform of Officer George Savage, eyes turned toward the approaching train.

Harry hoped George would see the note.

The train continued to slowly roll, and Susan continued to hold the note to the window. George appeared to be watching the locomotive.

Harry wanted to wave, but that would alert Lucille.

George continued to watch the locomotive.

Harry had to do something, but he didn't want to risk someone getting shot.

The train slowed.

Turn your head, Harry willed.

As if on command, George adjusted his gaze toward the first, then second Pullman car. His eyes widened, and he nodded.

When the train stopped, Harry realized he needed to distract Lucille. With his heart beating rapidly he shouted, "Mrs. Vickering, you won't get away with this!"

She aimed her gun at Harry's chest. "I certainly will, Officer McBride."

Harry tensed, wondering if he had overplayed his warning. Still, he needed to keep her attention for a few more moments.

"You should surrender your gun," Harry said. "It will be better for you than trying to escape."

Lucille gave a derisive laugh. "Ha. This is the last you'll see of me." She waved the gun left and right. "Everyone stay where you are."

She backed toward the door, pointing the gun in the direction of the passengers . . . and stumbled right into Officer George Savage, who clamped his hands around her wrist to direct the gun's barrel toward the floor.

A shot went off with a puff of smoke.

Allison Jacoby screamed.

Susan flinched.

Harry dashed to his feet and wrestled the gun out of Lucille's hand. Once he had it out of her reach, he said, "Mrs. Lucille Vickering, you are under arrest for the murder of Frederick Hammond. Officer Savage will accompany you off the train."

Professor Benjamin Sager jumped to his feet. "I'll hire the best defense lawyer in the city of Boulder for you, my dear."

Daniel Compton also stood. "I'll be happy to take on your

defense, Mrs. Vickering. I've seen what happened today. I won't let the police railroad you."

Benjamin glared at Daniel. "No time for one of your ridiculous puns. I said I'd hire the best defense lawyer, not you."

Daniel gaped, his mouth wide open. He shut it and spun away from the professor and dropped back into his seat.

"Unhand me, you brute." Lucille spat out the words.

"No, ma'am," George replied. "You're coming with me."

With his hand firmly on Lucille's arm, Officer Savage led her down the steps and into the station.

Harry looked down at the floor of the compartment to spot a neat hole. "Conductor Shultz, you need to notify the maintenance workers that a small repair will be required for this passenger car."

Shultz took off his cap and wiped sweat from his brow. "That was close. At least she didn't shoot any of us."

Harry turned to face the group of passengers. "This has been a most unfortunate incident. You may need to testify when a trial is held for Mrs. Vickering."

"I certainly will do that," Allison said. "The nerve of that woman." A tear rolled down her cheek. "What an awful way for Frederick to die."

"Since I won't be defending her, I can also testify," Daniel said.

Professor Benjamin Sager harrumphed. "I won't say a word against Lucille. I'm sure this was all a misunderstanding."

"I'm afraid not, Professor," Harry said. "She committed murder and will be tried and convicted."

Michael pulled his face away from the window and flapped his arms as he shouted, "Shoes! Mud!"

Allison patted her brother's hand. "That's right. You helped Officer McBride solve the puzzle of who killed Frederick."

Michael dropped his arms to his side. "Puzzle. I like puzzles."

"I need all of you to leave the passenger car while I wait for the coroner," Harry said. "Please exit through the front."

Professor Sager strode to where Harry stood. "I've had enough of this." He shook his right index finger at Harry. "I will see you in court." Then he marched out the door.

Daniel stood and faced Allison. "Is there anything I can do to assist you and your brother, Miss Jacoby?"

"No. We can get by fine on our own, Mr. Compton." She turned toward her brother. "Michael, let's go." She gathered her carpetbag, tucked her flowers in the top, took Michael's hand and led him toward the exit.

Michael glanced back one time and mumbled, "Puzzle. Shoes. Mud."

Daniel bowed to Susan and followed.

With only he and Susan remaining, Harry headed back to watch over the body of Frederick Hammond.

Susan gathered her flowers. "I'll meet you in front of the station, Harry."

"That's a good idea. I'll join you once I take care of things with the coroner. It shouldn't be long."

Susan went out the front door and disappeared down the steps. Harry stared out the window at the station. The crowd was dissipating as people returned to their homes or prepared to catch the interurban train to Denver. On this one trip into the mountains, lives intertwined, and a past grudge led to death.

In a few minutes the coroner, A. E. Howe, boarded the train. Harry led him to the body and pulled off the blanket. "We should be able to get fingerprints from the ebony knife handle."

A. E. Howe bent over and whistled. "Right between the shoulder blades."

"The amazing thing is that he made his way a considerable distance before the wound proved fatal," Harry said.

The two of them carried the body off the back end of the Pullman car and loaded it into a horse-drawn wagon. The coroner climbed into the front of the wagon, picked up the reins, flicked them and drove away.

Harry rejoined Susan, who sat on a bench in front of the station holding her wildflowers. "I wonder how long these flowers will last." Susan said.

Harry shrugged. He was lost in thought as he admired the station building, a strong stone gateway for travelers heading to many destinations. He wondered how long it would stand. Would it last longer than the young boy who sat on the platform watching the locomotive? Harry considered how fragile was the thread that held any one life, whether plant, animal or human. How long would any of them last?

His gaze turned toward the locomotive. There stood number thirty-three. As the professor had said, a most inauspicious number. It certainly had been a dangerous number for Frederick Hammond. The outcome wouldn't be bright for Lucille Vickering, either. Every one of the returning passengers in Pullman car number nineteen would remember this day for the rest of their lives. He knew he would.

Harry realized something else. This July Fourth marked exactly thirty-three years since, at the age of fifteen, he had set eyes on a beautiful girl in blond pigtails at a holiday picnic. He had watched her for half an hour and finally mustered the gumption to go over and speak with her. She was his age and had moved to Boulder a month earlier with her family. The two of them spent the rest of the day together and became inseparable thereafter. After completing school and once Harry had a job, they married. There was one good thing to go with the number thirty-three.

In spite of the troubles of the day, warmth passed through Harry's chest as he took Susan's hand and smiled at the woman who had outgrown her pigtails but now carried an armload of wildflowers to decorate their home.

CHAPTER 44

That evening, Harry McBride went to Frederick Hammond's room and found a telephone number for Frederick's brother, Robert. Upon placing a call, Robert declined to come to Boulder for any funeral service, so Harry arranged to have Frederick's belongings sent to Robert.

The next day Harry boarded the Switzerland Trail railroad at exactly eight-thirty, this time joined by John Penrod, the photographer who helped the police department on a part-time basis. The morning was already warm, and during the day, the temperature rose even higher than the day before.

Harry remained silent during the trip as they passed Orodell, Chrisman, Salina, Wall Street and Copper Rock. He almost made a comment when he saw the green-corroded stain on the rock face, but, even though it was a different color, it reminded him of the blood dripping out of Frederick Hammond, so he kept his thoughts to himself.

When the train stopped at Sunset, his companion asked, "Why so quiet, Officer McBride?"

Harry wrinkled his brow. "I've been thinking about the trip yesterday. It's the same but different today."

John Penrod looked askance at Harry but didn't ask anything further. The two of them remained silent for the remainder of the ascent.

Harry periodically turned to scan the back of the Pullman car, remembering the blanket-clad body. Today, an old man and woman sat in the back of the compartment, huddled close together. Would that be Susan and him in a few years? He could picture growing old with her by his side.

Harry had checked earlier, and the one Pullman car in use today was number twenty-two, not the one he had been on the day before. He expected car number nineteen was in the maintenance shop, having the hole in its floor repaired. A hole that could be repaired easily, not like having a knife stabbed in one's back.

When they arrived in Eldora, Harry led the photographer off the train, and they followed the still visible trail of dried blood from the station into the woods to the spot where the stabbing took place, identified by the flat straw boater lying in the mud. He also located the stump that Michael Jacoby had used, finding one hazelnut that had escaped the local squirrels and chipmunks. Harry made careful notes of what he saw while the photographer set up his equipment and took his pictures.

Susan's wildflowers lasted for a week. After petals began to litter the living room table, she finally threw them out.

Harry collected a good set of fingerprints from the ebony handle of Michael's knife, which had been used to kill Frederick. He subsequently matched those to the prints of Lucille Vickering. He also interviewed all the boarders at the Vickering boarding house, and two of them made statements that they had seen Lucille and Frederick Hammond together within the last week. With the photographic evidence, the fingerprints and Harry's notes from his interviews with the passengers of Pullman car number nineteen, Lucille was brought to trial.

This was a major event in town, with reporters even coming from the *Denver Post* and the *Rocky Mountain News*. The prosecutor methodically presented the evidence, culminating with testimony on how Mrs. Vickering threatened the passengers with a handgun.

Harry, Susan, Allison Jacoby, Daniel Compton and Conductor Shultz testified for the prosecution. The prosecutor built the argument of a premeditated crime whereby Lucille planned to kill Frederick Hammond on the stopover in Eldora. He stated that Lucille and Frederick had renewed their relationship, and Frederick had spurned her for a second time, causing her to seek revenge by killing him. She changed the time on Allison Jacoby's watch to prepare an alibi. When she came across the picnic spot, she remained in the woods, saw the knife left by Michael Jacoby, decided to use it rather than her handgun, picked it up and hid it in her skirt. She left a few of Professor Sager's nuts on the ground to divert attention to him. After asking Allison Jacoby the time to establish the misleading alibi, she went into the woods, crept up behind Frederick and planted the knife in his back. Then she dashed back to retrieve Professor Sager and returned to the train as if nothing had happened. The prosecutor pointed out that after Lucille had professed a desire to gather wildflowers, in actuality she never collected any flowers, another damning point. Several women in the courtroom nodded, obviously understanding the argument.

The defense attorney presented the case that there was a reasonable doubt of Lucille committing the crime. He tried to confuse the issue by indicating that two other people had been seen going into the woods right before the stabbing occurred and that either of them could have been the murderer. Professor Benjamin Sager testified on behalf of the defense, but his rambling statement did more harm than good for Lucille's cause.

After a calculated decision, the defense attorney called Lucille to testify. She tried to come across as a falsely accused widow. She wore a demure dark dress with a conservative hat and dabbed at her eyes with a cleanly starched white handkerchief.

She spoke quietly with sporadically spaced sobs.

While being cross-examined by the prosecutor, Lucille fainted. There was much speculation that this was a staged shenanigan to solicit sympathy from the jury. It didn't work, as she was found guilty of first-degree murder and sentenced to life imprisonment in the Colorado State Penitentiary in Canon City, in spite of the expensive lawyer Benjamin Sager hired for her defense.

It was unfortunate for her that she missed the discussion about fingerprints when she went to the back of the passenger car to speak with her friend in the climbers club, or she would have known to use gloves when she drove the knife into Frederick Hammond's back. That little oversight cost her dearly.

Lucille died in prison of influenza in March 1926, another year of an epidemic, although considerably milder than the one of 1918.

After the trial and in spite of his usual bluster, Professor Benjamin Sager never spoke again of that day of June 29, 1919. He managed to bore university students for the next ten years, dying of a heart attack while lecturing on the history of mining in Colorado. He was in the middle of describing the Boulder County tunnel at Cardinal, when his overtaxed heart gave out. Dr. Kellogg's regime did not help him live anywhere close to a hundred years.

Daniel Compton continued to practice law, with only slightly more success than in his attempts to woo Allison Jacoby. After the tenth and final rebuff from the young woman, he moved to California. He resumed his law practice, supported himself on meager earnings and never again returned to Colorado.

Michael Jacoby gained local renown as an artist who produced popular animal carvings. Homeowners through the county displayed his work in prominent places. He earned enough money to support himself and his spinster sister.

Theodore Shultz, after suffering unemployment due to the demise of the railroad, became a merchant, even selling a number of Michael Jacoby's creations to eager consumers. For years afterward, he regaled his children and grandchildren with accounts of his experiences on the Switzerland Trail.

Harry McBride's wish for a police motorcar was fulfilled in 1920, but it had a tragic consequence. On March 18, 1920, the first day of service for the new police vehicle, Police Chief Lawrence Bass was killed in an automobile accident involving the city fire engine. Some might say Harry could have benefited from that event, as he was one of two candidates to become chief of police. Although Harry considered it for a while, figuring Susan might enjoy the increase in pay, he ultimately withdrew from consideration, knowing he would see less of his wife if he undertook the added responsibility.

Fellow officer George Savage became the next Boulder police chief, a decision with which Harry felt comfortable.

Harry was left with the memory of this one case that flashed like a bolt of lightning and, as a summer thunderstorm, drifted away to dissipate over the plains of normality. He remained on the police force for three more years, and he and Susan even had a few opportunities to disappear into the mountains as on that one summer day, but using motorcars rather than a railroad. He retired and moved with Susan to a farm near Grand Junction, where they grew peaches, possibly even inspired by the comment made by Professor Sager about the good peach crop in 1919. Harry had good success, probably because he no longer had fingerprint ink on his fingers when he tended his fruit trees. He never again investigated a murder. You might say it was a once-in-a-lifetime event for him on June 29, 1919.

EPILOGUE

And the Switzerland Trail. I am still here, although a shadow of my former self. Other hands have plundered my rails, ties and rolling stock to nourish other railways all over the world. You can still find parts of me tucked between parcels of private land. Much of my body has disappeared, overgrown or covered by roads or houses.

Like Frederick Hammond, I survived the Great War and the tungsten boom and bust. My influenza was the flood of July 31, 1919. With 4.8 inches of rain within two hours, 700 feet of my track was washed away between Boulder and Chrisman, including eight places in Four Mile Canyon. Also like Frederick, I survived all of this, only to succumb to a stab in the back—my fatal wound being the motorcar, which reduced the earnings of the Boulder, Denver and Western railroad to the point that a profit was no longer possible.

Much like a wildflower from the bouquet in Susan McBride's living room, I withered away and was later tossed aside. Now my body lies broken and fallen as Frederick's did on that fateful day in 1919.

I never ran again after the flood of July 31, 1919, except for the crew that dismantled my track. The end of my story was quite simple. My skeleton was removed between February 20 and October 1, 1920. My parts were scattered within Colorado, to other sections of the United States and even into Mexico and South America.

I bled out 4,465 tons of rails, 600,000 pounds of splice bars, 450,000 pounds of spikes, 270,000 pounds of tie plates, 44,000 pounds of rail braces, sixty-four sets of switches, seventy-eight steel girder bridge beams, over 50,000 ties, six locomotives, six passenger cars, a baggage car, a combination car, two cabooses, one snow plow, twenty-three boxcars, thirty-five gondola cars, four flatcars, one coal-loading elevator, five push cars and seven wood water tanks.

Ninety years in the future, between Sunset and Sugarloaf on a dirt road that was once my railroad bed, a modern motorcar stopped, and the confused driver asked a group of people on the dirt road how to find the Denver airport. The hikers expressed surprise at how someone had strayed so far from the real highways that coursed through the hills. But then again, I always welcomed any visitors along the remaining parts of my route, whatever their reason for being there.

Unlike Frederick, I will never die. My disjointed remains now provide the path for hikers, snowshoers, and mountain bikers and, oh yes, even in some places, as that one lost driver, for my nemesis the motorcar.

ABOUT THE AUTHOR

Mike Befeler is author of six novels in the Paul Jacobson Geezer-Lit Mystery Series—*Retirement Homes Are Murder, Living with Your Kids Is Murder* (a finalist for The Lefty Award for best humorous mystery of 2009), *Senior Moments Are Murder, Cruising in Your Eighties Is Murder* (a finalist for The Lefty Award for best humorous mystery of 2012), *Care Homes Are Murder* and *Nursing Homes Are Murder*—as well as two paranormal mysteries: *The V V Agency* and *The Back Wing*. He also has another published mystery, *The Mystery of the Dinner Playhouse,* and a non-fiction book, *For Liberty: A World War II Soldier's Inspiring Life Story of Courage, Sacrifice, Survival and Resilience.* Mike is past president of the Rocky Mountain Chapter of Mystery Writers of America. He grew up in Honolulu, Hawaii, and now lives in Boulder, Colorado, with his wife, Wendy. If you are interested in having the author speak to your book club, contact Mike Befeler at mikebef@aol.com. His website is http://www.mikebefeler.com.